Can a past love become their future?

The Thorntons' mansion is full of timeless secrets waiting to be unraveled. When small-town journalist Ivy and ghost hunter Max are stuck in the forgotten, dilapidated house, they find more than just a haunting. Ivy finds herself dreaming of the former owners, Marcus Thornton and his lovely wife, Elizabeth. Their profound love was once the talk of the town, and the cause their mysterious, untimely deaths never found. When Ivy's dreams begin to become reality, the mystery starts to unravel and sheds truth on more than just the past.

Books by Rhonda Lee Carver

Dreaming Ivy
Castle's Fortress
Friends with Benefits
With Honor

Published by Kensington Publishing Corporation

Dreaming Ivy

Rhonda Lee Carver

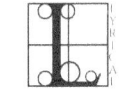

LYRICAL PRESS
Kensington Publishing Corp.
www.kensingtonbooks.com

B.A.--the beginning of forever

Foreword

Sometimes one must take a leap to see how far they can fly…

Chapter 1

"I must be hearing things. I've lost my mind. Or have you lost yours?" Ivy Kennedy eyed her boss, Marshall Deatrick, across the stretch of his paper-scattered desk. Her blood pressure rocketed. Sweat beaded between her breasts and on her upper lip. The air conditioning in the historical downtown building was on the fritz again. Tugging at the neckline of her blouse, she uncrossed her legs. "I could quit, you know." She swallowed back the bitter taste of reality. She knew it was a weightless threat.

"Well," he began easily, "you could quit, but we both know you won't." His lips parted with smug satisfaction. He lifted the lid from the antique box on the corner of his desk and took out a discount cigar. He laid his large frame back into his shabby leather chair as if he were relaxing into a bubble bath. He slid the cigar under his nose, taking a long, slow sniff like it was premium tobacco.

Ivy counted to ten. Her patience wore thin. "I hope you're not planning to light that while I'm here. The heat and your arrogance are all that I can endure at one time." The rotating fan on his desk squeaked as it turned, blowing hot air into her face. She pressed her fingertips to her temples.

"Don't push it, Ivy."

Dropping her hands into her lap, she sighed. Marshall was an intimidating man, but she'd learned over the years just how far to push. "Why this assignment, Marshall? Why stick me with a ghost hunter? You know I don't believe in ghosts and paranormal activity. It's amazing what people will write about to earn a buck."

He rolled the stogy between his fingers, then placed the cigar into his front pocket and patted it like a loved one. "Now, now, Ivy. There's no reason to get your panties in a bunch."

"That's a sexist remark," she snapped.

"Forgive me. Don't get your boxers in a bunch. Better?" He started to reach into his pocket but caught himself. Ivy knew he'd been making a

Rhonda Lee Carver

sizeable effort to stop smoking. It was putting him on edge, obvious by the tense set of his jaw and deeper lines around his eyes.

"Much better." She rolled her eyes. It was no use. Marshall didn't understand the concept of political correctness or treating people with respect.

"There are a handful of columnists and reporters in that room--" He flicked his thumb toward the outer offices. "--that would give their eyeteeth to grab this story."

"Oh really? Let's take a look at the handful jumping for this opportunity." She swiveled in the chair. She looked through the dirty window into the work area. Five desks filled the space, separated by short, gray dividers. One desk was occupied, not unusual for a Sunday afternoon. Jimmy Doyle, fresh from college with a golden journalism degree, had joined the Morgan Tribune two months earlier. The wet-behind-the-ears kid left a lasting impression of being an ass-kisser. She had nothing against the guy. In fact, she liked him. She respected anyone who had drive and passion matching her own. Too bad the ladder of success only had two steps above them. To get a better position at the Tribune, one would need to pry dead fingers off the rung.

She turned back to Marshall. He'd claw the eyes out of any person who dared to overstep him.

"Why not give this story to Jimmy? You don't see anyone else hanging out here on a Sunday, do you?"

"You are," he said.

She ignored his comment. She was always there. "Jimmy would get a kick out of staying in a haunted house for two weeks."

Marshall shook his head and scratched the top of his shiny, bald head. "Don't try it. It won't work."

"Try what?" She lifted a brow in dispute.

"To push this story off onto someone else. It's yours. Like it or not."

"Why me?" She shivered. Her voice was close to a whine. She didn't like to bellyache but there were moments. She considered herself a true journalist, open to all stories, but there came a time when she had to stand up for what she believed in. This was where she drew the line. "I've been here for five years, Marshall. Aren't I supposed to be above and beyond all of this small-time news? Hasn't my column doubled in readers in the last two years? Don't you like my articles? Isn't that worth something?"

"You want big? Go about two hundred miles upstate and you'll get your massacre headliners and your TV highlights. Here, you'll get what is available." He shrugged when she groaned. Maybe a silent apology?

"Look Ivy, you're my best journalist. I realize you think you've earned the right to call the shots, but you're not looking at the whole picture." He scooted forward in his chair. "For example, about that story you did last week. You know, the one about the stolen lawn ornaments. The day after the story ran, the thief was caught, thanks to your amateur detective work."

Why did his comment feel more like a slam than a pat on the back? He said it like it was something grand. It wasn't a prized moment for her. "Marshall." She leaned forward too. "The thief was a ninety-six-year-old escapee from the convalescent home. He had been suffering delusional outbreaks and thought he was a savior to all statues of the world. When he was busted, the deputy couldn't tell who was moving faster: the ornament or the thief. It wasn't a big-deal story and it didn't take a genius to figure out the culprit wasn't a clever thief with a devious, complex plan. The sheriff's office just didn't want to waste time on a pointless crime."

Marshall got up from his chair. He moved his large frame around the massive cherrywood desk and propped himself on the corner like it was his throne. "What do you expect, Ivy? Old men stealing lawn ornaments are the story here. If anything, you gave people a laugh. We're running a newspaper for a town of less than thirty thousand people, not a city with a population of drug users, felons and murderers. A tale like Thornton House with its ghost sightings and so-called haunting is news to these townsfolk. It has been the curse and talk of these parts since before you were the twinkle in your mother's eye. For an admired ghost hunter to come here from Chicago to investigate...Well, that is a huge story." He sighed. "I don't get why you're dragging your heels on this."

Ivy had a murderous urge to look Marshall straight in the eye and tell him where to shove this so-called story. With great control, she swallowed her pride. As much as she hated to admit it, and would refuse to say it aloud, he was right. Bigger stories than a ghost hunter coming to town wouldn't be on the horizon. "I'm curious why this ghost hunter thinks it's a value of his time and effort to come all the way out here to investigate paranormal activity. The house hasn't been lived in for years. Is he really in that dire need of snapshots of ghosts and goblins? You'd think they would have enough horror stories in Chicago."

"Tsk, tsk, Ivy." He clicked his tongue. "You're becoming cynical with age. Your hunger is growing into an evil beast."

At least she had hunger. "I'm just pointing out the facts."

"And you're saying you don't believe Thornton House is haunted?" One bushy brow popped up.

"We both know the story. I did a piece on the house and its history when I first started working here, remember? There were so many rumors swirling around town. My intention was to piece the puzzle together." She sat back. "People have lost sight of what's real and what's fantasy. They've glorified the house with stories of murder and mayhem. There is history there, but--"

"History of a rich landowner who died a lonely man," he interrupted. "A lot of people believe the spirit of Marcus Thornton and his wife still roam the halls of that old house. Others believe he buried his fortune somewhere on that property." Out of pure habit, he took out his cigar and took a few unlit drags.

"If that were true we'd have the whole town over there digging up the property. Now that would be a story." She laughed.

He shrugged. "Maybe it's time someone found a truth to all those rumors. And that's where you come into the picture."

"I've already been there and done that. There is no truth to the rumors. It's pure drama that keeps the rumor mill turning."

"But this will be different. You'll be there getting first glance."

"Why is this so important to you?" No doubt he had an ulterior motive. He always did.

"Imagine the publicity it will bring to our little town. We have to be a part of this, Ivy. We can't just let some out-of-towner come in and grab our story. We gotta get our piece of the pie. Not to mention that Mayor Tisdell and the owner of the Tribune, Mr. Parks, are breathing down my neck for me to make this work. Since they got wind of this man's arrival, Tisdell and Parks have been fired up, twisting and spanking this opportunity half past dead. We've kept it under wraps until the definite plans were made."

"All over a ghost hunter?"

"This ghost hunter's investigations are well known in his field and gobbled up by believers--and some not-so-believing. He's written a shitload of books on his observations and findings. They sell like crack hotcakes. Imagine all the tourists who'd want to come here just to get a glance at that old dump." His eyes sparkled dollar signs. "However, if my plan works…" He stopped.

She saw the mischief bubbling in his chubby face. "What are you up to, Marshall?" She narrowed her eyes. "Who is this man anyway?"

"Max Shepard. Heard of him?"

"Maybe, but once again, paranormal activity isn't my cup of tea." And then a thought struck her. "Wait… Isn't he the man who was in all the gossip magazines after he divorced that paper-thin supermodel? She walked the catwalk for those fancy fashion designers. When was that--maybe five, six years ago?"

"I don't know about all that nonsense." He snorted. "You know how those good-for-nothing tabloids feed off the crud of other peoples' lives."

"You mean the same sort of trash magazines you worked for before coming here?"

He didn't even acknowledge that. "Why he has chosen to come here and investigate the dilapidated Thornton House makes no sense to me." He rubbed his palms together. "What I do know is that Shepard made arrangements to stay at the old dump. The latest owner of that shack is all for this investigation. He sees this as a future sale in the making."

"You mean your golf buddy. Nice how that fits so comfy. Let me guess--you scratch his back, he'll scratch yours?"

"I have a lot of golf buddies, sugar."

"And what makes you think this ghost hunter guru would want some writer tagging along? Aren't most of those people loners?"

His eminent sneaky grin returned. "I'm afraid that choice won't be given to him. The property owner arranged for you to stay also. It's all been smoothed out. No worries. Just do your job."

"That's nice," she muttered. "Okay, let's say this man is worth a story. But what a waste of time investigating Thornton House for haunting. There's nothing to find but cobwebs and rats. I'd rather just skip the whole haunting buzz and go straight for a personal interview with Max Shepard." She grinned. "I bet I'd get a good one."

"Thatta girl." He stood up and straightened his tie. "And you never know, Ivy. From the photos I've seen of Shepard, he's a looker and known as a ladies' man. You may have to use those womanly wiles to convince him to give you an exclusive. Cozying up to him might be a blessing instead of a disaster." He winked.

"Oh…my…my…my." She surveyed him closely and her stomach twisted. "What are you thinking? You wouldn't! You couldn't!" she sputtered.

"What, Ivy?" He pretended innocence, which was a long shot. "Just remember us when you get that interview."

"I've never used seduction to get a story, Marshall. I won't start now."

He rubbed his double chin and shrugged a beefy shoulder. "That thought never crossed my mind. But just between the two of us, sex is not taboo in getting an exclusive. You could do worse things--"

Ivy jumped up from the chair, sending it hard against the wall. "Stop right there. There is no chance in hell I'd lower my values for a story. I will not go in there and seduce this man to convince him to let us publish his personal story. This is deplorable."

"Calm down, Ivy. I'm not asking you to seduce the man, for Christ's sake. I'm just asking you to go in and get a story on what he finds. Show Shepard how nice our townsfolk are. If he gives you an exclusive, that'll be icing on the cake. Look at it as a partnership. And being the journalist you are, think of the story you can get from him. And what if he picks up on a few freaking mysteries and ghosts? If we earn a story in one of his books, well hell, this town will no longer be stories of stolen lawn ornaments. Can you only imagine the boost such a story can give to a writer's career?" He pointed a stubby forefinger in her direction.

Ivy didn't respond. She toyed with the idea of an exclusive on Max Shepard. She didn't care whether there were spirits or walking dead. What she did believe in was finding an opportunity to make a name for herself. A story on *the* Max Shepard would be of interest to a lot of people, and definitely wouldn't hurt her lackluster career. "I think this Max Shepard is a phony. He claims to see ghosts? I bet he's never seen a spark of supernatural his entire life. Now that would be a story. To reveal a fake."

"A fake? Sure, go that route. I don't give a rat's ass what your storyline is as long as there is one. Find out what makes this man tick. Stay on him like white on rice."

"Desperate, are we?" Ivy raised a brow.

"When you get to be my age you'll know desperation." Something flashed across his face. Ivy couldn't read what it was before it disappeared. Was there more to this than met the eye? He turned toward the window and stared out. "Besides, you're a journalist. Journalists like to report. Maybe this is the story that'll get you that move into a big-shot newspaper. If not, you may be stuck in this small town for the rest of your life. Unless we both fail on this story and get fired."

She sucked in a deep breath. "That sounds like a threat."

"Well, one way or another, you may get your wish." He turned back to her. "You'll be leaving dodge by choice or involuntarily." He chuckled but it didn't quite reach his eyes. He returned to his chair.

"Marshall, you know I came back here to live for one reason and one reason only. My mother and her ill health. She needs me. I need this job until I have a backup plan." With her dismal thoughts burning a hole in her head, she told Marshall, "You should be glad that I'm still here doing your demeaning jobs. I bet we wouldn't see your star reporter, Jasmine, sleeping in a deserted haunted house for two weeks."

His scoff echoed off the empty walls. "You're a much better writer than Jasmine. Good looks, big tits and a tight ass can only get you so far in life." He thrummed his fat fingers on the desktop.

"And what am I? Chopped liver?" She scowled.

His face softened slightly. "Ivy, you don't need me to feed your ego. You're single because you choose that life. You've got the whole kit and caboodle. Looks, brain and future."

"I'll remind you of those sentiments later. And if I get this story and those photos, if he takes any, I better land a huge raise and a private office, you hear?"

"Does this mean I can count on you?" He was already smiling in success.

"On one condition. Well, two conditions." She smiled.

Chapter 2

"Why do you have to go, Max? I'm only in town for a few days before I leave for California. I can't believe you're leaving me."

Max Shepard eyed Renee. She was his comfortable, pleasing-to-the-eye diversion. He couldn't call what they had a "relationship." Maybe a friendship with benefits. "I'm not leaving you," he finally said. He turned to her, giving her tousled blond hair and slender body, outlined under the thin white sheet, a long, slow perusal. He slid her his most meaningful wink of appreciation before going back to packing his tattered leather bag.

"But why to Morgan Sites? Where the hell is that anyway?" Her words bordered on a wail. He clenched his jaw in reaction.

He swiped a hand through his hair and sighed. He didn't have a relationship, with her or any other woman, because of *this* very reason. He couldn't even understand why they were having this discussion. "Renee, you travel all over the country. You're gone most of the time on modeling shoots. When you do roll into town, every few months or so, we reunite, have a drink, share dessert--usually in bed. You haven't cared that I wasn't around before to keep you entertained."

"I thought you'd be happy that I visited. It's been months since I've been here last."

"Sure, I was happy. I was just surprised to see you." The words came out automatically. He instantly wished he could've snatched them back. Sugar-coating the truth wasn't his style--and for some reason he hadn't been pleased that she'd dropped by unannounced. Coming home late from a book signing, he had found her waiting, naked, in his bed. Only an ungrateful ass would have complained about a sexy, available woman. But, exhausted and spent, all he'd wanted to do was fall into bed alone and sleep. Her luscious body in his king-size bed hadn't even tempted him into adult playtime. Angry that he'd denied her, she'd gotten out of bed, stomped around the room and thrown a temper tantrum. He couldn't give a damn anymore at that point. If she'd called first he'd have told her he wasn't up for company. Sometime in the middle of the night she'd come back to bed.

"Can't you postpone your trip for one day?" She moved languorously toward the edge of the bed, causing the sheet to slide off her shoulder, in the process revealing her firm, expensive D cups.

Her body was definitely a weapon against a man's libido. Normally the sight of her nudity would result in a tent behind his zipper, but it just wasn't working for him. Was he ill? After all, she was good. Not just good, but skilled at seduction. That's what made her great at her job-- seducing the camera lens.

He glanced over her pert, pink nipples. Not one twitch.

There *was* something wrong with him.

He didn't have time for this. He certainly couldn't let Renee's passive-aggressive behavior deter him from his focus. "If it makes you feel any better, it's not a pleasure trip. I'm going to be holed up in some old, dilapidated house for two weeks. And to top it off, I have a rookie journalist shadowing me." He still couldn't believe he'd agreed to the tagalong, but in the scheme of things he really didn't give a shit.

An elegant groan escaped her throat. "I thought you were supposed to be alone?" She looked up at him through a perfect veil of false eyelashes.

"I did, too. That was the plan, but damn these people in these small towns. They find a way to bust a man's balls every time. They think their towns are separate from the rest of the world." He sighed. "I guess if I really cared I'd say 'screw it.' But hell, let the woman do her job. Everyone's got to get ahead somehow."

Renee's mouth opened into a faultless O. "A woman?" Lifting a thinly manicured brow, she made an expression that he was certain had taken her years to perfect.

It didn't do a thing for him. He continued packing. "Yeah. So what?"

"Should I be jealous?" She reached up and ran her red fingernail down his abs, stopping at the waist of his jeans.

"Not unless you want to push me away." He shot her a quick glance.

In a soft, sexy voice she said, "If you stay, I'll cook you a meal. Afterward, I'll cook you." The tip of her tongue came out, licking her plump bottom lip, as if to drive the hidden meaning home.

He chuckled. "You cook? You don't even know how to boil water, Renee." His words weren't mean to offend her, but she drew back and hammered him with a cold blue stare.

"Oh yes, I do." She huffed and covered her body with the sheet. He guessed it was a way of punishing him.

"Okay, maybe you do know how to boil water." He shrugged.

"Three minutes on high in the microwave," she snapped.

Closing the suitcase and clicking the lock, he sat next to her on the bed, kissing her gingerly on the lips. "I'm sorry." He meant it. He usually wasn't in such a foul mood. He didn't know what it was, but instead of exciting the hell out of him, Renee was beginning to repulse him.

Before he could move away, she shimmied closer and burrowed her bare breasts into his chest, whispering into his ear, "Stay."

"I'm going." Enough. His patience grew thin. He got up and grabbed his suitcase. "Don't forget to lock up on your way out."

* * * *

A prickle slithered up Ivy's spine as she approached Thornton House. The place gave her the creeps. Were the rumors getting to her? She laughed. Her trepidation had nothing to do with gossip and had everything to do with the idea of sleeping with creepy crawlies and whatever else lurked in the shadows.

The property was overgrown with weeds and sat back on a dead end road. If a person didn't know the country roads of Morgan Sites, they wouldn't know the three-hundred-year-old house existed. Seldom did anyone drive on the gravel road, by mistake or otherwise.

She drove through the broken, rusted gate and took in the view of the house. The red brick two-story was only a figment of the beautiful house it had once been. The windows were overrun with foliage and years of filth. There was no life, only darkness. Weatherworn shutters hung haphazardly. A place forgotten in time.

She frowned. Marshall said the owner had the house checked every so often for problems. There was a *big* problem. The house was missing underneath layers of grime and neglect.

Ivy climbed out of her car, fighting the urge to climb back in. She inhaled and exhaled through her mouth, gaining the strength she knew she had. Two weeks would fly by. She could tolerate it. At least the place had electricity, water and a roof. It could be worse.

She grabbed her bags out of the back seat and moved toward the house. "I must enter with an open mind." Ivy chanted the words over and over.

She came upon the weathered porch and stopped in her tracks. A few warped planks thrown together didn't classify as a porch. Many of the boards were missing and she didn't trust the ones that remained. With the toe of her shoe, she tested the first step. The board seemed sturdy. With slow, deliberate movements, she walked up the stairs and across the dry rotted timber as it creaked in protest.

Reaching into her front pocket, she pulled out the skeleton key. When Marshall had handed it to her that morning, she'd laughed, thinking it was a joke.

It took her three tries until the metal slid into the lock, but it still wouldn't turn. She struggled as irritation swirled in her stomach. She had a second's worth of patience left when the bolt finally clicked. The heavy door screeched with age as she pushed it open. It stopped halfway. She pushed, but it wouldn't budge. There was only enough opening for her to slip through.

Apprehensive, she peeked inside the two-foot-wide crack. She couldn't see anything through the dark. She skimmed her hand inside the shadows and felt down the wall, hoping to find a light switch. Nothing. Grabbing her flashlight from her purse, she switched it on.

She left her bags and slid between the door and the frame. Once inside, her lungs were accosted with a deep mildew scent. A string of cobwebs attached itself to every inch of her exposed skin. She resisted the urge to scream.

Ivy concentrated on the house as she turned, flashing the light around the hallway. Even in its state of decay, it was magnificent. She guessed the hallway, with its antique wood flooring and dark wood trim, was once grand. A stunning glass chandelier hung from the tall ceiling. She'd never seen anything like it before. She wondered if it still worked. She found the switch and lifted it, jiggled it twice, but nothing. Not even a spark. She hoped it only needed a change of bulbs.

She continued her perusal as she moved along the shadows like a thief in the night. It was so quiet she found herself instinctively walking on tiptoe.

Stopping at the next doorway, she peeked in and shined her light around the small space. She stepped into the room with caution. A ratty-looking settee, a small wooden chair and a wooden table on its last three legs filled the area.

She wandered down the hall. The next room was absolutely gorgeous. A huge stone fireplace covered one wall. The massive wooden mantel was lost beneath years of dirt, but a swipe of her finger told her it remained in good condition. There was another spectacular chandelier, not in working order--no surprise--but there was enough light filtering in through the two large windows that she could shut off the flashlight. She dropped it back in her purse.

Faded and shredded drapes hung from bent rods. She pushed them open and a huge cloud of ageless dust exploded. She stepped back, coughing, and covered her mouth and nose until she could breathe again.

The sun flowed in, giving the room a golden glow, a new life. The house had so much potential. It was a shame it had stood empty for so long. Her mind conjured up a list of possibilities. It would have made an elaborate bed and breakfast accommodation or the home of a wealthy historical enthusiast, maybe even a home for a family.

When Marcus Thornton built the house in the early eighteen hundreds it had been a grand place, designed for beauty and wealth. During Marcus's first marriage to Sarah Mitchell, there had been many social gatherings and parties with the most prestigious invited. When Sarah died, so had the social gatherings.

Ivy headed toward the modern French doors, guessing they were added by the most recent owner. Through the dirty glass panels she caught a blurry vision of the overgrown remains of a flower garden and a huge oak tree. There were several more small rooms, stripped of furniture, with no hints of past life.

Back in the hallway, she stopped and looked up at the winding staircase that seemed to sweep upward for miles. She couldn't wait to explore the upstairs. She climbed each step as anticipation made her heart beat faster.

In the upstairs hallway the carpet was faded and threadbare. The four bedrooms were beautiful and spacious. One room tucked away at the end of the hallway was locked, which ignited Ivy's curiosity. She tugged and pulled on the knobs of the double doors. They creaked but didn't budge. She pushed. No movement.

Frustrated, she shook the knobs harder. Still nothing. On the verge of giving up, she tried again. It turned. Her mouth dropped open. A prickly sensation coursed through her as she stared at the door in bewilderment. Had it been locked? She checked the knob for a keyhole. There wasn't one.

She opened the doors wide and looked in. She held her breath. The master suite. It was without a doubt the most elaborate, beautiful room of the house. The pink walls were faded but remained pretty. The three large windows overlooked the garden and out over the rolling hills. She wasn't sure how much work the current owner had done, but the massive four-poster, cherrywood bed remained, covered in a green satin comforter. She couldn't understand why it hadn't been sold or destroyed along with the rest of the furniture in the house.

The entire bedroom was in good, moderately clean order. It held a certain warmth--something she couldn't quite pinpoint.

She found the bathroom through a set of thin-glassed windows. It was fit for a queen. She could have fit her home bathroom into this one three times. The fixtures were lovely in bronze, the ceramic tiled floor and walls decorated with hand-painted flowers. The bath was vast. In curiosity, she turned the knob of the bath faucet. It gurgled twice, spat awkwardly, and then spurted a stream of water. The water was tainted a tan shade but she was sure if it were left running a short time it'd run clear.

She glanced at her slender watch. Her company would be arriving soon. With a twist of the faucet knob to off, she headed back into the bedroom.

Downstairs, Ivy turned the corner into the corridor. She stopped when she heard a creak. She listened. Out of the corner of her eye she saw a shadow sweep across the wall. She turned and looked as it disappeared. "Hello?" she called out. No answer. Was it Max Shepard? Hadn't he heard her? She stomped down the hall and burst into the room. "Hello--"

The room was empty.

Ivy swallowed the taste of fright. A shiver raced across her skin. She had seen someone, or had she? She rubbed her eyes and sighed. Maybe the shadows were playing tricks on her.

Another loud crack in the flooring behind her sent Ivy twisting in alarm. The sun coming through the window blinded her. All Ivy could see was the flash of bright light before she acted on impulse. She drew her fist back and punched--landing on something solid. The force behind her connection with skin and bone sent her off balance, flailing backward. A hand on her wrist pulled her hard against a steely frame.

She brought her eyes up and met a dark stare, just as she felt wobbling. The impact of her body had sent him a step back. He lost his balance and together they fell to the wooden floor. The air whooshed from his chest as Ivy landed on top of the stranger.

Ivy cringed as she closed her eyes. She remained very still. She wanted nothing more than for the floor to swallow her whole. Several long seconds floated by. Neither of them said a word. She finally opened her eyes.

Embarrassed and confused, Ivy laid her palms against his shoulders, pushing herself up. She looked directly into his not-so-pleased expression and gulped. Enchanting green eyes, prominent cheekbones, midnight hair...and a pissed-off set to his jaw. She'd made a mistake--a huge one. "Max Shepard." It wasn't a question. She already knew the answer.

He narrowed his eyes. "Ivy Kennedy, journalist and amateur boxer?"

She couldn't tell whether it was sarcasm or anger. She did notice the deep, rich tone of his voice did funny things to the pit of her stomach. His voice wasn't the only toned part of him. Their bodies being pressed together gave her an up close and personal testimonial of his physical assets. From broad chest, tight abs to long legs, she could feel tight muscles and a curious bulge behind his zipper. She scooted her hip around the swelling in his jeans. Heat spread through her body.

One corner of his mouth lifted. "It's my cell." Could he see straight through her?

"Cell?"

He reached into his pocket, pulled out something and held up his phone. Ivy was certain her skin changed into the perfect color of mortification. She wondered just how bad this could get. She could handle this. Pasting a smile on her face, she said, "Nice to meet you." The temperature rose between them into the triple digits. Their bodies seemed to melt together. Ivy's nerves made her heady, making her feel like she floated on a cloud. He didn't look like the pictures she'd seen on the internet. He looked more distinguished in person. "You're older than I thought," she blurted.

He curved his brow. "Older?"

Damn. "Older, I mean, in a good way." All humor left his face. She licked her bottom lip and nervously pushed her hair behind her ear. "My mother said I have a bad habit of saying the most awkward things and rambling--" She swallowed. "--like I am now."

She felt his heart race against her breast. His zipper started to swell again. Was that another cell phone in his pocket, *or*... Before her mind could complete the thought, he wrapped his large hands around her waist, and in one swift, easy movement he lifted her off him. He set her on her feet as he came to stand in front of her. "That's better," he said as he backed up. "Damn rug." He kicked at the lump that must have been the reason behind their fall.

He was a tall man. Ivy guessed about six-feet-two. She certainly had to roll her head back to look into his eyes. He was also more handsome in person than in his photos. Not bad. Not bad at all.

"What's that?"

She realized she had said the words aloud. She winced. "I mean, bad... very bad." She pointed to the redness and swelling quickly appearing on his cheek. "I'm sorry." Would he walk out? "I guess that wasn't the first impression I'd hoped for."

He stood there, silent. Awkwardly silent. This was a complete disaster. She'd humiliated herself and at the same time managed to give him a black eye to match the dark scowl on his face. Maybe she needed to start searching for a new job? Marshall would have her head for this.

Chapter 3

Max snorted. What the hell just happened? The tightness in his southern region had finally dampened. A strange woman had just given him a woody. He'd survive the hard-on and the black eye he was sure he'd have, but the lady Ivy Kennedy stood before him looking like she was on the brink of peeing her pants. He wanted to laugh but he resisted. Had he just gotten his ass kicked by a girl? The girl carried a wallop. He swiped his knuckles over the spot on his cheek. "I guess you taught me a valuable lesson, Ivy Kennedy. Never come up on a woman unannounced."

That should have been the end of it. What was done was done. He had to give the woman credit where credit was due. She could defend herself. He wanted to move on and forget it, but it wasn't happening. Ivy stood on her tiptoes, reached up and touched the place she'd socked him with the tips of her fingers. The gentle, warm touch made him jerk. "It's swollen." Her minty breath sweeping across his cheeks and the feel of her breasts brushing his chest pushed every arousal button he knew he had, and some he didn't. Not that he didn't like it--or rather, he liked it too much.

"No kidding," he answered. Was that quivering that he noticed in his own voice? No, not possible. Did she have to stand so close, though? His body was acting like it'd been neglected for months. Hell, he should be glad to find out he was still a man after the Renee incident. He was taken back by Ivy's touch and her closeness. Looking deep into her eyes, he was caught. They were crystal blue and surrounded by the longest lashes he'd ever seen. When had he ever noticed any woman's eyes? He sniffed loudly. Enough with the admiration. "That's usually the effect a hit has on the face."

"We need ice." She interrupted his thought. "I have a cooler. It's that way. I'll meet you in the sitting room, or whatever the room is with furniture. If I don't return in ten, can you come and save me? You never know what's hiding in these dark crevices. I keep thinking the floor is going to give out and I'm going to fall through." She laughed, which quickly turned somber.

His quiet wasn't in anger--only irritation at his body's betrayal. He'd left a desirable, naked woman in his bed, untouched and unwanted. Now parts of his body wanted action with a woman who looked as innocent as a newborn kitten, as skinny as a rail and who talked way too much. There was only one thing he liked more than a voluptuous body--silence.

"I guess we got off to a rough start."

"Guess so." Rough wasn't the word he'd use. Annoying was a better one. He was irritated with himself as much as he was with her

"Okay, I'm going now."

She walked away and he couldn't help but admire the swaying move of her firm backside. *Nice.* But Ivy Kennedy wasn't his type--if he had one.

The smell of honeysuckle lingered in the room as a reminder that she smelled sweet. He liked the smell. What the hell was wrong with him? He wasn't some wet-behind-the-ears schoolboy who got a rise every time a girl got close. What was happening to his male anatomy?

A sting in his cheek caught his attention. He touched the area and moaned. She couldn't be much more than five-feet-four, in a good pair of stilettos, and one hundred pounds dripping wet. He'd think she was the size of a linebacker by that punch. And what the hell did he need an ice pack for? He didn't need or want one, but if it made her feel better then so be it.

Max took off for the room with the furniture. He took a seat on what he thought was once a couch. A puff of dust surrounded him but he didn't give it much thought. He'd been in worse joints spying on the extraterrestrial. He laid his head back and closed his eyes. The stillness was deafening and yet he felt like he was being watched. Opening his lids to a slit, he saw that indeed he was alone unless one counted the massive spider crawling across the wall. He hated spiders. He certainly didn't want to meet up with the creepy crawly during the night.

Reluctantly, he got up and crossed the room. Using a pen from his pocket and his notebook, he trapped the spider. With one hand keeping the spider contained, he quickly opened the window and tossed the critter out. "Go find another home. This one isn't big enough for the both of us."

Light footsteps broke into his thoughts. He turned as Ivy rambled into the room. "Were you talking to someone?" she asked.

He shook his head. "Nope." He slammed the window back down. He'd keep his fear under wraps. He turned to her with every intention of denying the urge to take a leisurely gaze down her body, but he just couldn't help himself. He enjoyed the sensual perusal of her body, taking in every soft inch until he came to the pointed toe of her shoes. He swept up the same route and his eyes collided with her baffled blues. He made no effort to hide his admiration. This was dangerous, he knew, but even her you're-not-getting-any-of-this look didn't deter the heat in his loins.

"All of the ice melted in my cooler but I thought this would help. A leftover from breakfast." She held up a container.

"Blueberry yogurt? This is a snack. Not a cold pack for my eye."

"It's cold."

"I don't need it."

"It'll keep the swelling down."

"Whatever." He'd rather not fuss.

She tossed the yogurt. He caught it against his chest. "Has anyone ever told you that you're pushy?" he asked.

"A time or two," she said.

He'd forgive the fact that Ivy was trigger-happy with her fist. He'd also forgive her for being so damn attractive. He was capable of keeping the line drawn between his business and personal life. However, he wouldn't forgive the fact that she was annoying. "I guess we should be thankful for leftovers." He hoped she caught the sarcasm. He pressed the container against his face. "I don't see how this will help."

"It was either the yogurt or a banana. I went for the yogurt."

"Should I say thank you?"

"You should but I'm sure you won't." She went to the fireplace and stared up at the painting of Thornton House from years ago.

He was a good boy and let a minute pass before he lowered the so-called ice-pack. "So why are you here?"

She didn't take her eyes off the oil painting. "What?"

He shrugged one shoulder and juggled the container between his hands. "You're a journalist. Why would you waste your time investigating a haunted house?" He knew why she was there and it had nothing to do with ghosts. There was always a motive. He'd realized that the hard way. He set the container on the mantel.

"You use the word 'journalist' like it's dirty."

"I guess it's all in how you take it."

"I'm here for the same reason you are." The area between her eyebrows wrinkled. "To find whatever *you* find in this old place."

"You're a journalist. I figure *I'm* the story." No need to mince words. They were both adults. And if she could hit like a man then she could take the truth like one.

Ivy waved a hand in front of his face. "Are you okay? Are you going to keep repeating that I'm a journalist like you have to pound it into my head? I know what I do for a living."

"You chose your profession." He wasn't sure why he suddenly felt hostility toward her. Yeah, he knew exactly why. He was agitated by her being there. Their characters clashed.

She squinted her eyes as if she were shooting him with an imaginary weapon. "I'm beginning to get an idea of what people meant when they said you have a chip on your shoulder."

* * * *

Ivy could see by the thin line of his lips that she'd struck a sensitive chord in him. Was he good at dishing it out but not receiving it?

"I'd say I'd heard rumor about your reputation *as a journalist* but you're not old enough to have left a mark."

She smirked. He was rude, but since she had the patience of a monk, she'd let it roll off. She didn't need the drama. She had a job to do and the main idea was, what did he want at Thornton House? He may think it was none of her business but he was on her territory now and that made it her business. "I understand why you're annoyed. But it's best just to let it go."

"Oh, you think you understand why I'm pissed?" he asked.

She nodded. "Yes, I do."

"And why is that?" He challenged.

"Because you got your ass kicked by a girl. I guess that would play on most men's egos." Ivy knew it wasn't entirely true, and her words certainly wouldn't build a bridge between her and Max, but she couldn't resist the temptation to knock his egotistical attitude down a notch or two. At least she hoped she gave him something to think about.

Without another word, he stomped across the room.

Ivy watched him. It was only natural instinct that she'd notice his broad shoulders encased in the white cotton, back lowering to the perfect narrowing of waist, pausing a bit too long on his behind until she made a turtle's path down his long legs. Her gaze had landed on his boots when he stopped walking. She dragged her attention back up his tall frame and met his intense gaze. He'd caught her red-handed, or rather, red-eyed. She grinned in embarrassment.

"That might not be safe when we'll be holed up here together, alone, for the next few weeks. I'm assuming we both know the line between work and play." His voice echoed off the bare walls.

Ivy's mouth fell open in disbelief. Max Shepard couldn't possibly think she was trying to seduce him. True, anything that had the words

'Max' and 'seduction' in the same sentence didn't leave a bad taste on the tongue, but she wasn't interested. "You're safe, trust me. I'm not interested in playboys."

He faced her. "Playboy?" He appeared amused.

"Do the tabloids lie?"

"Never." He laughed and shook his head. "But you'd know, since that rag you work for is only a step above the bottom feeders."

She tried to form words that resembled a juicy comeback but all she could manage was a pathetic sputtering of, "Uhhh…" And to make matters worse, he turned and strolled out of the room. Anger charged up her spine. How dare he insinuate that she belonged in a group of 'bottom feeders.'

Ivy heard the voice in the back of her mind telling her to let it go. It didn't matter what he thought, did it? Of course not. But Ivy had no desire to allow him to think he could get away with such a despicable attitude. She marched after him, catching up to him as he stepped through the door onto the rickety porch. "I'll let you know, Mr. Shepard, what I write is called 'journalism.' If you haven't heard of it, then I'll explain. It's where you write true stories about true events. You wouldn't know what I'm referring to considering you write about extraterrestrial beings and ghosts."

She started to take a step onto the porch and he caught her with a hand on her elbow. "Don't step out here with me."

Oh, that man! She seethed. "Are you telling me what to do now?"

He chuckled. "Lighten up. What'd you eat with breakfast? A shot of speed? The boards won't hold our weight."

She knew her cheeks must have turned bright red.

"Ahh. Finally quiet." He snapped a pensive expression at her as he stepped off the porch and headed to his Jeep.

Time seemed to stand still for Ivy as he grabbed his bag from the back seat and slammed the door. When he reached the doorway where she stood with her arms crossed over her waist, he said, "Regarding your crack about my job, all I can say is that not everyone's a believer." He swept past her and tossed his bag on the floor inside the door. "You're a semi-believer."

She shifted in her heels. "What?"

"I'm getting a good idea which side of the fence you hang on."

Her muscles tightened. "Is that right?"

He scanned the entranceway and tried the light switch. It still didn't work. "I know you're not a fan of my work or my books, but I'm not convinced that you don't believe in the spirit world."

"I'd believe anything with proof."

He went back to his car, unloaded more equipment bags and slammed the lift gate with one hand. She didn't move from the doorway when he approached her. His gaze met hers in conflict. Tedious seconds ticked by until he finally snapped, "Excuse me."

She sidestepped. "Maybe we need to sit down and clear the air." Ivy closed the front door with a loud thud. Then a thought caught her. The door that had barely opened for her was now swinging without any trouble.

"Whatever." He brought her attention back. He started for the stairway. "I can explore and listen at the same time." He made his way up the stairs two at a time.

"Fine." She left the doorway. Her patience grew thin. The man's ego was enough to cause her exasperation. She stomped up the stairs behind him, huffing and puffing. "Look, I understand you're not keen on sharing this house with me for the next few weeks." No response. She shrugged. "You know, I don't find this a pleasurable experience, either. I think if we both want to survive this we should accept that we're here together and make the best of it."

At the top of the stairs he paused long enough to glance down the hallway, then headed in the first open doorway. She watched him give the space a quick inspection. It was simply decorated with a chair and nothing else, and he seemed satisfied. "Mind if I take this room?"

"It doesn't have a bed."

"I have a sleeping bag." He bent and unzipped one of the duffel bags he'd brought.

Momentarily sidetracked by the way his jeans fit his backside as he bent, she shook her head. "Fine by me. I had my eye on the master bedroom."

"Great." He pulled a small notebook from a side pocket of the bag and an expensive-looking camera from the inside.

Max stepped back into the hallway. She trailed close behind. "You didn't answer me."

"About?" He stopped to examine the wall, delicately pulling at the peeling wallpaper.

"If it's possible that we can find common ground between us and work together."

"We both know it didn't require a response." He scribbled something onto the notebook. "Do you have any experience in hunting ghosts?"

Ivy laughed. He shot her a sour expression. He was serious. "No, I've never hunted a ghost before."

"Then you're no use to me."

Ivy gritted her teeth. She squeezed her hands into fists until she felt the sting of nails biting into her palms. The man was incorrigible. A half an hour into this situation and she'd already had enough. She stopped walking and closed her eyes, taking a deep, calming breath. Eventually she'd verbally lay into him because no one could be expected to deal professionally with the likes of a man like Matt Shepard. He'd definitely give Marshall a run for his money. She opened her eyes in time to see that he'd come to a sudden stop, but not in time to keep from crashing into his broad back. She went bouncing backward and caught herself against the wall. He didn't seem to be troubled by her impact as he made a quick examination of another room.

Feeling slightly ignored, she squeezed between the space of the wooden doorframe and his large, muscular body. This room was much like the last. Insufferably bare. She opened her mouth to say something but stopped. She stared closer at the window. It had a thin horizontal crack. Along the top was a small vertical one, connecting the lines to make a T. Both lines were perfectly etched. "Did someone intentionally do that into the glass?" Ivy whispered as she strolled across the room and touched the splintered glass. It was odd. She couldn't feel the crack but it appeared to be broken all the way through.

The clicking of a camera interrupted her thoughts. She heard the soft shuffling of Max's boots against the wood floor as he came up next to her. He bent and inspected the glass. With the tip of his forefinger, he followed the long, straight line. "Interesting."

Ivy got a whiff of his woodsy scent. She started to lean nearer, wondering what cologne he wore, but caught herself. Definitely not a good idea. She cleared her throat and looked past the broken window into the captivating view. "Wow. Beautiful." A group of deer grazed along the edge of the woods. The clear blue sky seemed to go on forever along with the overgrown field dotted with purple wildflowers.

"Nice." Max snapped the view. "This is enough to make the blood pressure drop."

She started to nod in agreement when she realized he was latently referring to her as the reason his blood pressure was high. She turned and braced her hands on hips. "If you're still sore about me hitting you, remember I did say sorry. I'd hardly say that was enough to cause your blood pressure to rise. I have made an effort to end this ridiculous attitude you are airing in my direction."

His voice was calm as he said, "The cheek still stings, but I'm beyond that."

Ivy wanted to say something, anything, but his piercing glare held her silent and the amount of space his massive frame dominated in the room made her feel...different. It wasn't suffocating, but she had an uncomfortable, breathless feeling. His height towered over hers. No words formed on her lips. Her brain seemed to stop functioning.

"If you'd like for this situation to work, I suggest you do your work quietly and allow me to do mine by staying out of my way."

"For your information, Mac--"

One corner of his mouth twisted. "The name's Max. Not Mac."

"Excuse me, Max." She put blatant emphasis on his name. "You may not want my opinion--"

"I don't remember asking for it," he said frankly.

"You asked for it the moment you came in here presuming you could get by with being an ass," she stated firmly.

"Then please, by all means, tell me what you're thinking."

She bit into her bottom lip. Okaaay. He asked for it. "I think this ghost hunting, or paranormal investigation, is all an illusion on your part. You play into people's off-the-wall beliefs to sell your books."

"Now aren't you the one presuming a bit?"

"That you play off people's beliefs? Not at all."

"Aren't you presuming that I'm an ass? Maybe I should presume you're an ass. I've had warmer welcomes from evil spirits."

Her palm ached to slap him. She'd never hit someone in anger in all her life. She'd hit him earlier in self-defense. "Me? An ass? How dare you!"

"No, how dare you. You think you can dish up your subtle put-downs with a side of smile and a flash of blues and I'm supposed to grin and bear it. I have no doubt that you got roped into this assignment. Secretly, you wish you had more to write about than a mother giving birth to her baby in the back seat of a Honda Accord or a flasher giving the Mayor a shot of nudity on the lawn of the courthouse. Remember something, sweetheart, we may have to share this space for the next two weeks, but I don't have to like it. If you can't take the heat, I suggest you jump out of the pot."

"You'd like it if I got all flustered and furious and walked out of here, wouldn't you? Let me warn you, it isn't going to happen. I can tell you that much. While you're here, I'm here. Like it or not. I was just trying to be nice--to break the ice, so to speak." She started to walk away, and then stopped. She wasn't finished with him yet. "And another thing, you should feel lucky that your work sold two million copies. I'm sure it was simply because of people's rooted fascination in ghosts because if they met you and if first impressions had anything to do with it, you'd be selling peanuts out of a cart on some street corner." Her words dripped with ice and she didn't care one bit.

"For someone who doesn't know a lot about my work, you definitely know about my sales revenue. You sure you haven't read one or two?"

"Don't embarrass yourself." She crossed her arms over her chest. "I can appreciate anyone who can pick up a camera, point and click." She took a deep breath. "I won't drop to your level of insults." She sniffed.

He was undisturbed by her disaffection. In fact, he curved his lips into a smile as he went back to recording in his notebook. "Are you finished?" he asked without looking her way. He was casual about the situation, like he had smashed a bug and was flicking it into good riddance.

Ivy knew the squabble should end, but something inside her just couldn't let it rest. Getting everything out in the open absolved any chance that later she'd let him have it. "I haven't yet given my opinion of *you* yet," she stated.

"You could have fooled me."

She kept her tension in check. No sinking. "I think you hold a personal grudge against me because I am a journalist. Not me as an individual, but all journalists as a group."

"Okay," he tossed over his shoulder, unconcerned.

"I read the articles written about you and your ex-wife. They called you a man who used his wife's place in society as a ladder for success." The tensing of his shoulders and the tightening of his jaw told her she'd struck a chord. Had she stepped over some hidden boundary of human kindness? She did feel better--slightly. Now who was the bug being smashed?

He remained quiet. She'd given up on receiving a reply, but at last it came. His gaze connected with hers, and when he spoke it was eerily low and husky. "I see that my first impressions aren't award-winning but they sure are interesting. You've gained a lot of information about me in this ten-minute chitchat that proves to you the logic behind the mumbo-jumbo that filled those trash magazines. Most reputable journalists wouldn't cite information they'd found in a tabloid." He smirked. "You're like the fly that won't quit biting the horse's ass."

She laughed. She couldn't resist. "And you're the horse's ass in that statement? It's nice to see we agree on something."

He apparently didn't find the humor as she did. He threw his notebook and pen down onto the floor and took three paces toward her. She sucked in a breath. He came so close that she could smell his cologne and see that he had two different colored eyes. One was a lighter green and the other was darker. "You're a feisty one, aren't you, Ivy?"

His closeness was much like a sweet, cool breeze across her clammy skin. It felt good, and she didn't like it. She blurted, "It's no secret your life has been--" She carefully searched for the right word. "--*eventful* in the media." Had he taken another step closer? She needed to get away but the only way she had to go was out the window or through him. "Why are you standing so close?"

His eyes were focused on her lips. Did he want to kiss her? "How many times are you going to do that?"

"Do what?" Her words were a whisper.

"Invite me to kiss you?"

She opened her mouth and nothing came out. It took a good five seconds before the words traveled from her near-man-alert brain to her tongue. "I'm inviting you to do no such thing." Her voice cracked.

He reached up, took one silky strand of her hair, wrapped it around his finger and lifted it to his nose. Ivy thought men only did such things in romance novels. It especially didn't happen in her life. "I've lost count on the times you've looked at me and silently asked me to kiss you."

"You can't count very high, can you?" She couldn't believe he had the nerve to accuse her of such ludicrous nonsense. He could make her all hot inside, but she didn't want him to kiss her. Hell no. "Do you come with a badge of warning--insanely arrogant, converse with at your own risk?"

He dropped the wisp of hair. "In my attempt to prove a point to you the reason behind it is lost between my rapidly beating heart and the bulge behind my zipper." His eyes were molten. That should have been warning enough to stand clear. "Don't worry, Ivy. Although physically I am a red-blooded male, fact is, you're not my type."

She stiffened. Why had his comment been a direct hit to her ego? Why should she care what his type was and whether she matched the criteria? He was hot, sure, but not her style, either. She liked men who were kind, sweet and worth a damn. "What are you doing in Morgan Sites, Max? Shouldn't you be off in some other part of the country pointing and clicking your equipment?"

His jaw tensed underneath a five o'clock shadow. "I'm curious, Ivy, is it safe to take time away from your newspaper? Aren't there a few more leprechauns that are in need of saving from elderly criminals?"

She cringed but kept her back straight. No cowering under his ego. Men like Max thrived on other people's weaknesses. "It was a gnome. And it was only one story." Dammit! She knew that story would somehow come around to haunt her. Just why did it have to be from a man like Max Shepard? "I'll admit, it'll win no Pulitzer Prize, but it served its purpose."

"I bet it did."

She could not argue with him on this subject. There was no defense she could use. He'd been all over the world. He was known for his work. She swallowed the lump in her throat. "Divorce can make someone bitter--"

His face went cold. She realized immediately this was a point of contention for him. Wasn't she trying to douse it and not add flame to the fire? She'd only meant to say that he had a right to be angry, but she'd screwed that up.

"That explains a lot," he snapped. "You read all this information in a gossip column and that makes it all fact? That is one self-promoting, underhanded writer to another. There's no reason for me to indulge in your opinions or knowledge any further since you know all you need to know about me." He turned on his heel and started for the door. "Now, if you'll excuse me, I think we're finished convincing each other we belong here."

Ivy watched in perplexed silence as he stomped out of the room. He'd made her angry and she had unleashed on him. She didn't believe everything she'd read in the tabloids. No one would want something so detrimental to be slammed in his face, especially by a stranger. The media had already torn him apart.

But there was something more important going on here. Why was he in Morgan Sites? And something else…

This wasn't going to be easy. He was a dangerous man. He could wreak pandemonium on her senses with one look. She wasn't the type to fall for any man's macho tactics, especially one with an ego the size of a football field. If he thought he could bully her he was sadly mistaken. She may be younger and less achieved than him, but she was smarter, she'd guarantee that.

Chapter 4

Blowing off her frustration for the useless argument with a pigheaded man, Ivy headed straight for her food rations. She had a tendency to eat when she was upset. Chocolate was always top choice. She fumbled through her supplies and didn't find one ounce of chocolate. Her choices: a granola bar or an apple. Grabbing the apple and her cell phone, she went to explore her surroundings. She was certain if she looked hard enough she'd find something to satisfy her curiosity. And she'd get a big kick out of finding something before Mr. Ghost Detective.

The kitchen was the first room on her list. It was in dire need of a caring touch and a broom. Besides old-fashioned wooden cabinets, cracked countertops, and an old stainless steel sink, there was a small decrepit table.

Opening each cabinet door, she peeked in, did a brushing of her hand inside and was disappointed to find nothing except mouse droppings and a box of matches.

Next place: upstairs.

She was excited to explore the master bedroom. Passing through the bedroom the first time, Ivy had assumed the door by the bed was a closet. Now, she opened it and was shocked to find a nursery. The antique wooden bassinet and rocking chair looked desolate in the barren room. Lacy curtains yellowed with age hung haphazardly at the window. Ivy's heart pained. She knew the history.

Records showed that Marcus Thornton's first child had perished in a fire around the age of five, along with his wife, Sarah, in their home in Boston. Years later he had married his second wife, Elizabeth, and she died during childbirth a mere year and a half into their marriage. There was no written history of a live child being born, so it was believed that the baby had died too. Fifteen months later, Marcus died. Townspeople said it was from a broken heart. The entire heritage had died away.

The story was a wretched and sorrowful history of loss and tragedy.

Ivy opened the door to the closet. A strong whiff of dust came barreling out. Coughing, she started to close it. She almost missed seeing something in the far corner. She stepped into the small space, opening the door as wide as it would go to allow light in. She saw it was a painting. Kneeling down onto her hands and knees, careless of her clothes on the grimy floor, she lifted the frame only to realize there was another behind it. Her heart raced.

"What did you find?"

She jumped. The deep voice behind her had startled her. She turned and eyed Max with fury. She hadn't heard him come into the room. "Do you have to sneak around?" she snapped.

"A little jumpy, are you?" He cocked an eyebrow. One corner of his mouth lifted as if he were happy to see her unsettled.

The man had the ability to scrape her nerves like fingernails down a chalkboard. She wasn't sure if it was because of his overinflated ego or the fact that every time he came near she felt an unfamiliar tingling down her spine. "Make yourself useful."

Ivy fumbled with the paintings until they could easily be pulled through the doorway.

She lifted the first painting to Max. He stared down at it with narrowed eyes. He blew his breath across the dusty frame and a cloud of dirt surrounded them. She coughed again as her lungs filled with the particles.

"Nice," he said sarcastically.

Then came the second. It was in worse condition.

"I can't believe these paintings were tossed into a closet." She swiped her dirty hands across the legs of her pants. They were covered in cobwebs and grime. It was too late to worry about cleanliness.

"It seems they should be hanging up instead of shoved into the darkness." Max set the paintings against the wall and they stood back to stare at their find.

The first painting was a portrait of a beautiful woman. Her raven hair cascaded like swirling waves over her bare shoulders and along the exquisite green lace gown she wore. The ornate gown was the only sign of wealth. She was bare of expensive jewelry and the kind of trendy hairstyle that most women of riches would have adorned their bodies with, especially for a portrait. The woman's enchanting green eyes spoke volumes in the finely painted portrait. It was Elizabeth Thornton.

The next painting was of a man. Ivy knew it was Marcus from an old picture she had seen of him. However, his exquisite good looks, intense dark eyes and hair like the midnight sky all seemed oddly familiar. He was standing by the fireplace downstairs, his chin rested on his fist. He carried an expression of a man in deep thought.

Both paintings were superb.

Ivy turned each of them over. To her surprise, scrawled in one corner on each painting was the name *Elizabeth*. "Elizabeth painted these. Marcus's second wife was an artist. A good one, so it appears."

"The paintings seem--" Max seemed perplexed. "--haunting."

He was right. There was a quality to both paintings that exuded deep emotion. Ivy was overcome with such sentiment. Tears sprang to her eyes. She swiped them before they fell to her cheeks.

A draft of cold air passed through the room. The hairs on the back of her neck rose. She wrapped her arms around her chilled body as she kept her eyes on the paintings. She felt Max's eyes on her. Minutes seemed to pass in slow increments until he finally asked, "What do you know of this house's history?"

She swallowed as she searched for her voice. "I really know so little about Marcus and Elizabeth. There was only a minuscule amount of research I had luck in uncovering. Most of the information comes from years of rumors passed down from generation to generation. Each tale gets juicier and further from the truth, I'm sure. There is probably only a figment of fact left to any of them. But one legend still remains the same." She looked up at him, hoping he couldn't see the remnants of tears left in her eyes. "Marcus was known for his kindness. History labeled him as quite the charming gentleman who'd had more than a few single, and married, women interested. He was roguishly handsome, as we can see by his portrait--" She darted a glance back at the man in the painting. "--passionate, and exceptionally wealthy."

"But as you said yourself, they could have molded his memory into a kind man. It seems a man can be shaped by the untruths of others."

Ivy understood there was hidden meaning to his words. He was referring to himself and how the media had dogged him for months until he disappeared from the spotlight. And then he was criticized for running away. "I find that if a yarn gets twisted it's usually to make the person bad, not good." There was a flash of something that passed over his features. It was gone before she had time to investigate it. "Some of Morgan Sites's oldest residents said that Elizabeth's father worked here, on the farm. Marcus established his riches through an inheritance but acquired his fame by way of farming and real estate. The details of his career are vague, but he was known for building the economy of the town."

"Do you know any particulars about his and Elizabeth's marriage?" Max took a step closer to Elizabeth's painting. He lifted it, holding it out for closer examination.

"Elizabeth was said to have been in her late teens and Marcus in his thirties when they married in the late 1800s. Age wasn't of much concern, I'm sure. It hadn't been unusual for an older man to marry a young woman, especially a man as wealthy as Marcus. He was probably the prime catch for young and old." Aspects of the story that she'd heard and read became clearer to her. As if it had been only yesterday that she'd learned the facts.

Max set the painting back against the wall. He strode to the window and stared out. Ivy wondered what thoughts crossed his mind. She brought her attention back to the portraits. She couldn't deny that she found the intensity of their eyes mesmerizing. It was almost as if Marcus and Elizabeth pulled her into their paintings, tugging her into the molten colors. Although it didn't appear that Elizabeth had painted herself with the intention of seduction, Ivy thought that the young woman staring back at her from the canvas was bewitching by nature. Any woman, with even the slightest amount of pretension, would have been bejeweled with diamonds and gold in her own portrait. Marcus could have afforded to adorn her with the finest jewelry. Elizabeth had deliberately painted herself as a simple, demure woman. Her beauty was enough embellishment.

"I wonder what type of person Elizabeth was," Ivy wondered aloud. "Was she madly in love with her husband? Was he crazy in love with her? Did they share great happiness before tragedy struck? Did Marcus die a heartbroken man after losing all his loved ones?"

Max's chuckle reverberated off the bare walls. "If you believe in all that romantic bullshit."

Ivy turned on her heel and swiped a stray tendril of hair off her cheek. "Some people do believe in love."

He snagged her with a cold stare, then pushed away from the window and started for the door. It slammed shut before he reached it.

Ivy's breath swooshed from her lungs. "Did you do that?" She wasn't sure if what she saw was accurate.

There was a slight hesitation before he muttered, "What the hell?"

* * * *

Max had seen a lot of strange things over the course of his career as a ghost hunter. He'd seen enough outlandish events that he'd written books on haunting and mystical spirits, sold millions of copies, but he'd never been invaded with the kind of deep-rooted sense of unease he felt at that moment.

But even with everything he'd seen over the years, he still didn't chalk anything up to paranormal unless he had proof. A slamming door wasn't enough to have him calling it a ghost at work.

He jiggled the knob, but the door didn't open. "It's locked." He gritted his teeth. "Damn old house. It must have been a draft."

"Yeah, must have been."

He could hear the speculation in Ivy's voice. She looked a bit green around the edges. He laughed. "You scared?"

She turned her lips down at the corners and she shot him her priceless "I could slap you" stare. "No, I'm not scared." She blew a long breath through tight lips. "How will we get out of here?"

"Relax." He gripped the handle again but it wasn't giving. Just when he thought he couldn't be more miserable, something happened to prove that things could always get worse. When Ivy started tapping her foot in frustration, he knew it had gotten bad. He wanted out of the room.

Running his hands along the frame, he quickly realized that he wasn't going to break the door. It was solid wood, thicker than doors made now. He turned and looked at the window. He sighed in irritation. "I guess I gotta do what I gotta do."

"Through the window? That's what your big idea is?"

"Do you have another way out in mind?" She remained quiet. "Didn't think so."

To his luck, the window rolled up easily and was large enough to accommodate his size. Once he placed one foot on the roof, he silently hoped that it would hold his weight. He didn't trust its durability.

With both feet planted firmly on the wood, he tapped lightly and stomped and checked out the best way down. Nothing looked safe, but he'd been in tougher situations. Satisfied that he wouldn't fall through, he made his way slowly across the unevenly-shaped shingles toward the edge.

And there he stopped. The only way to the ground was either jumping, which risked death--not going to happen--or the rickety trellis that looked to be a relic from when the Thorntons called this place home. The paint had chipped and parts were broken. Bending, he pushed the lattice and investigated its strength. It didn't move, but that didn't mean anything. It was nailed to the side of the house securely but he wasn't sure how decayed the wood was. With great caution, he scaled the lattice, securing his footing with each step. The old wood creaked and cracked under his weight, warning him that an apparatus meant for a climbing bush wasn't built for this.

Half way down, a loud splintering sounded seconds before he felt shaking and the loosening of the boards. "Shit."

The lattice completely separated from the house.

* * * *

Ivy heard the stomping of Max's footsteps long before he opened the door. She had a feeling something was wrong. When the door swung open and she saw his bitter expression and the disarray of his clothes, she had a good idea what had happened. "Are you okay?" she asked.

"As happy as a pig eating slop." He had pieces of foliage in his hair. A long scratch ran down his cheek.

"Thank you for opening the door."

"Was there another option?" With a turn on his heel, he marched back down the hall. She could hear the thumping of his boots all the way.

Her cell rang and she saw the ID was her mother. "Mom, you okay?"

"I'm fine, dear. Just checking in."

"Great."

"Is that old place safe enough for you to be staying in?"

"Besides a few cobwebs, I think it'll suffice." Ivy hoped.

"Where will you be sleeping?"

Ivy smiled at her mother's sincere interrogation. "In the master suite. You wouldn't believe how lovely it is."

"Take pictures. Is there electricity? How will you eat? You'll eat properly, right?"

"Yes, Mom. I'll be fine. The house isn't the problem. I have a much bigger issue."

"Oh no, you sound miserable. Is it that bad? And *please,* don't leave out the juicy details." Her mother's chuckle vibrated the phone line.

"Juicy details? I'm not sure they could be referred to as juicy," Ivy said. "Although, we did have a small disagreement." She glanced to make sure she was still alone.

"Oh really?"

"Now I understand what 'bighead' means. Max is the most egotistical, arrogant jerk I've ever met. I should have just let his arrogance slide in one ear and out the other, but you know me. I get long-winded when I'm upset or nervous. Why am I such a big-mouth? Is there something in our gene pool that causes us to talk too much?"

"That's certainly not a bad thing, dear. Sometimes it's necessary to tell others how we feel, to shine light on their bad behavior, just as long as we don't lash out as a way to hide our own issues."

Ivy didn't want to ask her mother what she meant. She had a feeling she already knew. "Max and I just have to get along for the next two weeks. I don't want to be here with him any more than he wants to be here with me. He is the most deplorable man I've ever met."

"This is your biggest lesson as a writer. You have to grin and bear it, even when you think it's impossible."

"At least he's nice to look at." Ivy admitted. She would definitely enjoy watching him as long as he didn't open his mouth. But good looks didn't make someone nice. If a person was ugly on the inside it didn't take long for the nastiness to seep to the outside.

Finishing the call, she went downstairs and into the sitting room where she found the devil himself sitting on the floor, slumped over his camera equipment in concentration. He either didn't hear her enter or he was just simply ignoring her. If she had to bet she'd go with the latter. She saw that he had changed his shirt and picked the foliage out of his thick, dark hair.

Ivy meandered over to the fireplace and stood there for a few minutes. He still paid her no attention. She couldn't understand why he was pissed at her. She hadn't caused him to fall into the bushes.

With a dramatic sigh, she moved over to the small, flowered sofa, patted the cushions and took a seat. It was actually quite comfortable. She tucked her feet up and leaned her chin against her propped-up hand.

Ivy made an attempt to keep her eyes off Max's profile. She found it impossible. Somehow the man was like a magnet drawing her attention. She watched his long, lean fingers as they moved deftly in unscrewing the converter lens from the camera. He had nice hands. Large, and his nails were clean. She wondered what those fingers would feel like on her body. Was he as much of an expert on lovemaking as he was hunting ghosts and writing about it?

She swallowed with difficulty. Was she crushing on the delusional man? She would never--nor did she want to--know what making love with Max Shepard would be like. So why would she even drift down that impossible path? She liked gentle and kind men. Would a man like Max take his bed rules as seriously as he did his work rules--serious and raw? Or would he rush through lovemaking like an adrenaline junkie needing a fix? *Wam, bam, thank you ma'am.* No thank you. She could imagine that he was skilled at sex but not in communication.

It did strike her that, while maybe she was being a little presumptuous regarding Max's character, she doubted she was too far off target. She'd seen a few of his pictures in the tabloids since his divorce. He seemed to enjoy women who had more beauty than brains. Once he dated a popular actress who was known for her role as "the dumb blonde" on TV and off.

It wasn't all his fault, she was sure. He probably had more than a few women who would find nothing more pleasurable than hitting the sack with him. He exuded masculinity and sexuality.

So why then did she notice these tempting qualities? She wasn't interested in accompanying herself with fast men. Ivy had a clue why. She didn't believe it had anything to do with his appeal. It was the bad boy attitude. It was intriguing. He was nothing like the men in Morgan Sites.

She gave a stretch of her arms over her head and sighed. It was starting to get dark outside and the room was falling into a shadow. The silence was irritating. "I guess I should take my bags upstairs to the bedroom." No response. "Hmm, it's getting late." Just as she suspected, he still didn't respond. "So no issue with me sleeping in the beautiful master suite, I hope?"

"If you talk in your sleep as much as you do when you're awake, I'll be happy that you've chosen the room farthest away from mine."

She narrowed her eyes. Could the man say anything without proving he had a hair up his ass? "I don't talk in my sleep." At least she didn't think she did.

"Good." He took a soft cloth and rubbed the lens.

"Will you be up late taking pictures?" she asked.

"Yes." He looked at her strangely. "There you are, trying to smooth things again."

Ivy refused to allow him to anger her. "I guess I should ask, do you snore? I can't stand to hear anyone snoring." She pretended interest in a loose string hanging from the frayed material of the settee.

Max went back to cleaning his camera. "Why? Do you plan to sleep with me?" His voice held not even an ounce of humiliation.

She'd walked right into that verbal trap. He wasn't even looking at her when he said his words and the sexual innuendo made her squirm in her seat. She was ashamed. Her body betrayed her.

She was beginning to expect everything and anything from this man who apparently had no mortification. "Only in your dreams, Max," she stated firmly. "I must tell you, I don't sleep around on the job. But no worries. I'm not your type, right?"

"Thanks for the clarification. I'll remember that." He set his camera down and looked her directly in the eye. Her breath quickened. "I have a rule that I don't sleep around on the job either, especially with someone who I'm not even sure I like, but if you don't quit looking at me like that I may change my mind. Now, you wouldn't want that on your conscience, would you?"

His voice was smooth and confident. She eyed him curiously, wondering if he were joking. The set of his jaw went hard. "I think you're forgetting that I'd have to be interested, which I'm not."

"Oh, you're interested." He lifted the corners of his mouth into a perfect mocking smile.

"Go ahead and poke fun. Some people would think this situation could get a little awkward. I just wanted to make things clear and to let you know that I don't plan on allowing intimacy to become an issue."

He sighed and rubbed his eyebrows. "Do you feel that you must make everything clear to everyone as it pops into your mind? We are just here to do our individual jobs, not to share every aspect of our existence."

"Oh, I'm sorry that I'm not as seasoned as you are in proper etiquette in a situation like this. I guess it's the huge age difference that makes us so different." She smiled. "No response?" she pushed.

"I'm not about to encircle myself in a verbal duel over age. I'd be the first to concede that I am older than you and have lived more life. If I had to guess, I'd say I'm older by at least ten years. So, I figure, since you're expecting me to tolerate your non-stop chatter and candor, you should be willing to accept my solitude. If you'd like to rationalize it's a matter of an age difference, I'm fine with that."

Silence fell between them as he finished his work. She bit her bottom lip, controlling her words, but she hated the quiet. And the cold. The temperature was dropping and the room was growing bitter. "Wow, this place is really cold."

He responded by clearing his throat.

"Alrighty, then." She got up and went to the fireplace, busying herself cleaning out the cobwebs. The alcove looked to be in reasonably good working condition. It was obvious the place wasn't insulated. She wanted to start a fire, but there was a problem. She'd never used a real fireplace before. At home, they had a gas fireplace and the flames came alive with a flip of a switch.

Grabbing a look at Max, she saw that he was still putting away the equipment. She supposed he was capable of starting a fire but she wasn't about to ask him to lend a hand.

There was a stack of wood in a large wicker basket sitting next to the fireplace. She didn't remember seeing it there before and wondered if Max had gathered it while she was upstairs. So, he did have some sense of responsibility and gentlemanly deeds.

She remembered watching a documentary on survival on a cable channel. There was a military man who demonstrated the best way to start a fire. Although she had no flint or dry grass or any other means that he'd used, she knew it couldn't be that hard. All that she needed was a box of matches or a lighter. She had a lighter in her purse.

Retrieving the lighter, she strategically placed wood in the bay.

Chapter 5

Max smiled as he watched Ivy's best effort to attempt to get a fire going.

He tried to ignore her, but damn, he found her amusing--in a good way.

He figured a gentleman would offer his help because it didn't seem that she had the slightest clue on how to get the fire to stay lit. He had to give her credit on two points; one, she was attempting to make a fire. He didn't doubt that Renee would freeze to death before risking breaking a nail. And, two, Ivy looked sexy as hell bent over at the waist with her hair falling in silky waves around her face. She'd taken it down from the earlier style and he hadn't realized how long it was.

How was it that some women didn't have to do anything to make a man's heart beat out of his chest? Did Ivy have any idea how the curve of her bottom brought images of her naked and him standing behind her doing what he hadn't stopped thinking about since the moment she landed on him upstairs? With any other woman he would have already gotten the sexual tension out of the way and showed her how skilled he was in bed. But not Ivy. Not now. Not ever.

There were just some women one didn't have to sultry sex with unless the third finger had a ring on it. Ivy was one of 'em. She was innocent. He had known that the moment he'd cornered her in the bedroom upstairs and she had gotten the look of a frightened deer caught in headlights.

Point was, she was certainly not the type one slept with without a solid commitment.

Especially by a man like him.

She thought he was rude and an introvert. He was exactly that. He was a self-proclaimed recluse. Especially when he was on a job. He liked to work alone. That's how he'd always done things and that's what he preferred.

Loner or not, he was a healthy, red-blooded male who was attracted to the opposite sex, particularly when they were fervid and fiery like Ivy Kennedy. A woman who didn't know her own power. Her impetuous attitude kept him on his toes while her inadvertent sexual come-ons kept him rock hard. And it was only day one.

Ivy was definitely nothing like Renee, nor his ex-wife. Both Renee and Marie were models: tall, dangerously beautiful, and dangerously fake. Ivy was natural, and she gave the persona that what one saw was what one got.

And he had read her work.

No doubt she was wasting her time on two-bit stories, but she had a good writing style. He may have hounded her earlier about the leper--*or rather, gnome*--but he had found her column to be humorous and deeply motivational. Her style reminded him of an old friend he'd known from school who wrote best-selling novels. His friend had started her career as a columnist.

He guessed there was a lot to learn from Ivy. He'd bet during the next few weeks she'd allow him a glimpse.

He watched Ivy reach for the wood. She jerked her hand back. "Damn," she mumbled. The injured finger went into her mouth. A heated tingle rushed through Max as she suckled the finger. He needed to do something soon to cool his head before he crossed a proverbial line.

Doing something smart was shot to hell, he thought, as he got up from the floor and crossed the room toward Ivy instead of away from her. "Splinter?" he asked.

She nodded. "A big one."

He took her hand into his. It was only minor to him, but she was acting like it was a gash instead of a small sliver of wood. He'd seen people impaled with chunks of material after an explosion so it was hard to have compassion for one little splinter. But, surprisingly, he did feel something odd and unfamiliar. He found himself wanting to take care of her.

That's when he dropped her hand like a hot potato. No way would he allow himself to be drawn in. Gaining his equilibrium, he stuck his fist into his front pocket. His indecision reminded him of a rat trying to make it through a maze. "Do you have a needle?" he asked. She shook her head. He didn't carry needles with him in the field. Splinters were easily dealt with by other means. He wasn't sure she would be delighted with the resource he used. "Does it hurt?"

She nodded. Her eyes were curious. He wondered if it hurt that bad or if she was shell-shocked from the feeling of his touch.

"Will you trust me to get it out?" he asked. He took his hand from his pocket.

"Ok."

"Be right back." He went and grabbed his pocket knife from his camera bag. He came back to her side and took the lighter from her. He opened the knife. She looked up at him. Her eyes widened. He held it above the flame of the lighter.

"What... What are you doing? And what in heaven's name have I agreed to?"

"I'm sanitizing the blade." He snuffed the flame, satisfied that the knife was clean.

"I kind of got that but why are you sanitizing your blade?" She gulped.

"To remove the splinter." He wasn't a bit put off by her fear.

He felt her eyes on his face. "You're serious."

"Yes."

"Oh, no you're not." She pulled back her hand.

He resisted the urge to smile. "I've done this a million times and I'm good at it. I promise."

He saw sweat bead on her upper lip. "Promise until the cows come home, but you're not using that--" Her eyes lowered to the sharp blade. "--on this tiny splinter."

"I never would have guessed." He shook his head.

"Guessed what?"

"That you're a coward."

"You're good, real good, I'll give you that. You know just the right words to push me, and even though I know you're pulling some form of psychotherapy mumbo jumbo on me, I won't be labeled a coward." She glanced from him to the knife then back to him. "Keep in mind, if it hurts, I scream."

"I have no doubt. I bet those vocal chords are good for more than just talking a lot." He ignored her snort. He took her hand into his larger one and examined the piece of wood lodged into the flesh. It wasn't too deep, but it was a long slice. He glanced at her and she winced. "I haven't started."

"I know." She peeked at him through one narrowed eye.

"Don't watch," he advised her. The last thing he needed was her to pass out. She did as he asked. Working quickly, he used the tip of the knife to lift the splinter. His fingers were too big to grab hold so he brought the finger to his mouth. He heard the sharp intake of her breath as he used his teeth as tweezers. He spat the splinter into the fireplace. "All done."

"All done? That's it?"

He smiled. Was there disappointment in her voice? Her blue eyes were bright and her face flushed. She was not a woman who'd had a splinter removed, but instead one who was turned on. He knew that look. He hardened and his breathing deepened.

Her eyes dropped to the crotch of his jeans. She must have read his thoughts. Her tongue darted out and swept across the soft curve of her bottom lip. Damn--the look and the lick were enough to drive him to the edge.

He swiped his palm down his leg and cursed the fact that his libido was as active as always. This was one circumstance he needed man's worst fear: erectile dysfunction.

What was the attraction? He swept his eyes along her high cheekbones and mouth, which now seemed full and luscious. Her breasts pressed against her shirt as she breathed in and out. They weren't large--hell, not even close. But that didn't deter his palm from wanting to mold them to his touch. Her body was thin--too thin. Yet she had curves in all the right places.

Was he losing his mind?

Ivy was like a breath of fresh air to him. Maybe that was the attraction. Some sort of conundrum. She was completely the opposite of his "type."

The woman had managed to bruise him, infuriate him, verbally insult him, and attain his enticement all in a scarce day's time. He agonized to think of all the time they still had together under one roof. What could happen next? He didn't like this rise and fall of sensation, yet somehow, it intrigued him. And he wasn't a man easily moved.

She arched her mouth into a smile. It set her eyes aglow. The woman was an open book. She wanted his kiss, he knew it. Why did she leave her feelings open for everyone's perusal? The big-bad-wolf disorder climbed his veins and settled into his conscious. He was the wolf and poor little red riding Ivy played her innocence like a fiddle. What was worse--she *was* naive.

Yep, that had to be the appeal for him. Incorruptibility. He didn't see that too often. He'd get over the lust.

Lust. Powerful enough to take over any man's mind and body like a swift and forceful subsistence. He wasn't immune.

* * * *

Ivy breathed in deeply. The unspoken attraction between her and Max was like a suffocating blast of heat. She wanted him to kiss her, oh how she wanted it, but he wasn't making the move. She even waited, giving him what she thought was her best smile.

Nothing.

Irritation swept over her like needles pricking her skin. "Thanks for helping me." She kept her eyes on his face, not allowing them to drift down again to his obvious sign of arousal. Yes, she'd thought he was aroused. But then why hadn't he kissed her?

Her head still reeled from his touch. She'd never been more turned on at something so minuscule as seeing her hand held in his much larger one. The calluses on his palm and the slight rough skin on his knuckles were evidence that he worked with his hands a lot. The warmth of his fingers had engaged her thoughts as she imagined them on her bare skin, flicking her hardened nipples and following with his mouth. She'd felt no pain as he wedged the splinter from her skin, but what he'd done after the knife would be a memory embedded inside her mind. She'd thought maybe it was part of her seductive daydream until she opened her eyes and saw her finger in his mouth. She was certain now she'd gotten extra special attention. He'd swirled his tongue around the flesh, and gently guided his teeth down the skin, removing the wood. He'd awakened new senses inside her body. He'd triggered a stirring between her legs followed by a moistness in her panties.

But now he pulled back--way back. She saw the cold surface in his eyes. She needed to let it go. "Are you that good at starting a fire?" she asked.

"I'm good--at a lot of things."

What did that mean? Was he flirting with her? Could he really move from hot and cold that fast? She grew even angrier. "Can you prove it? A gentleman would."

"I never said I was a gentleman," he stated.

"Are you going to make me ask?" She sighed heavily.

"Asking would have been a nice effect."

"Offering without my coaxing would have been nice, too." The man deserved an award for annoyance. "Are you going to quit acting like a ding-dong and start the fire?"

"Ding-dong? Are we in the fifth grade?" He laughed.

"Okay…stop acting like a dick. Does that better suit you?"

He laughed harder. Did anything bring down the man's ego? She didn't say another word and neither did he. She stood there, next to him, and watched him effortlessly start a blazing fire. She almost felt like it was a blow to her ego. He didn't rub it in but she guessed he'd wanted to.

When the fire was alive, warming the room, he said, "I hope you like beans."

She eyed him curiously. Her mind was still stuck on sex, not food. "Yes. Why?"

"Beans are my specialty in the field."

Ivy laughed. She'd guess a lot of things were this man's specialty, just as he'd hinted earlier, and none of her thoughts were decent.

* * * *

Several hours later, after sharing a meal of brown sugar beans and roasted marshmallows, Max and Ivy sat in front of the fire. He poured cups of coffee for them while she relaxed on the small sofa. The night had fallen and the only light came from the golden flames. The house seemed unusually quiet. Ivy was surprised Max hadn't set up his equipment yet. She couldn't deny her interest in wanting to see how the hunting took place. She'd seen movies based on paranormal activity hunts but nothing in person.

She glanced at his profile, fighting the urge to ask about his work. Did she want him to know that she was fascinated? As he stared into the fire, she followed the lines of his prominent features. He looked like a warrior with dancing red eyes reflecting the fiery blaze, his thick dark hair and square jaw covered in a shadow of beard. His legs seemed to stretch for miles. His boots and jeans were worn, telling her he had on his favorite clothes.

He turned and their eyes met. Instead of pulling away, she held steady. A moment of tense silence passed until he moved and grabbed a plastic bag from his backpack. He held it up. "Jerky?"

She refused the first but graciously accepted the coffee. She sipped the hot brew and the bitter taste enlightened her taste buds. "Wow, strong."

"Sorry, no fluff coffee with all the flavoring and whipped topping that people like these days. Just honest to goodness black joe."

"It's good. So were the beans. You must be a pro at cooking over the fire."

He looked at her. His eyes were like sparks of ember. "It's amazing what a person can do when they're hungry."

She ran her finger around the rim of the paper cup. The steam warmed her palm. "I read that you were in the Marines, and after your service you went straight into journalism. Do you miss being a journalist?" She dared to pry, half expecting that he'd snub her investigation into his personal life.

He shrugged a broad shoulder. "There are times, but now isn't one of them."

"Because you enjoy ghost hunting?"

He seemed to toss the question around. "Great job." He curved his mouth into a perceptive smile. "Who wouldn't like it?"

She didn't answer.

He read into her silence. "I think we've already established that you don't think much of my career choice."

"I guess it's just one of those things I don't understand. It's similar to people who believe that snakes hold healing powers. What do these people prove but only that they enjoy playing with snakes?" She stared back into the flames.

"Don't think anyone has ever compared my job to a snake handler's."

"I wasn't comparing the two." She was a bit embarrassed. Seeing his disbelieving expression, she sighed. "I said that, didn't I?"

"You actually said that," he said.

"I'm sorry." She was apologizing not only for his sake but hers as well. "You are a bestselling author with enough fans to fill this house a hundred times over. That proves you have the ability to reach the public."

"But you still aren't a believer?" He lifted a dark eyebrow, challenging her.

She couldn't mince her words. "No, I'm not a believer."

Max leisurely extended his six-foot-two frame in front of the fire and relaxed on his elbows. He turned his head slightly to look at her. "It was a fluke that began my career in hunting. I had been doing investigative journalism and a buddy of mine, Pete, who was also a journalist, was doing a story on a missing girl who'd been kidnapped from her bed during the night. Pete had been following the story closely for months and he told me that the child's family was so distraught that they'd called in a psychic to help in the search." His chuckle bounced off the wall. "Pete and I thought it was the biggest waste of time for this family to rely on a clairvoyant. Out of curiosity, I went along with Pete to check out what crap this psychic would pull."

Ivy unconsciously moved further on the edge of the seat. His voice and the topic of conversation drew her in.

He continued, "Let's just say what I saw that night changed my mind. I saw a complete stranger lead a family to the very place where their daughter lay dead." He paused a long moment. She was certain he didn't want her to hear the emotion filling his voice. "Being the curious investigator that I was, I wanted to learn more about the spirit world and if there was such a thing. What started as a story that I followed for maybe three months, four months tops, turned into a career of ghost hunting. The fascination and intrigue is always there."

He hadn't said more than two words to her since the splinter incident, or since he'd arrived, for that matter, and she found she liked hearing him talk. "Why this place, Max? Why Thornton House?"

"Why not?"

"This place--" She moved her hands through the air, encompassing the room. "--is small scale considering the highly publicized specials you investigate."

"Ivy, I began my investigations in places just like this."

She nodded. There wasn't much defense she could find, but she still didn't believe his intentions and purpose regarding the house were strictly ghost hunting, but to find out the truth she'd need to get on his good side. "Max, it wasn't fair of me to bring up the past, your past, earlier, especially when it's none of my business." She wasn't too proud to apologize.

"No problem."

"Yes, it is." She needed for him to hear her thoughts. "It bothered you and it wasn't right. We all have turmoil in our lives."

"Let me get this straight." He brought his eyes back to meet hers. She couldn't see them, but she could feel their laser heat. "You're arguing your apology for our earlier argument? Why not just accept that I said it's all okay?"

"I'm not starting another argument. I only want to get things out in the open. I feel bad that I was so mean. I read the articles written about your divorce. They were awful. At a time in a couple's life where things are going south, they don't need it run through the media."

He remained quiet.

"There was one writer who threw most of the dirt. Dan Archer."

He clenched his jaw. "Dan's version was one of the first printed stories on my divorce. I counted thirty lies in one story. No one took into account that the bastard was known for his lower-than-scum stories." He sighed. "Those bastards enjoyed slamming me to earn a buck."

"But not all journalists are the same, or have the same moral code." She finished off the last sip of coffee. "I don't think you're a cold-hearted bastard, Max, like the papers said."

There was a long release of breath. "You believed it.'

"Okay, maybe I did think that at first. I was wrong. You do have some good qualities."

"And what are those qualities?"

A cold draft swept through the room and Ivy hugged herself. Even the blazing fire didn't take away the chill. "I'm pretty sure you are just a man with hidden emotions and kindness bursting to get to the surface. You can only exist so long before that layer of ice melts and the true you springs into life."

"Lord, Ivy, you're a Hallmark commercial. Word of advice, don't hold your breath." There was conviction to his words.

"I'm pretty sure you're not a psycho ready to snap with a wee little push."

"Pretty sure, eh?" Humor laced his tone.

"Yup, I'm fairly confident you're not psychotic. However, I won't change my mind that you have an ego the size of the Atlantic Ocean."

"That's okay. I'm still questioning your mental and emotional state as well."

He was joking, right? She wasn't clear. "I'm not such a bad person. I do speak before I think. I'm actually just your average girl next door."

He laughed. "I'd bet you're anything but an average girl."

She bit her bottom lip in thought. "Well ..." She carefully selected her words. "I'll just let you find out on your own." Did she just invite him to get to know her better? Geesh…what was in the coffee?

"I already know a lot about you, Ivy." The burning wood popping and cracking was the only sound in the room. "I'm beginning to get the idea that you're not as innocent as I first thought. You're a bit of a mystery and a tease."

Her breath caught in her lungs. Where was this conversation headed? Was he turning the tables and teasing her? Did he truly care who she was and what made her tick? "I'm not as mysterious as you may think. What you see is what you get. And a tease? I wouldn't know where to begin."

"Just what I expected you to say. You're more perplexing than you give yourself credit for. And that is why you need to go to bed before we delve much deeper into this line of conversation. Some things are best left undisturbed."

She was curious; what exactly did he mean? Was he afraid that something would happen between them? He didn't seem like the type to be afraid of a woman, so what about her had spooked him? "One thing, Max."

"What's that?"

"Why are you really here?"

"Same reason as you, but the difference is, you're looking for a story and I'm looking for a ghost."

"Too elementary." She tapped her short fingernail against the cup. "I'm here because you are. That's obvious. If you're interested in this old place for more than ghosts, I want to know why. You're hiding something."

"I hate to tell you, but there's nothing left on me that hasn't been written or told already. And I won't be your story, Ivy."

She sighed heavily. He was a hard nut to crack. Fumbling with the lacey edge of her shirt, she hesitated in thought before saying, "You haven't given a personal interview since before your divorce. Why not? I'm sure you've been asked."

A dark cloud filled the room. "I hate giving interviews. And if you're askin' for me to give it up, the answer's no. The story's been told," he stated blankly.

She'd let it rest. For now. She'd learned that Max Shepard wasn't a man who liked being pushed.

The chill was seeping deeper into her bones and her eyes were becoming grainy from lack of sleep. Without a word to him, she got up from the couch and headed for the stairs. She had her purse light and had started to turn it on when she heard Max say, "The electric works."

Examining the wall for the light switch, she found the plastic knob. The light hanging from the ceiling came aglow. "That's strange."

"What is?" Max asked.

"The lights here weren't working earlier. Did you fix them?"

"Sure, I took out my twelve foot ladder, climbed up and somehow fixed the lighting unbeknownst to you. I'm just good like that."

She smirked. "Just asking." She started up the wooden stairs, each step creaking in protest. If one didn't know better they'd think the house was ready to fall to the ground. But Ivy had a feeling this old place could withstand much more than two people spending a few nights in it. Before disappearing around the top of the staircase she stopped and looked down at him. He was staring into the fire. "Will you be up late investigating?"

"Sure will. Wanna help?"

"Really?" she asked with bated breath.

"No. I work alone--at least when it comes to using my equipment."

"I hope you enjoy that fire I started for us."

"If we'd waited for you to get the fire going we'd have frozen to death." His words followed her down the hall.

Inside the master suite, Ivy stood admiring the lavish bed. She was certain the mattress had been changed, but she felt rather sinful knowing that she'd be sleeping in the bed where once upon a time Marcus and Elizabeth had slept and made love. The atmosphere in the room was sensual and passionate and every time she entered she felt a rush of sensation down her spine.

She'd brought fresh sheets and blankets from home and she'd made the bed earlier. This room wasn't as dingy as the rest of the house, but it could use a nice sprucing. She put that on her mental to-do list for tomorrow, among investigations of her own.

She changed into her gown, a modest tunic style with lacy hem. It wasn't anything romantic. In fact, she hadn't owned a sexy gown in so long she'd forgotten what it felt like to dress seductively. She guessed her Victoria's Secret bra and panties would be considered a seduction luxury, but she had no one in her life to impress.

She went to the window and pulled back the gauzy curtain. She couldn't see anything through the darkness except for the twinkling stars in the purple hazed sky. She imagined that Elizabeth had stood in that very same spot, gazing out into the yard. Had Elizabeth loved her husband? Had Elizabeth felt a stirring of emotion every time Marcus came into the room? Had she felt a fireball burst inside her stomach whenever he left, knowing she'd miss him?

Ivy's curiosity spiraled through her mind.

She pondered what it must have been like for a girl entering womanhood to have an older man as her lover. Had Marcus been a gentle lover?

Her thoughts traveled to the man downstairs. She had no doubts that Max would be a skilled lover. There lay the danger.

Ivy shook her head, hoping to erase such thoughts. If she allowed her mind to play out Max and her making love she'd end up smack dab in a pile of foolishness. She did not, nor would she ever, have an attraction for him.

She moaned. Too late. She couldn't deny how he made her head spin.

She'd passed that invisible line of no crossing. She wanted him. Why? She wasn't quite sure. Max was a cynic. She liked compassion. He was disconnected. She wanted someone who was filled to the brim with emotion. Emotionally, he was as dead as a tree stump. Wasn't he?

So, if he had all of these bad characteristics, why did he evoke such strong emotion within her? She'd felt more frustration and excitement with him than she had her entire life. One minute she was insanely angry with him. The next minute she wished he'd open up and tell her all his stories.

Maybe her attraction issue was obvious. She was tormented by him because he was unrefined and indelicate. She wasn't used to his type.

She assured herself that tomorrow would be different. She had to remain indifferent and disengaged from him. No more flirting. No more asking him about his past. And most definitely, no more fingers in his wonderful mouth. *Gosh!* She knew what she would be dreaming tonight. Dreams never hurt anyone, did they?

She took her phone and punched in a number. When Jimmy Doyle's voicemail asked for her to leave a message she said into the phone, "I could use your help here, Jimmy." And then she hung up. Jimmy would be a damper to the fire igniting between her and Max. With a third person hanging out there would be no opportunity for close calls for kisses.

The room was getting chilly. She quickly jumped into bed and covered up with the blanket. She started to turn off the reading light she'd brought with her, but decided against it. She wasn't afraid of the dark, yet she did feel uncomfortable sleeping in strange houses. Who knew what went "bump" in the night and what creepy things hid in the shadows? From the rumors she had heard about the house, a lot went "thump" in the night.

Her own eerie thoughts made the hair stand up on her neck. She was being silly, but she couldn't keep her mind from wandering. There was nothing to be frightened of. In fact, the house was quite hospitable. And this room, this dynamic room, was something of a time machine. Relaxing into the mattress, she closed her eyes and sighed in restlessness. As comfortable as her body was in bed, her mind wasn't. She conjured up images of a tall, devilishly handsome, egotistical man with eyes that penetrated her very soul. She could not deny her tranquil mind the satisfaction and thrill of drifting in the areas of naughty thoughts. After all, it was *her* mind, so she could do whatever she wanted in secrecy. In her slumber, she could have Max doing all sorts of delectable things including and not limited to lowering himself to hands and knees and begging her forgiveness for his bad behavior.

She smiled broadly at the thought. Rolling over, she buried her face into the pillow as if it were possible that Max could somehow see her bright eyes through the walls. He probably wouldn't even call it a night for some time. She wondered, simply food for thought, what he slept in. Did he wear tiny bikinis? Or did he prefer boxers? She doubted he was a tightie whitey kind of man. He could be the wild and free type and sleep in nature's best, completely naked.

She shivered impulsively at the mere thought of him lying in his sleeping bag, nude--*ahem*--stop right there, Ivy.

Her mom had been right when she said Max would not be one to take with a careless hand. He would definitely keep her on her toes and she'd be profoundly aware that she was a woman who had been living a life of celibacy for the last year.

She wasn't even sure why she wasted her thoughts on him. She wasn't even sure she actually liked him. But there was a connection and she couldn't quite pinpoint it.

****

Max set up his full-spectrum camcorder, the ghost meter, tape recorder, infrared thermal scanner and a still camera. He was ready.

But maybe he wasn't.

He couldn't concentrate. He was supposed to be watching for paranormal activity but he couldn't get his mind off the activity upstairs. A blue-eyed, dark-haired woman had his brain in a clutch.

He needed to relax. Putting on the earphones of his iPod, Max found his favorite music by Bob Marley. Listening to the timeless tunes, he felt his muscles unwind. He laid his head back and watched the blank screen of the monitor.

Max's eyes blurred and his mind detoured to Ivy. Wrong place for his thoughts to be.

He rubbed his eyes and dropped his hand to his lap. His gaze landed on the framed paintings that Ivy had found in the closet. They were leaning against the wall and drew his attention like a neon light. Especially the woman. She was beautiful.

A flash on the screen got his attention. He tore off his earphones and waited. The screen remained blank and the sensor hadn't picked up anything. Had he imagined it?

He was tired. Why the hell had he made this trip? Was it a waste of time?

Max sighed heavily, as if releasing a head full of tension. Ivy was right. He'd came to Morgan Sites to do more than shoot some rolls of film and search for a ghost or two. Thoughts of Thornton House had perplexed him over the years. His grandfather's contact here and the mystery surrounding it had captivated him.

He took an envelope from his pocket. He opened it and took out the piece of paper folded neatly inside. He didn't need to see it to know every line and mark. He'd looked at it so many times over the last years after he'd found it tucked away in his grandfather's study. It was a drawing of Thornton House.

The drawing had haunted his dreams. He wasn't sure why but it had lured him to come. Maybe once and for all he could solve the mystery of his grandfather's connection to the Thornton family. Why did his grandfather, while lying in his deathbed, tell Max to find the envelope? His grandfather had been on morphine shots for pain and had a weakened state of mind. But the drawing was proof there must be a correlation.

After a couple of hours with no tremors in the equipment, Max called it a night. He went upstairs and into the small room he'd be calling his bedroom for the next fourteen nights.

It didn't take long before Max was sound asleep. He was a quick sleeper, but not a deep sleeper. It was a habit from many nights sleeping in unsavory locations trying to catch a few winks. So when he heard a scratching noise he was fully awake in a millisecond and ready to attack.

Moonlight filtered in through the window. Once his eyes adjusted he could see that the room was empty. Nothing was amiss. Lying back down on the sleeping bag, he closed his heavy eyelids.

A loud bang bounced off the walls, bringing him off the bed again and onto his feet in alarm.

He counted twenty feet straight from the corner of his mat to the location of the light switch. He knew this because, out of habit, he'd counted how many steps it was to the mat before bed. Amazing what four years in the military could burn into a fellow's mind.

He reached the wall and flipped the switch to the overhead light. The light flickered once, zapped, then sparked alive. It was dim but it was on. He couldn't ask for much more, considering the lighting was ancient.

The room was still empty. There was still nothing to concern him. No sign of activity. He was beginning to think he was ensnared in paranoia. He rubbed his jaw and shook his head. His equipment was downstairs. Tomorrow he'd have to set up the gear in here.

Tonight it was a lost cause.

Shutting the light off, he stumbled back across the room and climbed under the blankets. He closed his eyes and fell asleep.

Chapter 6

Ivy stretched languidly, arousing from a deep, restful sleep. The blanket fell carelessly to her waist. It was the best night's sleep she'd had in years.

She looked through the window and blinked at the bright sun. The sky was pale blue and not a cloud was in sight. The birds chirped their morning "hello" music. "It's going to be a wonderful day."

She heard rustling followed by, "What was that?"

She shot her eyes to the open doorway. Her body tensed from the top of her head to the tips of her toenails. Max stood there, watching her. Impulsively, she slid a perusal down his broad, bare chest and to the waist of his low hung jeans that were unbuttoned. Her gaze caught on the bulge at his crotch. Was it a morning woody? Heat invaded her blood. She jerked her eyes to his face, which was shiny from a recent shave, and his hair was damp. She swallowed. "What are you doing in here?"

He gave her a whimsical smile that showed a line of white teeth against olive skin. "You called out my name."

"No, I didn't!" she stated firmly. Or had she?

"I was coming out of the bathroom and I heard you call my name."

"How could you hear through the closed door?" She wasn't falling for it.

"Your door was ajar. I thought you were awake and out of bed."

"I closed it before I went to sleep."

"Whatever. I'm sure you did." His tone dripped sarcasm. He really believed she had called out to him.

This frustrated and embarrassed her. "You could at least knock before you enter a bedroom." She glared at him.

With a shake of his head, he said through thin lips, "Okay, Ivy, I'll knock before I come in again. But, a word of advice, close your door before you start accusing someone of opening it." He began to turn, but then stopped and looked back at her. "And another thing, the nights are cold here so if you don't want to catch your death you may want to wear something that is not see-through." His eyes skimmed her chest.

Ivy quickly drew up the blanket to her neck and planned to retaliate when he shut the door, cutting her off. She fell back into the bed with an exasperated moan. She could dress however she wanted to dress. She hadn't expected him to see her in her gown and it was completely his fault if he found her indecent.

She pushed back the blankets and finger-combed her hair. "This could have been a lovely day until the beast had to ruin it."

Thirty minutes later Ivy rambled into the kitchen. She'd pulled her hair into a ponytail and her teeth were brushed. She'd been tempted to come downstairs wearing her nightgown simply to prove a point to Max, but decided against it. A man with his ego, he'd have thought she was coming on to him.

There would be no coming on to Max. Not now or ever.

She ate her words when she saw him. It didn't take more than a minute to get her blood warming. He'd put on a shirt, but what good did material do when the snug fitting Polo clung to his tight body, showing off toned abs?

Her mouth began to water when she got a whiff of the bacon frying in the pan and the rich scent of brewing coffee. She liked a man who cooked. "Did you bring that two-burner stove? And the bacon?" Did the man carry everything but the kitchen sink?

"Yes. I wouldn't have minded using the fireplace but I had the burner in the back of the Jeep so I pulled it out. The bacon and the fruit came from a market a few miles down the road. I hope you're hungry."

"I feel like I've awakened in another house." She looked over his shoulder. "There's just something about the smell of bacon that brings a house alive."

"The house certainly has a different feel to it."

His eyes caught hers. Was there a latent meaning? She swallowed the tightness building in her throat as she remembered how he'd come into her bedroom and run his eyes over her.

She snapped her thoughts back onto a safer path. "I'm starving. This is very nice of you to make breakfast." Her stomach growled in agreement.

He shrugged. "Maybe the smell of food will drive the ghosts out of their hiding places."

"Don't hold your breath." Ivy laughed and went to the coffee maker. "Just what I need. A cup of coffee." She grabbed a paper cup and helped herself, adding a liberal amount of powdered cream and sugar. She felt his eyes drilling a hole into her. "What?"

"Sugar? I can't remember seeing a woman use real sugar since, well… forever. Isn't there some unwritten rule that a woman have to use the pink packet sweetener?"

"What kind of women have you been dating, Shepard?" she replied. By using his last name she drew the line between professional and personal, one she wasn't crossing. She wanted to keep their relationship strictly business-related. And, it was in keeping with her new rules of 'what not to do with men who wreaked havoc on her nerves.'

"Did you sleep well?" he asked.

"Like a baby," she answered. She hopped up on the counter and watched him through the steam of her coffee. "You look right at home, Max." Damn! Double damn! She'd broken her own rule.

"A man's got to eat, doesn't he?" He divided up two plates of bacon and sliced apple. "Keep in mind, I *can* cook but I never said I was good at it." He handed her a plate.

"It looks delicious."

He sat down at the table and she chose to keep her backside plastered on the counter. Distance was good, and abided by her second rule, no close contact.

They ate in pleasant silence. It was nice to not feel like the quiet had to be monopolized with conversation. Finishing, they cleaned together, which was also nice, but then they went their separate ways.

Ivy had a morning planned for exploring.

Her first stop was the beautiful outdoors. Stepping into the fresh air, she breathed in the smell of country: cows, grass and pine trees. The yard was in need of the tender loving care of a landscaper, yet it was visually soothing and the quiet had a calming effect. As she looked out over the tall grass and purple wildflowers dotting the land with color, she imagined that she could get used to this.

She lingered underneath a huge oak. It appeared as dilapidated as the exterior of the house, yet solid. It reminded her of a wicked tree from a scary movie, with its misshapen limbs as arms and chipped bark as eyes. The birds didn't mind her as they sat happily perched on the tree's oddly angled branches.

She looked toward the rickety barn, which looked like it was pulled from the three little pigs' story. One strong puff and the matchstick shack was history. Ivy guessed the only thing holding up the four cracked walls was a nail and a splinter.

Rhonda Lee Carver

She knew that once upon a time the farm had been impressive and modern, probably the best any farmer had ever seen. Other than the few remnants of farm equipment, too rusty and mangled now to distinguish what role they had played, there wasn't much to prove that people had lived on and farmed this land.

Ivy wondered if Elizabeth had loved the land as much as Marcus. If Ivy owned this land she'd have a flower garden outside the French doors. She'd cut a colorful arrangement every morning and place it in the crystal vase that still sat on the small table in the sitting room. She would then sit for hours reading a book in that one room while watching through the window waiting for her husband to arrive. The daydream seemed so real.

Ivy shook the thought from her mind. She had never been a hopeless romantic. Here she was creating images of a man and woman whom she'd never met--and a romantic life for herself.

She decided to walk into the field and pick wildflowers. Who took the time to pick their own flowers? She bet Elizabeth did.

Taking the bouquet inside, she filled a vase she found in the sitting room with water and placed the rustic collection of flowers inside. She heard Max's heavy footsteps and turned in time to see him eye the bunch with what looked to be a snarl. She held up the vase for his consideration. "Won't this add a perfect touch to the room?"

He crinkled his nose. "They stink."

She flung him a look of disbelief. "Are you cynical about everything?"

He shrugged.

Ivy ignored his attitude and set the vase on the table in front of the window. She stepped back and admired the touch of color it added to the dull space, making a mental note to pick some for the bedroom.

When she turned, she caught Max watching her, not the flowers. A warm tingle spread through her body. She squirmed. How could he affect her this way? He was sitting in the shabby chair, eyes on her, his expression blank. She went to the settee and sat down, propping her feet underneath her. "Are you trying to make me feel uncomfortable?"

His eyes remained on her. "How so?"

"By staring at me."

He brought his hand up and scrubbed his eyes. "Sorry."

Her jaw dropped. Did she hear right? Did he actually say 'sorry'? She liked it. It encouraged her to have a conversation with him like a normal person would. "How much do you know about this place, Max?" She broke her own rule again and used his first name, but she didn't care. He had apologized and somehow that made him seem more human. "Do you know how many families have lived here since the Thornton family?"

"I'd guess two, not including the current owner."

"Good guess."

"Good research." One eyebrow wiggled.

"But I'm afraid not accurate." She shrugged unrepentantly. "Four families have changed the deed to this property. The second owner, who bought this place after the Thorntons, lived here for a few years. The family complained of mysterious noises and happenings. Personal belongings disappearing. Sightings. They sold it to the third family. That family lived here for a short time with their two children but moved away, saying it was haunted by a child's ghost."

"A child?"

"That's what they said. The place stayed empty until Everett Barnard's father bought it years and years ago. In his attempt to sell it and make a sizeable profit, he repaired the plumbing, the roof, added the kitchen and the basic necessities. It didn't sell."

"People don't want large houses like this. The cost of heating alone would be sky high," he said.

"True, but there are possibilities here."

"So what did Barnard do?"

"After growing impatient, he sold parts of the land. He gave up on selling the house and it's stayed empty. He has a cleaning crew come in once in a great--" She sympathetically glanced around the layers of dust. "--*great* while to clean." She took a deep breath and exhaled slowly.

"Interesting." Max leaned his elbows on his knees. "Can you tell me any more about these mystical happenings people talk about?"

His eyes were on her again. Bewitching and profound. Like he knew a secret. She slid her fingers through her hair and breathed in deeply. "There were different complaints of the unexplained happenings. Like I said, missing personal items. Keys, shoes and jewelry all just vanished. Then the sightings began. One woman said she saw shadows in the hallway. Another said the ghost they saw was a small child."

He shook his head. "Most sightings are false. The mind has a way of believing something that isn't there--illusions. But for the true sightings, which are rare, if one doesn't understand how to accept it, the visions can play tricks on the mind of even the sanest people," he said in a low voice.

She wasn't sold on the theory of sightings, but decided she'd keep an open mind. She did find it intriguing to listen to Max talk about the subject. "Maybe it takes a certain person to connect with the next world."

He flipped an eyebrow. "Are you changing your views?"

"No." At least she didn't think so. She swallowed. "I had a friend who saw a fortune teller two, three times a month. She believed everything the woman told her."

"Did you ever go?" he asked.

She looked over at him, hesitated, then said, "Once. It was creepy instead of informative. The gypsy woman told me I wouldn't find love until I found my meaning in life. Whatever that meant." Ivy rolled her eyes. "Some things she knew, like I had been close to marrying an ex-boyfriend, and some things she was way off mark, like what I did as a profession. She told me I was a house designer. Boy was she wrong."

His lips curved into a smile. "Was that recently?"

"The reading?"

"The boyfriend."

"A year ago." She lowered her eyes to her lap. Talking to him about past boyfriends wasn't at the top of her list of good conversation.

"No one since?"

She shook her head. This definitely crossed the professional lines.

"Really? No dating?"

She wondered if he was trying to push her buttons. "Let's drop this subject." She buried her bottom teeth into her top lip. She'd rather eat pickled pig's feet for a week than tell him she hadn't gone on a date in months, and worse, she'd been celibate for far too long.

He sat forward in the chair, his eyes holding her as he said, "Why stop there? You are open about everything else."

Was he purposely making her wriggle in her seat? She turned the table. "What about you, Max? Is there a little woman waiting back at the ranch for her cowboy?"

"The only time I've been called cowboy was in the sack. 'No' to your question."

Her stomach twisted. This conversation was going entirely the wrong direction. She got up. "I think I'll have a look around and see what I can find. You never know, maybe I'll find a hidden treasure. There must be something here," she said in more hope than belief. "I once read that ghosts linger when they have unfinished business. Maybe that's what it is. Elizabeth and Marcus have unfinished business and they are trying to reach over from the in-between life."

He looked at her and curved his lips. "Then you believe that the house is haunted?"

"I'm not saying that. I'm only laying out all the facts, whatever those are. Who's to say what actually took place and what didn't?" She glanced at the portrait of Elizabeth hanging on the wall above the fireplace. She had brought down hers and Marcus's portrait and hung them where they rightly belonged. "Some say that Elizabeth was sold to Marcus for a good sum of money. Her family was poor and they did what they felt was necessary."

"Unfortunately, people have a tendency to romanticize history, don't they?" he said.

"Maybe they thought that Marcus would make a great husband for her. He could afford to pay. In the late 1800s it wasn't unheard of for a woman to be sold into marriage, willing or not."

"Sounds like a form of slavery."

Still mesmerized by the portraits, she said, "She looks happy and peaceful." She paused. "I believe she loved Marcus and that he loved her."

He gave her an incredulous look. "And you can see that through a painting, can you?"

She ignored his flippant remark and continued, "I wonder how they met. It definitely would seem they had socialized in different circles. I wonder if it was love at first sight?" She gave him a challenging look. "Do you believe in love at first sight?"

His laugh was harsh. "I don't believe in love at first sight, second sight, or even last sight."

She shook her head. "You're unbelievable, Max." *And it's very sad,* she added silently.

"And you're idealistic. Your world is candy-coated."

She caught him with a narrowed gaze. "Can't you believe people can be happy in this world? There are those who have found satisfaction even after their hearts have been wounded. Some people, like Elizabeth, could have fallen in love, even under the circumstances of being sold into the marriage. It shows in her eyes."

Max's eyes paralyzed her, unraveling her senses. "You're seeing what you want to see." He looked up at the painting. "She was a great artist, no doubt, but I don't see satisfaction. I see something much deeper. An unspoken longing. Much like the longing I see in you, Ivy. The longing for something or someone. Perhaps it's romance that you're longing for?"

Her heart did a cartwheel. While his words were soft and warm like melted chocolate, it sounded too close to mockery. She didn't like being studied or examined by him. She'd keep her longings to herself. She was certain a man like Max Shepard would love to rip her desires apart. "You're wrong," she stated through tight lips. "Are you sure you're not seeing a reflection of your own needs and wants?"

"I get all the romance I can handle."

If his words were meant to irk her, they did. "I bet you do, cowboy. I get plenty myself."

He laughed. "You can't lie. Your eyes don't allow it. It must be such a handicap in the line of your work. Your eyes will tell the truth even when your lips say something different."

"I won't deny that I like the thought of romance. I also won't lie and say that I don't hope to find true love, a nice home, kids, happiness. But aren't those generic dreams? Who doesn't want someone, a companion?"

"I don't," he snapped a little too quickly.

"Are you sure about that?"

"As sure as I am that my nose is in the middle of my face."

Why did she care that he wanted to be alone? She denied it had anything to do with the lost chance of finding out what it would be like to have his lips on hers. But did she need commitment to allow herself a taste? Probably not. "Your eyes are cold. I see it's your soul that's tormented. You push people away on purpose. I'm sure you've broken a heart or two." *But it won't be mine.* "I know deep inside you want a woman who is the right woman, a woman who means it when she says she loves you--unconditionally. You haven't found her yet. Until you demolish that wall you've managed to build around your heart and emotions, you're going to miss her. You're going to miss out on the one true love of a lifetime." Ivy wasn't sure where her impractical words came from but she had found them falling from her tongue as easily as water through a sieve.

"Thanks, Dr. Phil." He stood up and took a step toward her. She stood her ground, keeping her eyes glued on his face. "There isn't much to add or delete from your hypothesis. You speculate that I want love, but that is far from accurate. Love is the last thing I need or want, if it even exists. I have my doubts. I'm happy being who I am. Dating is good. When it's over, we go our separate ways. No hearts broken. No emotions left raw. No assets to divide."

His powerful eyes were on her, digging into the recesses of her mind. She felt vulnerable.

The silence became loud and intolerable. When he leaned closer, she stopped breathing in anticipation. Would he kiss her? She hoped he would.

But the kiss never came.

"You're insufferable," she spat. She turned and marched out of the room, feeling him drilling his eyes into her until she disappeared.

In the safety of the hallway, she sucked in a deep breath. Max was a commitment-phobe and that, without doubt, made him a dangerous, reckless man. He'd made it clear he wanted to tease her. She would not think of him kissing her or touching her ever again.

She'd concentrate on doing her job--and on investigating Marcus and Elizabeth.

In her heated state, she let her mind drift to Marcus and Elizabeth making love. Had their love been exquisite? Had the couple made passionate love on the floor in front of the fireplace? On the settee? Had Marcus treated her like a seductive vixen, rough around the edges, or had he been tender and giving?

The love and the tragedy here in the house were palpable. It enveloped her and she couldn't explain it. It was bittersweet torment.

Ivy debated her emotions. She grabbed her phone and headed outside.

Chapter 7

Ivy punched in a familiar number on her phone. She walked to the twisted oak tree and sat down. Marshall's secretary answered. "Hi, Maggie. It's Ivy. Is Marshall around?"

"Hello, hon. He's a bit occupied at the moment. An afternoon delight," Maggie said in a lowered voice.

Ivy rolled her eyes. Figured. "Do me a favor and tell him to pick up, okay Mags?"

"Anything for you, Ivy." Her laughter flowed across the line until she put it on hold.

A few minutes later Ivy heard a click followed by Marshall's breathless voice. "Hey, Ivy. Any ghosts in the ol' house?"

"Sure, Marshall. In fact, I'm playing checkers with one at this very moment."

"Yeah? Who's winning?" Marshall chuckled.

"I am. The poor ghost says she can't focus with your negative aura blocking her concentration."

"Quit playing, Ivy. Get to the point. I'm in a meeting." He sounded gruff.

"You're always in a meeting. When are you going to stop using conferences as a smoke screen so you don't have to talk with people? Now, tell Jasmine to close her legs, zip her dress and leave your office." Ivy would have given anything to see his expression at that moment. Everyone knew the boss was sleeping with Jasmine. How else would that nitwit reporter have gotten the top job unless she was taking care of Marshall behind the scene? The mere thought sent waves of nausea through Ivy.

"I'll pretend you didn't say that, young lady. You know I'm a married man. Talk to me about the house. I hope you and Shepard are having a good time. Did you enjoy your first night?"

She cringed. She caught his underlying meaning. "Sorry to disappoint you, Marshall, but no ghosts, no goblins and no sex. However, there's lots of excitement in regards to the dust mites. There's a whole army."

"Dust mites?" He moaned. "Unless 'dust mites' means lowdown, dirty secrets involving a ghost hunter named Max then you're not talking journalism." His voice was a growl.

"I told you, there are no stories here. Max isn't going to agree to an interview," she said. And anything they'd already shared was off record.

"Shit..." The word snapped through the phone. "I'm detecting some optimism in your voice. Does this mean that things are warming up between the two of you?"

She caught his sarcasm. The man had his ears tuned for self-satisfaction. "Not in the way they are in your office at the moment." She bit back laughter. "Tell Jasmine I said hello."

"You're a pushy one, Ivy. Now get your ass back to work and get me a story." The line went dead.

That's what Ivy liked most about Marshall, and about the only thing. His words were quick, simple and to the point.

She closed her phone and tossed it to the side. She was content at the moment, even after talking with her boss. She'd also rankled him as a bonus. Oh well, that served him right for keeping his mind in the gutter and his man parts where they didn't belong. She pushed all thoughts of Marshall from her mind and relaxed against the tree. Her blood pressure dropped at the sweet sound of nothing. All worry faded.

She thought about calling Jimmy Doyle and hounding him about his nonappearance. Was he ignoring her? Why hadn't he called after she left him a message last night? What would Max say if he gained the company of another journalist? He would be livid, no doubt.

Ivy couldn't even wrap her brain around any thought but the tranquility. She felt alone, but not alone. There was a sense of security within the stillness.

She closed her eyes. She drifted, imagining for a moment that she was Elizabeth. She envisioned herself as a woman living long ago. What had it been like for Elizabeth? How had she lived each day? Ivy wanted to understand Elizabeth's and Marcus's way of life.

A heavy, warm cloud fell over her like honey, comforting her in a nice blanketing sensation. The heat spread from the tips of her toes and slowly traveled through her entire body, coating it in harmony. She allowed the sensation to consume her, and then she drifted into an abyss of complete softness.

* * * *

Elizabeth stood beneath the oak tree looking out onto the endless grassy plot, mesmerized by the colorful array of flowers that bloomed in the fields. The sweet scent of the blossoms encompassed her. She loved nature's garden. Life should only be as lovely and as peaceful as the land. She was newly married to Marcus. Only a month. No comfort or love cloaked her in its kindness, at least not the giddiness that a recently married bride should feel. Marcus's attempts at gentleness were lost on her. She was failing him and their covenant. She was at fault.

With a sigh, she plucked a golden wildflower and brought it to her nose. She wanted her husband to be happy. His pleasure was her duty as his wife. Even if she'd been forced into the marriage against her will, she still had an obligation. The future that she'd planned for herself had been very different and her wishes had come to a bitter halt when things had turned disastrous at her family home. Her father becoming ill had sealed her fate.

When Elizabeth was sixteen, her father had gotten sick and became so frail that he couldn't labor on the farm any longer. To survive, her mother had taken on jobs cooking and cleaning in rich homes. That's where her mother had met Marcus.

Marcus had always been kind and courteous to Elizabeth and her mother. Through his generosity, he made it possible for Elizabeth's mother to support her family and ill husband.

One evening, Elizabeth's mother had come home with important news. Sitting Elizabeth at the table, she had told Elizabeth that Marcus had asked for her hand in marriage. Elizabeth had argued that she was too young for marriage, especially to a man who was quite older than her and seemed very sad. There were numerous possibilities for her life that didn't include getting married.

In the end, her new life as Mrs. Marcus Thornton had been carried forth. She was traded for a generous amount of money, a fact that she had overheard her new husband and mother discussing during a private conversation. Elizabeth hadn't been surprised, only deeply hurt. She'd hoped that her life meant more to her mother than a large bounty.

Marcus had brought her into his home and treated her well, even when she'd rejected him and asked for her own bedroom to sleep in.

It wasn't that Elizabeth detested the idea of being intimate with her husband. She did find him physically attractive. Forty years had not worn his good looks. If anything, age had improved him. When he sat across from her during dinner she'd steal glances at him. She found him intriguing and wondered about his trade. He obviously had money. That was all people ever talked about. She didn't care how much he had but she was curious how he earned it. But he never talked of those things.

Elizabeth turned away from the beautiful scenery with a serious sigh. Her long velvet gown flowed about her legs. It was a divine dress, certainly, but she wasn't used to the heavy fabric and the confines it placed on parts of her body. It made it rather difficult to walk in her garden with such a trail of material to protect and cart around. One day she hoped women could appropriately outfit themselves in britches like men. It seemed insanely unfair that men had the freedom of comfort.

Elizabeth followed the worn path along the edge of the thick foliage where she'd walked on many occasions. She was deep in reflection and had forgotten about the root obstructing the path. Her slippered foot entangled in the root, causing her to fall forward. Luckily, she was not alone and a man caught her in his strong arms.

* * * *

Ivy jumped up in alarm. She awoke in the shade of the oak tree but sweat beaded between her breasts. Confused and unsettled, it took her a long moment to identify where she was and realize she'd only been dreaming. Her dream had felt so genuine, so physical. Her heart raced. She instinctively laid a hand against her chest. She'd walked in Elizabeth's shoes, or at least it had seemed like it.

Gaining her composure, she got up from the resting spot and carefully made her way through the thick grass.

The scents of the flowers, the warmth of the sun and the security of a pair of arms still consumed her.

She had met Elizabeth.

Chapter 8

Max stared at the paintings of Elizabeth and Marcus. Secrets loomed here. He felt it. He'd learn the crazy mystery surrounding Thornton House and move on once and for all. The quicker the better. He needed to get back home. But for what? He had nothing in Chicago to go back to, so why was he in any hurry? Did he really want to get away from the house? Or was it someone.

Ivy.

The way she'd looked in bed that morning--sexy and inviting--was etched in his mind like burn marks. Her hair had hung loose, tousled around her tender face. Her eyes had still held that innocent sleep-induced glaze.

Max wished he had something to keep his mind off Ivy and on business. What was wrong with him? Whatever was happening, he needed to douse it before things went any further.

Max heard Ivy's light footsteps on the wooden floor as she came back into the house. He listened as she came up the hall until finally she appeared in the doorway. He instantly noticed her radiant eyes and rosy cheeks. This look was sexy too.

Shit.

Max had checked on her while she slept. Except for the occasional twitch or fluttering of an eyelid, she'd seemed to be resting soundly. She'd looked lovely lying underneath the tree, surrounded by nature. How could he resist the temptation? She was like a breath of fresh air. Or water to a thirsty man. But there was something more. It'd been a long time since he'd felt anything for a woman other than something merely sexual. There was something pulling him to her, and fight it as he'd been, he was losing control.

She stood there looking at him. She appeared delicate and fragile, but he knew better. He saw the fighting spirit in her blue eyes when she was peeved. Her skin was creamy fair and smooth with a hint of crimson from the warm outdoors. Her shining hair was falling haphazardly in soft tendrils around her face. Was it darker than he first thought? He ached to touch her face, her hair, but dared not to. He came to Thornton House to terminate thoughts of an abandoned house, not to embark upon a complicated relationship.

"Did you have a good sleep?" he asked.

"Amazing." She stretched and smiled, as if the mere thought made her ooze with warmth. "I feel like new." Her shirt lifted slightly, revealing a sliver of her flat stomach. The twitch behind his zipper was completely against his will.

"Great." The last thing he wanted or needed was for Ivy to see just how she affected him. He just couldn't help himself.

* * * *

Ivy felt tingly under Max's close scrutiny. He looked at her like he actually liked her. Interesting. There was a new softness around his eyes and mouth. What had come over him while she was outside?

He was a strong-natured man who dripped vigor and masculinity. His eyes were so fierce they could impel fire within her soul. He was a man who dictated his world, and for this, she was quickly becoming frightened of her unbridled feelings for him. She believed him to be a man who became interested in a woman only to discard her when the fascination ceased.

She didn't wish to be another score in his game. As long as she kept this in mind she couldn't be played. On some level she believed he was frightened of her too.

She could not, nor would she, deny the attraction to him. It would be no use. She wore her emotions for the world to see. But would she give in to these emotions?

For now, she needed to work.

"I'm going upstairs to explore," she mumbled and left the room.

Ivy was certain that somewhere in the house were hidden documents or belongings of Elizabeth and Marcus. There were secrets here. She knew it at her very core.

Her first suspicious hideaway: the attic.

In the master bedroom she found the trapdoor entrance to the attic. She had her flashlight in hand and in working condition. Light it would give, but protection from creepy crawlies it wouldn't. She hated spiders, and mice even more. She heaved a sigh in her silliness. *Get a grip!* Spiders were more afraid of her than she was of them. It was time she got rid of the childhood fear.

Ivy reached for the door. She was too short. She went to the nightstand, gave it a quick inspection and a firm shake, and decided it was stable enough to hold her weight. It wasn't in the best condition. Nothing in the house was in the *best* condition except for, amazingly, the bed.

She dragged the piece of furniture over and situated it underneath the door. She climbed onto the wood, gained her balance and reached for the latch. Giving it a tug, she found it wouldn't budge. She guessed it'd been years since it'd been open.

The situation seemed hopeless, but she couldn't give up. The door would just have to cooperate and open because she wouldn't accept not exploring the attic.

With another yank, and all the steam she could muster, she heard a sharp snap. The door jolted open to an unexpected, and very startled, Ivy. It was heavier than she'd anticipated. The burden caused her to lose her balance. The shift of her weight was too much for the dilapidated nightstand. She heard a splintering of wood seconds before it staggered and leaned. Ivy was unable to hold steady although she attempted to maintain her stability while still containing the heavy door.

She cursed as her foot slid and her body tumbled backward. Instead of falling hard onto the wooden floor as she'd expected, she was caught by a pair of strong arms. She brought her gaze up to meet the deepest eyes. Max.

"I had a feeling you were up to something," Max said through a lazy grin.

Their faces were within inches of one another and all she could do was stare up at him in utter disbelief. He couldn't have picked a better time to rescue her. She wanted to say thank you but she wasn't sure her voice would work. She stayed statue still, afraid if she squirmed out of his arms she'd fall flat on her face because her limbs were like jelly.

No coherent thought entered her mind. The enchantment of being in Max's arms, cuddled protectively against his broad, warm chest was enough to cause her paralysis of the brain. She was struck with the strongest emotion, something between torment and sweet, sweet pleasure. She took in everything. His masculine scent. His minty breath. His secure arms. She imagined that she could give in to the childlike fervor and drop her head onto his shoulder.

* * * *

Max was tempted.

He wanted to lower his mouth to her pink lips and kiss the hell out of her. Just to get it done and over with. It crazed him to know she was off limits. *Isn't she?* Maybe if he got a taste of her, a little sampling, he would get it out of his system and he'd be done with the torment. He ached to have her but his convictions warned him that there'd be hell to pay for tasting something so damn sweet. It was like the devil thinking he had a chance with an angel.

She was light in his arms and he could have held her forever, but his hunger was growing heavy. He was a mere man with needs, and his was growing hard against her side. He carefully set her down onto her feet. Feeling her wobble, he steadied her by holding her elbows. "You okay?"

She nodded. "I wanted to look in the attic."

"I see that." He couldn't take his eyes off her. "You shouldn't explore this old place alone. You never know what you may come across."

"I'm a journalist. I'm used to investigating sticky situations and places. I feel this place is safe," she stated steadfastly. "I'm fine alone."

He lifted his eyebrows. "Then I guess I should have let you fall flat on your backside because, well, you're a journalist and you can do everything alone. A few scrapes and bruises can only add character, right?" He liked the way her mouth lifted on one corner in a dry smile.

"I thought you were finished acting like a ding dong."

"You were hoping to change me with one glance of those eyes, but just keep in mind who you're dealing with." He wanted to kiss the sassiness right out of her. She had felt good, better than he thought possible, in his arms.

She actually smiled. A beautiful smile that could have lit the street. He was as good as fucked. He could feel it in his bones. He ambled across the room for some well-needed space. "What exactly are you looking for?"

"Ghosts," she answered mockingly.

He gave her a sober look, wondering if she'd ever been spanked. He'd get real pleasure in bending her over his knee and...damn! He tore his mind away from that thought. He needed an adjustment in his jeans but her eyes were on him. Sucking in a breath, he blew it out between tight lips. More in control, he said, "I was under the impression that journalists didn't believe in anything they couldn't see for themselves. Unless you saw something you're not sharing."

"I'll leave the ghost hunting to you."

"I don't mind the help. That is if you can handle the apology after."

Her eyebrows scrunched. "Apology?"

He nodded. "Yep, the one you'll give me when we find out this place is as haunted as The White House."

Her mouth opened. "The White House is haunted?"

"Abraham Lincoln is known to visit a few times a year."

She stared at him, curiosity marring her flawless features. "Are you lying to me?"

"I wouldn't lie to you," he said.

"What are you hiding, Max Shepard? Don't delude yourself into believing that your secret is safe from me. I may be 'small town' compared to you, but I'm damn good at uncovering details."

"If you're a damn good journalist then why are you vegetating in this no-news, forgotten town? A journalist, one who truly wants the scoop, doesn't wait for it to come to them, but instead goes where the story is." She squinted. He realized his words were a bit harsh. "I can't sugar-coat the truth, sweetheart."

She placed her balled fists on her hips. She nailed him with a vicious glare. "Sometimes a story isn't all that matters."

"The impression I got from you is that a story *is* all that matters. You're too young to be tied up in an unknown town. Think of the career you're giving up," he said without apology for his candor.

The corner of her lip quivered slightly. "And aren't you just a bit too old not to have some stability in your life? How long do you think you can bounce around the world catching ghastly photos? When you give up everything, you have nothing to hold on to." There was an icy bite to her tone.

He leaned against the window frame. He moved his gaze along her slender body, sizing her up. He liked her saucy attitude. If he gave her the truth dry and straight he expected the no-holds-barred approach in return. Problem was, how did they always end up bickering about his personal life like it was an important topic? "I don't need refining in my personal life, Ivy. It's just the way I want it. Alone and loving it." He slid her a wink. "At least I've had the guts to take chances and explore the world and the risks. When you're old, to use your word, like me, will you be able to say the same? Will you regret not having spread your wings and conquered the world?"

"Trust me, I'll be just fine. I've got more character in my little finger than you do in your whole body. Will you look back on your life lived and feel you've taken risks to be happy? I mean, come on, Max. You say you're a risk taker, but actually you're hiding from life."

He beheld her flushed skin and satin hair. Pleasing to the eye but a poison to the bloodstream. The woman never ceased to amaze him with her psychoanalysis bullshit. "My character is deep enough. Quit trying to save me."

"Sure!" She snickered. "Could have fooled me."

"Consider yourself lucky that you've gotten to know only the top layer of my personality. I'm afraid you couldn't handle the rest."

"Don't count me out just yet, cowboy." And there was the challenge, laid out on the table like sparkling jewels. There wasn't even a stutter or hesitation before she used the nickname she created for him. "Now, if you'll help me into this attic I'll share my treasure with you."

He smiled smoothly. "Is that a promise?" It took her a second, but the spark in her eye told him she realized what she'd offered. And just how he took it. "I'd be happy to share your treasure."

She shook her head. Her cheeks turned a pale shade of pink that made her eyes glisten. "You know exactly what I meant. And anyway, I'm not your type."

He sighed. That one statement he made in ignorance would live to haunt him, he just knew it. He'd never known a woman who could forget something bad said in the heat of the moment.

Time to move on. *The attic.*

He eyed the pathetic excuse for a nightstand and knew there was no way it'd hold his weight. He was tall and could manage the reach to the ceiling. He pushed the broken table out of his way. He shot a look at Ivy over his shoulder. "You first?"

She sighed. "Yes, step aside and allow me to do my job."

He didn't say a word, just laughed. He lowered the ladder, checked it for safety and moved up the wooden rungs. He lifted himself into the small opening then threw out his hand for her to take. She climbed up and he easily helped her up. "Flashlight?"

She grabbed the light from her waistband and clicked it on. They scanned the sour-smelling darkness with matched interest.

There wasn't much to explore, Max thought bleakly. Very little occupied the space, except layers of age. Boxes of empty canning jars lined the wall, an antique cherrywood cheval mirror with a broken glass, a rattan rocker and a few miscellaneous items.

"Hey, flash that light over here. In the corner." Max obliged her. "Looks like a big box... No, wait..." Ivy grabbed the light out of his hand and investigated closer. He could see her smile beaming in the dim light. "A trunk."

Chapter 9

Ivy could barely contain her excitement as she knelt beside the trunk. She swiped the thick layer of dust from the top and her anticipation grew.

"Does it open?" Max asked from over her shoulder.

"Let's see." She tried the handle but it was locked. Her enthusiasm dampened. "No."

"Let me see." He took the light back and investigated the outside of the trunk. "There are no initials, no marks, nothing to show ownership." He rattled the rusted bolt. "It's old and fragile. It won't take much to break it."

"Do you think we could lift it downstairs?" she asked.

He examined the worn and tattered edges of the leather. "There are no handles." He picked up one side, as if to gauge its weight. He handed her the flashlight. "It's more awkward in size than in weight. I could scoot it across the floor." He maneuvered it across the rough floorboards.

Ivy joined the effort. They both worked at getting the chest to the edge of the opening.

Max lowered himself out of the attic and Ivy then pushed the trunk closer to the trapdoor. With brute strength, he was able to heave it down onto his shoulders and drop it to the floor, making a resounding thud. Ivy was surprised that the thud didn't break the chest into pieces. It remained intact.

Ivy allowed Max to help her down, but he didn't keep his hands on her any longer than necessary. She was a bit disappointed but they certainly didn't need to test their control.

"Are you trembling?" he asked.

"No," she answered too quickly.

A mocking smile curved his mouth. He moved closer, so close that she could smell a hint of musk. The beads of sweat on his forehead appeared like small crystals. She moistened her bottom lip and closed her eyes-

-waiting in logical desertion. And then…nothing. Feeling his fingers digging in her hair she jerked her lids open. "What is it?"

He removed his hand and held up his fist. He opened his palm and a black spider crawled across his fingers. Staring, she blinked twice and swallowed a scream. "You…you…found that in…my hair?"

"You okay? You look pale."

Her stomach lurched. She could no longer hold back. She squealed. She jumped up and down while raking her fingers through her hair, shaking it over her shoulders. "Anything else? Look!" She twisted and turned. She saw the humor in the twinkle of his eyes, but she didn't care.

"No. You're fine. Spider-free."

She faced him. "I. Will. Never. Go. Back. Up. There."

"Suit yourself." He dropped beside the trunk and wiggled the lock.

Breathing under control, Ivy asked, "Can we open it?"

"Shouldn't be a problem." He let go of the lock.

They both stared at the trunk for the longest time, as if invisible chains kept them from breaking it open. The mystery held them. Ivy finally broke the silence. "I wonder who it belonged to." She explored the outside for any signs or markings indicating who the owner was. "You're right. There's nothing to show ownership. Sometimes leather trunks had symbols or initials branded into the material. This is definitely from the mid-1800s."

"Is that a good guess?"

"Not a guess as much as a hope, maybe." She continued her perusal.

"Do you see anything?" he asked.

"Actually--" She ran her finger over a spot on the lower left side. "This could have been initials or possibly a crest. It's too worn to get a good visual. There's a chance that one of the previous owners found it, opened it, then locked it back up." Her heart sank at that possibility.

"There is no sign of tampering. It's an old-style lock clasp. You can tell it's been a long time since it's been opened by the rust and the chipping around the clasp. No one could have fussed with it and put it back in the condition it's in."

She nodded her agreement. "You do have a point. Isn't it strange, though, that none of the others who have resided here found it?"

"It was hidden in the attic. Someone could have easily overlooked it tucked away in the dark corner, just as we almost did. Then again, there aren't many people who like exploring dark spaces in old houses."

"Another good point."

Silence held them again. Before them was a piece of history and yet neither of them wanted to hurry into unlocking it. Ivy wanted to savor the treasure.

By his hesitation, Max obviously felt the same. Shouldn't they be tearing into the trunk? Was it because she'd be disappointed if they found nothing? Was she nervous because maybe, just by chance, they would find something from the past? Her emotions were all in an upheaval. She still trembled.

Max's cell rang. Grabbing it from his pocket he flipped it open. "I gotta take this,' he said.

Ivy folded her arms over her chest. "What about the trunk?" she whispered.

He covered the mouthpiece. "It's been sitting in that dingy attic for over a hundred years. Another fifteen minutes won't kill us." And he left the room.

Ivy sighed in frustration.

She remembered the spider Max had found in her hair. The thought sent tingles of fear and disgust through her. She needed a bath. She could take a quick one and be done before Max came back.

In the master bathroom, she started the water in the tub. It was still a little rusty so she let it run a few minutes before turning the hot water on. Placing her hair into a loose bun, she slipped off her clothes and tossed them aside.

She moaned in satisfaction as she sank into the water. The warmth pooled around her like a comforting blanket, easing the tension in her neck and shoulders. She slid further in until the edge of the water skimmed her chin. She let go of all her stress. Even the trunk with its contents drifted from her mind.

Mesmerized by the complete quiet, she fell into a semi-conscious state.

Ivy wasn't sure how long she'd been out. She heard someone whispering into her ear. She fluttered her eyes open. A tickling sensation on her foot brought her eyes downward. A hand--someone's hand--clutched her ankle. She jerked up in the tub in response. Water splashed over the sides.

"Elizabeth?" The deep voice of a man invaded her state of relaxation. She waited. "Elizabeth?"

She jumped up. The tub was slippery, causing her to lose her footing. She started to fall when everything went fuzzy.

Ivy awoke and realized she wasn't in the tub any longer. She darted her gaze around as anxiety gripped her. She was lying on a plush burgundy couch. Her legs were in Marcus's lap. She jolted away from his touch. He watched her curiously.

"Are you okay, Elizabeth? Why do you move away?" There was a hint of hurt visible in his eyes.

"I…uhh." She was lost as to what had happened. "Why were you touching me?" Her words were breathless and panicked to her own ears. She drew back into the corner of the couch, tucking her feet up under her bottom and covering her body with her arms. The last she'd known she was naked. Now she wore the beautiful velvet gown that she'd seen on Elizabeth during the time she'd dreamt of her before, in the garden.

"I was only examining your foot. It's bruised from getting caught in the root along the path."

Ivy peered down at the hem of her dress. Moving her toes out, she saw that her stocking was halfway down her foot. The ankle was bruised and swollen. Marcus must have caught her as she started to fall on the path. At the time she'd thought it was a dream…"I remember," Ivy whispered. Was this another dream? It sure didn't feel like one.

Marcus shook his head and scrubbed his jaw. Ivy wondered if he was irritated. "Elizabeth, why did you agree to come here? To be my wife?"

Her throat constricted. She was shaken and confused. How had she gotten here? How had she become Elizabeth? She remembered soaking in the tub, closing her eyes…and then a touch.

"You can't ignore me, Elizabeth. Why did you come here?" It came out as a rough accusation.

Ivy searched her mind for an answer. How would Elizabeth answer? "It's only appropriate for a wife to live with her husband." Would that suffice?

"But no one forced you into this marriage. Sometimes, the way you look at me, I feel like your prison guard instead of your husband."

She lowered her eyes to where his hand rested on his thigh. His fingers were long and his skin was olive. She brought her gaze back up. He was devilishly handsome. In fact, he looked…familiar. His thick dark hair. Prominent cheekbones. Intense eyes. She caught her breath and brought her hand to her lips to keep from cursing. Max…Marcus resembled Max. They could be father and son, or brothers. The resemblance was that strong. Her mind reeled.

Marcus looked at her with a curious, narrowed eye and she dropped her hand to her lap, trying to control the shaking in her limbs.

"Even now, you tremble being near me. Am I that ghastly?"

Ivy moistened her lips. She felt trapped. "I did what was expected of me. I could not have stayed at home with my family. Mother explained that it was the only way." The words fell freely from her lips. She couldn't tell him the truth--who she was. He'd never understand that she wasn't Elizabeth, but instead a woman from the future. He'd have her locked away and she'd never get back home. She took in a deep breath and forced a smile to her lips. "And no, I do not find you ghastly at all."

That seemed to satisfy him. One corner of his mouth lifted. "Great. Now let me see that foot. I can call for Dr. Rhoads if necessary."

She swallowed. What would he think of the red nail polish? If he removed her sock the rest of the way she'd be in trouble. Ivy wasn't sure when women started using polish. "My ankle is fine. I assure you."

"Let me be the judge of that, may I?"

Denying him would only cause more drama. Reluctantly, she slid her foot out from hiding in her skirt folds. Before she could stop him the sock was gone. Her breath held as she watched his features. There really wasn't a change. He tapped her big toenail with his forefinger. "I've never seen such a thing before." She pulled her foot back, but he caught it with a gentle hand. He met her eyes and she felt her heart race. "I like it," he said.

He placed her foot back in his lap and began massaging her tender ankle. His fingers had just the right amount of pressure. She enjoyed his touch. She swallowed. She needed to get her mind off his sexy fingers and back to finding a way to get away from him and back into the bathtub.

"Are you unhappy?"

She wasn't the least bit unhappy. In fact, she wanted his fingers to travel further up her leg… But that wasn't how Elizabeth would feel. "It feels good," she said. *Yikes.* She chastised herself for having said the first thing that popped in her head.

He grinned and his face lit up. "I mean, in the marriage. Do I make you unhappy as a husband?"

"Oh." She had to get her mind out of the gutter. If she wasn't careful she'd screw up things for poor Elizabeth and he'd send her back home and call the marriage off. "I am not unhappy, Marcus."

"Then why are you always frowning?"

He continued his attention on her skin and it was hard to play a role that required a certain amount of concentration. She hoped that any moment this dream, or whatever it was, would zap her back home. Stilling her nerves, she looked at him, keeping her voice steady when she spoke. "Is it wrong for me to have wanted to marry a man I love? I was traded for an amount of money. It was so little. My mother could have gone to the corner and bought a cow for less hassle."

"Would it have been more gentlemanly for me to have not given the money?" he asked, one thick eyebrow cocked. His dark eyes were bright and questioning. His expression looked sincere.

"Did you wish for a wife or a cow?" Ivy wasn't sure that it was appropriate for a woman to speak to her husband with such a brazen tone, but it was never right for a man to buy his wife.

He looked into her eyes; there was a sharp angular line to his jaw. "I wanted you... Damn, I still want you!"

She turned her face toward the window to hide the unease in her eyes. Emotion wedged itself inside her heart. Where did it come from? Why was she emotional? Surprisingly, he reached out and gently turned her face back to him. His fingers were tender. "Look at me, Elizabeth," he demanded firmly, but there was gentleness in his tone.

She shyly brought her eyes up to meet his, afraid of what he may see there. If he peered close enough would he see that she wasn't his Elizabeth? Their gazes connected and the energy cut through her like a bolt of electricity. She sucked in a deep breath at the stirring of passion she saw in his eyes.

His face softened and his Adam's apple jerked as he swallowed. "You were a young girl when you started coming here with your mother. I thought nothing more of you than the content child who would run the halls, singing, laughing, innocent. I was a bitter man who had lost his wife and child and was so deeply filled with anguish. I didn't mind you drifting here and there, flitting about like an unmannered monkey in the wilds. You had a fascination for my things and your mother would apologize that she'd brought you along. I would tell her not to worry. This house deserved to know the sound of a child at play." He sighed, as if to relieve himself of deep agony. "She stopped bringing you. Then just last year you came back, and the curious child had grown into a beautiful woman. I hadn't realized you'd celebrated your eighteenth year."

"I had stopped coming so that I could help at home with my sisters." Ivy searched her mind for what she knew about Elizabeth.

"Your mother always bragged about how mature you were. When I saw you again, after so long, my heart opened wide and allowed an unfamiliar emotion to enter. For the first time in a long time I felt something other than sorrow and it was because of your bright smile."

"You must have loved her very much."

"Who? My first wife?"

"Yes."

"Once I did, or so I had thought. The feeling of love was once reflected in her heart, too, I suppose." His voice grew low and enveloped in sentiment. "Alyssa and I were both young when we married. She was thrilled at becoming a bride but her idealistic fantasy of marriage was far from reality. Soon after, she became fatigued with the matrimony. It was all boring to her." He looked off as if he could see into the past. "After years of me pleading with her, she finally agreed to have a child. We had our daughter, Cecilia." A smile formed on his tight lips. "Cecilia was an angel cast from above. Her eyes sparkled and her skin was fair. From the moment she came into the world, crying, I was filled with pleasure and she meant the world to me." His words dropped off into an eerie silence.

Ivy wasn't sure what to say, but she felt she should help. "I'm sure she was a pleasure. I don't know what happened but I'm sure you must have been devastated."

"By the time Cecilia was five, Alyssa and I had grown apart. She spent much of her time at our manor in Boston. She loved Boston and the socializing much more than I did."

"And your child?"

"She was here with me. Alyssa came back to visit on occasion, but each visit grew shorter and shorter. Eventually, she quit coming all together. A year went by without any interest from her, until one day she appeared to say that she was staying here with Cecilia and me. For a while I thought she'd come to her senses and wanted to be a mother to her daughter." A ruthless smile edged his mouth. "I was wrong. One day I came back to find Alyssa had taken Cecilia. Their belongings were gone as well. There was a simple note left on the bed. Its candor was so nauseating that I wanted, for the first time, to hurt Alyssa like she'd done to me for so many years."

Ivy watched him. Empathy filled her. "A note?"

"The terms were simple. If I wanted to see Cecilia again I would bring a certain amount of money to our home in Boston. Money was of no object or concern so I packed a cache and headed there." His eyes turned a shade darker. "By the time I'd arrived I found nothing more of the house but a huge pile of bricks and ash. It had burned, and Alyssa and Cecilia had perished."

Ivy felt her own eyes mist with tears. "Do you know what caused the fire?"

"Alyssa had been involved with an insane man. The housekeeper said this man grew uncontrollable in his rage when Alyssa refused him. My daughter was an innocent bystander. My life changed forever that day."

Ivy choked back a sob. This man, Elizabeth's husband, had lived through an unimaginable tragedy. She felt that no matter what she said it would not do justice to his pain.

"Well, your ankle appears to not be broken. I only see a small bruise and slight swelling. How does it feel?"

She was still rooted in the emotion of his story and it took her a long moment to oblige him an answer. "Uh...yes, sure, it's fine." She quickly dropped her shoeless foot to the floor. "Thanks for your attention, I mean, your help."

"I'm glad I could be of assistance."

"Why were you coming into the garden? Was it to see me?" she asked. She looked for her lost stocking.

"Lunch. I was coming to ask if you wanted lunch. Sally has whipped up something delicious and I thought we could picnic under the oak tree by the garden, if you'd like."

"Sally?"

One brow shot up. "The cook."

"Oh, I just wondered if mother would be stopping by today to help out." She spotted the sock on the other side of his thigh. She debated whether she should ask him for it.

"Elizabeth, you know your mother no longer helps here. That wouldn't be appropriate. If you miss her we can ride over and--"

"No!" Ivy realized she was making a mess of this. "I mean…I miss her, but I don't wish to visit her today. Maybe tomorrow."

"I believe the heat has gotten to you, my dear. Why don't I ask Sally to bring a tray upstairs?"

Ivy knew that upstairs meant in the bedroom. She needed to stay as far away from that master suite as possible. Ivy doubted that she'd have the same concern about sleeping with her husband as Elizabeth did. "No, I'd like to sit under the tree and have lunch. I'm fine. Maybe a bit hungry and parched."

"Shall we go and see what Sally has prepared for us, then?" He got up and lent his hand for her to take.

Ivy placed her hand into his. He clasped his finger around hers and helped her to her feet. He gave her an odd expression and she felt self-conscious. Had he caught on to something? "What is it, Marcus?"

"You smiled. That's the first time that you've smiled at me."

Ivy cringed. Now she couldn't even smile without coming across as suspicious. To Ivy, Elizabeth was drowning in her misery without any clue of the wonderment the future held. Ivy felt sorry for Elizabeth, but knew within time the lovely young woman would fall madly and deeply in love with her husband. Yet, a part of Ivy remained solemn. Their happiness would last for such a short time under fate's hand of death.

After eating a delicious spread of Irish stew and freshly made bread while sitting under the cool shade of the oak tree, Ivy and Marcus got up and decided to take a walk in the sunshine. They walked side by side, content with the silence. Ivy caught glances of Marcus's profile. It was amazing how much he reminded her of Max. Their prominent features, their long slender hands and the smooth sway of their walk. This certainly made her more suspicious of why Max was at Thornton House.

Ivy's mind wandered back to Max. Did he realize she was gone? When would time sweep her back? What if the path home was lost? What if she stayed here? She couldn't do that...

When they reached the edge of the voluptuous garden overlooking the grassy hills of the countryside, they both stood in admiration of its beauty. The fields seemed to stretch for miles under the blue sky. The wind billowing through the trees sounded like secrets being whispered to eavesdropping ears. Soon it would all be covered with a blanket of shimmering snow. The beauty would not alter from the hand of frost but change into something as magnificent.

Standing there, she felt more of Elizabeth's emotions. Strangely, Elizabeth's thoughts were embedded within Ivy's own. Was she becoming Elizabeth? It was as if she were transformed.

* * * *

Marcus looked down at his lovely wife. Her cheeks were rosy from the warmth of the sun and her eyes were like the image of the clear sky. "The flowers have bloomed wonderfully under your care, Elizabeth."

"I love working in the garden. They are like creating a new life of color."

"Is Sally working out well?"

"She's wonderful." The answer came promptly.

"Good." He was silent as he thought over his next words. He turned to her and said, "I'm going up north for a few days. I have business to tend to. Are you okay to stay alone?" He noticed her hesitant expression. She seemed different. He wasn't sure how, but there was something. Her eyes seemed brighter and she had smiled for the first time since she'd come to the farm. She almost looked happy.

"I'm not afraid to be alone, Marcus. There are things I can do to occupy my time. I'll be fine," she muttered.

"Has something changed, Elizabeth?"

He could have sworn she tensed. Finally, she answered, "Nothing has changed. Why would you suggest such a thing?"

He shrugged. His day shirt seemed to shrink in size against his tense muscles. He wanted to hold his wife's hand. Before he could attempt to make his move she darted from his side, as if she read his thoughts. She ventured down the path between a row of peonies, stopping every so often to brush her fingertips lightly over the blooms. She was so tender and familiar with the blossoms that he felt a tad envious.

He watched her from the border of the garden. He feared he was an intruder in her private domain. "Are you afraid of me?" he asked.

She glanced over her shoulder at him. A smile crept over her mouth. "Afraid? Why would you think that?"

"The way you look at me. I am confused. I don't know what you're thinking or how you're feeling. There are moments when you look at me with such distrust and anger that I'm afraid I'll never earn your faith. Then, like now, your eyes are warm and agreeable."

She didn't answer. He was disappointed. She instead turned back to face her quiet flowers. He waited, not wanting to pressure her. She finally said in a soft voice, "I'm not angry with you. I... I just need time. This is different for me."

"Is it so wrong here, Elizabeth?" He was going insane. He'd always been a confident man but when it came to Elizabeth he felt weak and befuddled.

She sighed. "I guess I believed there should be more, much more, to a marriage than a bought wife for a bored, lonely man."

"What?" His throat went dry. "Is that what you think? Do you believe I brought you here to save me from boredom? That's asinine! Trust me, if all I wanted was a woman to entertain me and keep me warm I could have found plenty willing bodies to fill my time and my bed." And although he found that she didn't need to know, he'd found comfort in the bed of a stranger on occasion. But that's all it had been. A warm body to satiate his male needs. Since he first saw Elizabeth as a beautiful adult woman he'd not thought of anyone but her. He hoped one day to share his bed with his wife. There would never be another woman lying beside him but her. "And why do you keep bringing up this laughable statement that you're a bought wife? For heaven's sake, I wish I knew what was going on under my own roof." He threw his hand up in frustration. Irritation boiled his blood.

She turned to face him, stomping down the path toward him. "You wish you knew what was going on? You're the one with all the control and the discretions in this marriage. You come and go as you please. You do what you please, yet I sit here expecting to be the person you want me to be surrounded by things that are not mine. I don't even know how I'm supposed to be or what I'm supposed to do because I don't know you and what you want of me." Tears fell to her cheeks. As if she'd realized her outburst, her mouth fell open and snapped shut. "I'm sorry. I'm not sure what came over me. Or why I said such things."

Marcus was disturbed at what he heard. He was speechless. He heaved a gigantic sigh and shook his head. At the same time, if this was how she felt, he didn't want her to feel the need to apologize to him. "Come, Elizabeth. We need to have a long talk. Apparently one we should have had long before now." He stuck out his hand to her.

She eyed his hand as if she debated whether he were friend or foe. He was beginning to think she'd refuse him until finally she laid her hand into his. Together they followed the haggard stone walk to the wooden bench. He'd had it specially made for her so she could sit and look out over the garden. He sat down first, then tugged her gently down beside him.

"Fill me in, my dear. Why do you believe that I have brought you here?" he asked.

She didn't answer right away. She seemed to be looking for the right words. "You gave my family money, a vast amount, for my hand in marriage."

His laughter grated the silence. The birds in a nearby tree stopped chirping. "Is that what you've been told?"

She lowered her eyes and stared down at her clasped hands in her lap. "Mother said you offered her money for me."

Burying his face into his hands, he dragged his fingertips along his tired eyes and shadow of beard. He looked at her in insult. "Hearing your side of things makes me appear nothing more than a boorish pig."

"And makes me appear nothing more than property," she added.

"You are nothing of the sort, my dear sweet Elizabeth," he said. "You must think I'm an oaf but if you listen to me, what I have to say, it may lighten your disapproval of me." He breathed and exhaled slowly. "The money was only a gift from me to your family. Your mother explained how wretched things have been since your father became ill. When she told me you were betrothed to an evil man in Boston I knew I could not allow it to transpire. You deserve more than an old man who was well known for beating his late wife."

A delicate whimper fell from her shell pink lips. He wondered, had they always been so pale? "Betrothed? I do not even know of such a man in Boston."

Marcus's jaw dropped. "No?"

"No!"

"I was told you would marry me if I offered so you wouldn't have to carry out a marriage to this oaf and move away. I was more than willing--no, gladdened, for a better word--to take you as my wife. I must confess, I would have given my fortune to have you in my life. I did not offer the funds for you to be brought here as my property. I was under the impression this union was an agreement and that your reproach of me was only uncertainty."

She touched his arm and he met her gaze. She leaned her body closer. He could smell her scent. It was unlike anything he'd ever smelled before. "Marcus, I'm not sure I understand. Why did you want me as your wife? I'm sure there are others."

He gently took her chin with his thumb and lifted her face. "There is no other, Elizabeth. You are my wife and I respect you. I am loyal to the commitment that we have made. You, my dear--" he pulled his hand away from her chin and dipped his fingers into the silky strands of her thick hair. "--make my heart sing. I wasn't looking for rapture but somehow in the midst of my torment I've found it. I did not bring you here to suffer as my wife and it seems that suffering is exactly what this marriage is causing you." He dropped his hand from her mane and lifted himself off the bench. He turned to stare down upon her flushed features. He extended his hand to her full lips and ever so faintly ran a finger along the soft curve. "I'm sorry that this union has brought you unhappiness. I had hoped for so much more for us, but if your hopes and dreams are not here then I don't want you to stay. I've lived in a problematic wedlock before. I don't wish to be responsible for another." His chest ached as he said the words. "You are free to leave, my dear, but all I ask is that you do it swiftly before it's too late for the manacles to be detached." He gave her one last look of longing before starting to ascend the path.

She remained silent, as he had guessed she would. He turned and said, "I'll be back in two days. That should give you enough time to pack and leave."

Marcus climbed into the carriage awaiting him. He looked out the window and into the garden where Elizabeth still sat. Her fingers were to her eyes. Was she crying? He dismissed it as his own futile hope. He told the driver to pull away and he kept his gaze forward. There was heaviness in his heart and he clenched his hands into fists.

Chapter 10

The bathwater had turned chilly. Ivy climbed from the tub, shivering and perplexed. She remembered falling asleep. And then…something had happened. Her mind was blurry but certain memories flooded through. Marcus. The garden. An argument. But it was nothing more than an intense dream, wasn't it? It had felt so…*right*. She breathed in and a musky scent lingered in her senses. Marcus's scent. Her stomach fluttered. She was as emotional as a girl who'd just encountered her first kiss from the man she loved. For a breathtaking moment she had lived Elizabeth's life--*again*.

Depleted, breathless, Ivy was overwhelmed.

What was happening?

Was she going mad? Was there something--or someone--in this house sending messages to her? Was she time traveling?

It was all too much to think about.

Ivy pulled on her robe, snuggled deep into its warmth and comfort and headed out of the bathroom. She stopped long enough to listen for Max. She could hear slight rumbling and thuds. Knowing he was there made her feel surprisingly content.

The chest was still sitting and waiting. She stared at the piece of history. Starting to turn around to go get dressed, she turned back. Interest held her steady. She should wait for Max.

Ivy bit into her bottom lip. She was mesmerized by the trunk. With more deliberation and less guilt, she stepped closer, glancing over her shoulder to check if Max was watching. He seemed to have an intuition that never ceased to amaze her.

She bent next to it, feeling the top. With the rough trunk beneath her fingers she slid her hand until the lock was in her palm. She shook it twice and gasped in shock when it broke. She hadn't expected the metal to crumble in her hand.

A thought bombarded her. Was it possible that Max had already snooped inside the box while she was in the tub? He could have wanted to get there before she did.

The notion drove through her brain at a speeding rate, becoming more logical and possible.

How dare he! She seethed in anger. They had made an agreement. Apparently he had decided not to keep his promise.

Any guilt or restraint about opening the chest vanquished. If he could look inside then so could she.

She lifted the lid easily. Each creak of its rusted hinges was like a scream echoing off the bare walls. It was nothing to deter her, though. She peered inside with excited fervor. The first thing she saw was green velvet. She gently took the fabric from its resting place and laid it upon her lap. It was a dress.

With a twist of her wrists she spread the dress out before her onto the floor, its heavy fabric covered in dust and sending a cloud above her.

It was elaborate, although worn and soiled. She fingered the delicate lace on the collar, yellow with time. She followed the velvet material all the way to the edge of the skirt, which was also trimmed in the antique lace. The material was faded. She imagined it was once a deep and rich color…

Ivy's breath whooshed from her lungs. The dress. It was the one Elizabeth wore in the portrait downstairs. A tear came to her eye. This dress had been worn by the beautiful young lady years before. How could it have survived being shredded and mildewed over time?

"You just couldn't control yourself, could you?"

Absorbed in her find, it took Ivy several seconds to realize she was no longer alone. She turned and focused on Max, who stood behind her. Her heart skipped a beat. Standing above her, he looked so much like Marcus. The resemblance startled her. His rich dark hair, sharp jaw and intensely mysterious eyes. It was all uncanny.

She was speechless, but he was not. "I'm shocked, Ivy. You were waiting for the first opportunity, weren't you?" He stepped around her and over the dress.

"What are you talking about?"

"The trunk, of course. I thought you would respect the fact that we agreed to open it together."

She stood to her feet and set her chin at a determined angle. He'd pushed a button.

* * * *

Ivy stood up and Max swallowed. Her attire, or rather the lack of, didn't go unnoticed by him. Draped in a white robe that opened to reveal her long neck, she was sexy. The swollen tops of her creamy breasts were visible and inviting. The enticing curve of her hips and her firm nipples pressing against the material made his mind travel downward, onto a road he shouldn't be voyaging. One that could only land him in deep trouble.

He moved away. He was tired of hiding his desire. He didn't know why he couldn't control it.

"Max, don't you dare suggest that I've done something and then turn away from me. How dare you scold me like a child who has misbehaved. You're the one who broke the commitment we made."

He laughed. He couldn't help himself. She could almost pass as an innocent nymph with the way her eyes sparkled. Her lips reminded him of cherry pie. Her hair was now drying. It hung in wayward strands down along her smooth face and one silken shoulder. Denying that he found her undeniably intriguing was useless and tiring. Even while she was eyeing him like she could pitch a fork into his ass, his cock was still in high alert.

Max did realize that she was turning the tables on him to defend her actions. She was desirable enough that he could have easily allowed his man parts to override his judgment and forgot all of his mistrust and irritation. He could've made love to her in a way she'd never forget. Yeah, he could have.

This was dangerous, his mind warned. He raked his hand across the back of his neck as his muscles tensed and sweat beaded on his upper lip. Had the temperature turned hell-hot? He was boiling internally. He laughed. This woman was going to be the fall of his sanity.

"Go ahead, Max. Laugh all you want. That's the juvenile in you rearing its head. At least one of us is honest." Her infuriation seemed to seep through every pore and zap him with its singe.

"I'm afraid only one of us is living in the land of reality." Giving her a spanking sounded sweeter every second.

"Oh, that explains it." She threw her hands up. "Your reality allows you to believe you're superior to everyone around you. You can abandon and forsake people at your will. That was my first impression of you. Apparently it will be my last."

"First impression? Have you forgotten that you've found me attractive and interesting from the first moment we met?"

"Now *that's* something to laugh about." Her laugh was harsh and very fake. "There's that reality issue rising up again. If you can figure out what fact and fiction is in that little self-involved mind of yours, now would be the time."

He watched her. He saw the way she looked everywhere in nervous apprehension but kept her eyes off him. "It's true, isn't it? You've wanted me from the beginning."

"Are you on drugs?" She rolled her eyes.

"If you really detested me, Ivy, you could've walked out the door. It was evident you didn't want to be here in the first place. What angers you the most is that you're attracted to me. It's almost like you're losing control, right sweetheart?"

She shook her head sharply. "Attracted? Why would you think that?"

"You felt the captivation between us immediately, didn't you?" He took a step forward, closer to her. He caught a whiff of her womanly scent. He wanted to breathe her into his lungs. "There is a force here. I'm not going to bother denying it. Don't be frightened." With each word he took one more step. She blinked and the fluttering of her lashes swept across the tops of her cheeks.

"Sure, I'll admit there is an attraction between us. But frightened?" He caught the tremor in her tone. "There's no reason." She fumbled with the belt at her waist, closing it tighter. "If anyone is terrified, I'd say it's you. After all, you're the one who has spent a lot of years building a wall of armor around your heart. Maybe you're a little scared that what you're feeling, your emotions, could bust down that safeguard."

"Wow." He dramatized the tone of his voice. "That's a sweetened description. Most people would simply say that I'm a cold-hearted bastard not worth the effort."

"I'm not *most* people." Her words were said in a whisper.

"Well, I guess even cold-hearted bastards can seize a woman's desire." He appreciated the way the corner of her mouth quivered. "Ain't that right?" Her tongue came out to moisten her bottom lip. The movement triggered his naughty thoughts.

"Yes," her answer was throaty.

Max couldn't resist human nature any longer. If he were bound to hell then he'd go straight south doing something he'd wanted to do since he met her. He reached out and ran his thumb over her moist bottom lip. "Tell me, Ivy. Are you a good girl? Or are you a very bad one?"

"I... I don't, I mean, maybe a little of both."

His body ached for her, turning rock hard--solid in need. He wanted to slip his hand inside that silly robe and touch every heated inch of her. He knew she'd be as soft as satin. He couldn't remember ever feeling so damn desperate. "Good girls don't have sex with a man they only met yesterday." There she went licking her bottom lip again. His erection twitched in urgency. Hell-bound indeed.

"And what would a bad girl do?" She looked at him through the veil of her long lashes. Her lips were parted slightly and her eyes were glazed.

"Bad girls would say screw propriety and give in to whim." He lowered his face within inches of hers, breathing in her sweet scent.

"Then I guess I am, without a speck of doubt, a very, very bad girl." Her lips curved into a wicked smile.

All the oxygen was sucked from the room. Max knew at that very moment that he was tangled in a web, and just like a fly, he didn't have enough brains to realize he was about to be devoured by the black widow. Brains or not, he wasn't thinking with his.

Sliding his arm around her waist, he pulled her hard against his body. In the process, he lifted her inches off her feet. His mouth fell to hers in a deep requirement for release.

Max wanted every part of her. He was like a sponge and she was the liquid that he absorbed into every pore. His mind skipped on the heat of passion. His heart raced without constraint. He couldn't remember ever feeling so damned buried in need for a woman. It was like a drug that he couldn't resist although he knew the consequences.

She wrapped her arms tight around him. She pulled herself closer. He moaned. Her mouth opened to allow his tongue full entrance. A deep needful sound came from within her throat. He took that as complete invitation to take it a step further. Oh, he knew he certainly would. There was no turning back. Sometimes two people were just meant to connect.

In one swift, smooth motion he positioned her petite frame against the wall. He pressed his body against hers, holding her steady. He dropped his hand to the opening of her robe and plunged in.

He needed to taste her beauty. He stopped kissing her to lower his mouth to her exposed flesh. Her breasts were creamy smooth and the nipples erected for his pleasure. She arched against his mouth as his lips enclosed around the pearly pink areola. The robe slipped further off her shoulders.

"Max." His name fell from her moist lips like a butterfly fluttering across a flower. Her fingertips dug into his scalp as he nibbled gently on her silky skin. "Max..."

"Yes, baby. I'm here."

* * * *

Ivy could have resided in the ultimate bliss Max inflicted on her. But it wasn't going to happen. She heard her name through a fuzzy tunnel. She thought she'd imagined it. But when she heard a muffled pounding and Max's head snapped up, she realized, although too late to respond suitably, there was someone in the doorway.

"Oh no." The words fell from Ivy's swollen lips as she grasped for the robe to cover herself. Thankfully, Max had been quick and was keeping her nudity covered with his body.

Jimmy Doyle. A look of confusion and surprise marred his boyish features. Ivy

was still pressed up against the wall because Max hadn't moved. Jimmy's mouth fell open.

"Hi, Jimmy," Ivy said. She tried to laugh but it sounded more like a gurgle.

There was no laughing this off.

"Are you okay?" Jimmy's voice sounded similar to a frog being strangled.

"Of course." Ivy tapped Max on the shoulder as a silent request to step back.

Max lowered her to her feet, but she still clung to his shoulders. Her legs were too weak to support her weight. "I'm fine," she answered in a similar choked tone.

"Who the hell is this?" Max asked. His jaw tightened. If looks could kill then Jimmy would be dead.

Ivy reached up and held the front of her robe tightly closed. Her cheeks must have been the color of crimson because they burned like fire. "This... this is Jimmy…umm--" Her mind went blank.

"Doyle. Jimmy Doyle." Jimmy pushed his fists into his pockets and shifted in his tennis shoes. "I work with Ivy."

"That explains who he is, but it doesn't tell me why he's here." Max's eyes swept from one face to another. Ivy realized he was the only one who seemed calm.

Ivy cast Jimmy a glance. He was green around the edges. Ivy felt sorry for him. "He's here for me, Max." She stumbled over her thick tongue. "Not for me, exactly. I thought I could use his help." And in case she needed a third wheel for company, Jimmy would be the perfect buffer. Jimmy had the worst timing.

Max narrowed his eyes on Jimmy. "You look barely old enough to stand up and piss let alone to be Ivy's chaperone."

Ivy shook her head. She heard Jimmy's swallow. "Max, he's not here to chaperone. Like I said, I thought I could use his help." The man had the instincts of a wild animal.

"I know I look young for my age, everyone says so, but I'll be twenty-two next week." Jimmy was a thin man and his Adam's apple bobbed when he spoke, especially when he was nervous.

Max slid Ivy an expression as if asking, "Are you serious?" Then he looked back at Jimmy. "One question. Do you talk as much as Ivy?"

Jimmy glanced from Ivy to Max. "No." Ivy flung Jimmy an evil look. He quickly added, "I mean, I like to hear her talk a lot. No, I meant, only that she doesn't ramble on and on and on."

"You can stop now, Jimmy. Pull your foot out of your mouth," Ivy said. "Now, I'm going to go change if you think you can be a good boy?"

Max appeared offended. "I think we know who the bad one is, don't we?"

Ivy didn't allow Max to embarrass her. She was still flaming from being caught with her lust hanging out. She stopped in front of Jimmy long enough to say, "Don't worry, his bark is much bigger than his bite."

Grabbing her clothes, she headed back into the bathroom where she quickly changed. She couldn't leave the men alone too long--it was like a tiger sitting with a squirrel. Max was definitely the tiger.

She glanced in the mirror. Her hair was already dry. She laughed at her appearance. Had she stuck her finger into a light socket? There wasn't much else she could do to save it at this point. She pulled it up, leaving soft tendrils falling around her face. Her skin was noticeably red and flushed from Max's kisses. There wasn't much helping that, either. She lathered on rich, tinted moisturizer.

Surprisingly, her inner thighs tingled and ached, as if they had been touched right up until the breaking point then discarded like yesterday's news.

If Jimmy hadn't walked in at the most inopportune time she would have made love with Max--not just once. She was sure it would have been time and time and pleasurable time again.

She closed her eyes as the sensual thought embraced her.

She was a bad girl. What would her mother think of her?

A smile came to her. She knew exactly what her mother would say: *Go for it!*

When she went back into the bedroom she stopped in her tracks. She was surprised to find Max and Jimmy laughing and chumming it up like two old pals. She looked from one to the other then focused on Jimmy, the safer of the two. "I see you tamed the wild beast." She was only partly joking.

Jimmy gave Max a buddy pat on the arm. "This guy here, well, let's just say, he's my hero."

Max shrugged. Was that a smug smile? Ivy cringed. Just what the man needed. Another rung to his ego. "Actually, Jimmy, I'm just your average Joe that has been lucky to find extraordinary situations."

Ivy wanted to barf in her mouth. Here she had been in the bathroom, holed up, imagining what could have been happening if they hadn't been interrupted. She'd been close to throttling Jimmy for his untimely arrival. And why hadn't he called first? Now the men were acting as if nothing awkward had just transpired. How did the male gender do that? Ivy wondered how it was that when a woman got caught in a sticky situation, she lived with embarrassment. If a man got caught, he was suddenly a hero. Ivy wanted to scream.

"Average Joe?" Jimmy shook his head in disbelief. His pale eyes shone in amazement. "No average Joe could get the pictures that you do, man. A ghost hunter. How cool. Most photographers would walk away with their balls... I mean, afraid," he tossed an apologetic glance at Ivy,--"after witnessing the things you have."

There was another meaningful buddy slap and a smile of manly attraction. Jimmy was straight as a popsicle stick but it was obvious he had a male crush on Max. His voice lowered as if to keep his words from Ivy hearing. "Did you really date that hot supermodel, Candace Martin? She has those enormous--" Jimmy formed his hands into two large invisible mounds, representing a part of Candace Martin's anatomy.

Ivy quickly interrupted before Max could answer. "If you two are finished ass kissing and telling, I'd like to get back to business." She intentionally kept her eyes off Max. Why did she suddenly feel jealous that he'd dated Candace Martin? So what if Candace was a hot blonde with large breasts? What really bothered Ivy was the notion that, if Max dated hot supermodels, then what would he want with her? He hadn't been joking when he said she wasn't his type.

Ivy reminded herself she wasn't chopped liver. She believed she was in good shape. She didn't work out every day but three times a week in the Pilates studio had made her derriere firmer and legs longer and leaner. In the looks department, she could hold her own. Supermodel or not, she was talented. Done with the pep talk, she said, "Let's get back to the trunk."

"Trunk?" Jimmy asked.

Ivy pointed at the leather trunk with the velvet green dress hanging out. "That trunk." Ivy did not hide her sarcasm. Her patience was growing thin. She denied it had anything to do with sexual tension. She then gave Max a quick glance. "Well, Max, you may as well tell us what you found the first time you searched in it."

"Ivy, I didn't open the damned box." His voice was cool but his lips were thin. "This is crazy. Why are we even arguing over this?"

Lifting her chin defiantly, she narrowed her eyes on him. "Crazy? It's about something more than the box, isn't it?"

Jimmy's nervous laugh made them both dart a look his direction. "Wow, you guys have some kind of love-hate relationship, don't you?"

"Those scales are tipped." Ivy folded her arms around her waist.

"Tipped?" Jimmy's brow popped up.

Ivy didn't respond. Her crossed arms and frown must have spoken volumes.

"Wow, man." Jimmy elbowed Max. "When the babe hates you that's the hottest."

"Jimmy." Ivy lowered her tone to a dangerous level.

"Yes?" Jimmy still had a smile curving his lips.

"Can it." Jimmy was a good kid, a hard worker, and Ivy considered him a friend. But if he couldn't control his mouth it would be a problem. It was bad enough that he'd walked in on one of the most passionate moments in her existence. On top of that, had he seen her partially naked? Max had covered her, but had it been in time? It burned her that Jimmy snuggled up to Max as if he were the next best thing to a teddy bear.

"Okie dokie," Jimmy said.

"If you didn't open the trunk then why did the lock fall into my hand when I barely touched it?" she asked Max.

He stooped to the side of the trunk and looked at the lock. "It's in three pieces, Ivy. There is no way, even though it's rusty and worn, that I could have broken this without making noise. You would have heard me."

Jimmy glanced from Ivy to Max. "If Ivy didn't open it, and you say you didn't--" He pointed a thin finger in Max's direction. "--then who did?"

"Were you here earlier?" Max asked Jimmy.

He shook his head, sending ear-length curls rustling. "Nope."

Ivy and Max looked at one another but didn't say a word. Ivy thought what Max had said was true. If he'd been in the bedroom pounding at the lock, she would have heard the racket. However, she had drifted off--if that's what she could call it--for a short time. She tapped her lips with the tip of one finger, confused at the situation.

Her eyes were drawn to the dress. Bending, she picked it up and carefully folded it. "This is the dress Elizabeth has on in the portrait."

"Shouldn't it be dry rotted?" Max asked.

Ivy shrugged. She had wondered the same thing. "I would think."

"That's some garment, dudes," Jimmy chimed in.

"You're right. This is some garment," Ivy agreed. After setting the dress down on the end of the bed, she peered into the trunk, and disappointment seized her. "Well, there's nothing else."

Max's heavy sigh bounced off the walls. Without a word, he left the room.

Ivy listened to Max's fading footsteps as he made his way down the stairs. She looked at Jimmy, who was watching her apologetically. "I'm sorry, Ivy. If I'd had any idea what I was walking into I would have run the other way while kicking myself in the ass. What a bummer."

She smiled and shrugged. "It's okay." Not really.

"Wow, I'm glad you forgive me." Relief crawled across his face.

"I didn't say I forgive you." Seeing his confused expression, she finally said, "Can you blame me?"

He bobbed his head in a nod. "I'm not into men or anything, but he's a hot dude. Of course," he said, flashing his pearly whites and turning up his collar, "he's no match for me. What does he have that I don't have?"

Ivy tucked her hand into his elbow and gently said, "Twenty years in age, equal time in knowledge and skills, and Candace Martin in his list of achievements. You know, the woman with massive--" She mirrored his earlier hand motion.

"Ahh, come on, Ivy. Candace Martin has nothing on you. If you were my girl even a woman like Candace Martin couldn't turn my head."

She patted his hand appreciatively. He seemed serious and it touched her, slightly. "Thanks, Jimmy. Even if you're a big liar I'm still flattered. How about if I give you the two-cent tour of our haunted house?"

"Is it really haunted?"

"I don't know," she said.

"Can I spend the night? I'd love to watch Max work."

"Come on, Jimmy. A true reporter would stay a night in hell to get a story." Maybe it was a good thing to have Jimmy around--to keep the lines strong between her and Max. The match had been ignited and the burn was slow. She wasn't sure she could resist the magnetism alone with Max.

"I'm only an apprentice. I don't get paid the big bucks like you do for a front pager."

Ivy started to laugh at his disenchanted words but caught herself. He was serious and she didn't want to burst his imaginary bubble. The money never got better, no matter which position or story a journalist landed at the Tribune. She just couldn't do it to him. "As we're walking, let's talk about that new girlfriend of yours. The pretty brunette who just started at the Tribune."

"Delilah? How did you hear?"

Ivy smiled. She felt sorry for Jimmy. She believed him to be the most naïve man she'd ever met. No secrets were safe from a group of journalists.

Chapter 11

Max went downstairs, grabbed his camera and headed outdoors.

He believed himself to be a man who could conquer anything that came his way. While in the Marines he'd experienced war-torn countries, AIDS-plagued villages and hungry children who begged for a crumb of food. Many times he'd sat quietly around a fire scared out of his wits and with little or nothing to eat.

Once upon a time he'd been a different man. Certainly he'd always been tough and rough around the edges; after all, he was a military man. He had lost the simplest forms of human kindness and compassion.

Stepping into the bright sunlight, he blinked as his eyes adjusted. It was the right amount of light for perfect pictures. He had wanted to snap some of the house and a few around the property. Not to mention he needed to ease his inner turmoil.

He was still dazed over what had transpired between him and Ivy. The shocker wasn't in the act itself, but the raw magnetism that drew him to her. He found her sexual appeal amazing. What was sexiest about her was the sheer fact that she didn't try to be sexy. She just was. There was nothing sexier than a woman being confident in herself and her abilities.

Max knew he shouldn't have allowed it to go that far. They were two consenting adults who could make love without strings attached, but with a woman like Ivy it could be as deadly as playing Russian roulette.

Life was how he wanted it. He liked having no one to answer or explain himself to. He was a happy man. He chose to live alone because it was easy. He didn't need a warm-hearted, talks-too-much woman coming along and trying to cast a spell on him.

Max explored the property until the sun started to drop. He ran down to the small corner market and grabbed more food supplies. When he got back the house was shadowed in complete darkness. He didn't hear Ivy and her cohort as he started a fire.

The quiet didn't last long. Ivy and Jimmy gathered around the warmth of the fire, too. The two were busily chattering about the mystery surrounding the house. Max listened, not wanting to interject his thoughts and opinions. It was obvious Ivy was ignoring him. If Jimmy caught a hint of the tense predicament he didn't let on. When Ivy became silent, staring into the fire, Jimmy turned his attention to Max and bombarded him with a hundred and one questions about Max's travels.

Max wasn't a man who enjoyed conversation, especially an interrogation about himself, but he was happy enough to tolerate and be patient with Jimmy's interest.

A knock came at the door. Max looked at Ivy in curiosity but she appeared as surprised as he was. They both looked at Jimmy, who lifted his hands in a guilty action. "I hope you two don't mind that I invited Delilah." He looked at Ivy sheepishly. "You know, she didn't want to be away from me one night."

Max shook his head in disbelief. "Damn, boy, you better go and answer the door before she decides you're not worth waiting for." His eyes impulsively slid across the space to Ivy. Did she realize that he wasn't worth her wait?

Delilah wasn't what Max would've expected. Her hair, dyed jet black, was pulled into a severe bun. Her eyes appeared like two small slits beneath layers of thick blue eye shadow and black eyeliner. She had a line of six earrings in each ear and a small piercing in her nose. She wore a spiked dog collar around her neck, a chain around one wrist and a tattoo of a barbwire around the other. And she was very sweet and entertaining.

Max could see that Jimmy was fascinated with Delilah. He couldn't keep his hands off her, from simple touches like fingers in her hair, to quick kisses on her cheeks, to holding hands. Young love--nothing like it. Max inwardly cringed.

Ivy was like a magnet for his gaze. She'd been quiet most of the evening. He wondered what consumed her. Once in awhile he noticed she'd look over at him but she made it seem like an accident.

It wasn't long before Jimmy and Delilah excused themselves. It was obvious they had more in mind than sleeping.

Alone, Ivy broke the silence. "Max, about today--"

He waved a hand to dismiss it. "There's nothing to say."

"But I believe there is. If Jimmy hadn't walked in we would have made love. I know it's wrong but I don't think I would've regretted it."

His eyes found hers through the dimly lit room. Those weren't the words he'd expected to hear from her. He wanted to deny that it would've gone that far but there was no credible defense. She echoed his thoughts. He was used to feeling numb. Ivy was taking his senses for a ride.

"Why can't you open up and tell me what has made you so distant?" Ivy coaxed.

"By 'open up' to you, you mean why don't I open up and tell you the story. Once a journalist always a journalist, right?" His words weren't bitter but simply direct. "You want the story? Well, here's a story for you. There was once a man who met a beautiful girl. He fell for her, whole heart and soul because he thought their relationship was golden, or at least it appeared to be. They married and were happy with a nice, abundant group of friends--her friends--and they had good, praiseworthy jobs. The foolish man didn't want to believe that his wife wasn't the woman he thought she was and that the love wasn't what he thought, either. One day the senseless man came home early from a business trip to find his wife in bed with another man. Apparently his lovely wife had become bored and lonely and had asked a male friend to keep her company."

"Max, I didn't--"

"I'm not finished. I'm at the good part now." He couldn't stop. The words flowed like water from a faucet. "Instead of going berserk like the foolish man wanted to do, he instead ran off onto some remote island for solitude. One would think then the story would've fizzled, right? *No*. A quick divorce wasn't in the cards. The wicked wife wouldn't be pleased until she had everything--and I do mean everything--that the foolish man had worked his whole life to achieve." He paused to take a deep breath, then released it through his tight lips. "She had the cars, the animal, and even the friends, which didn't really matter because they were her snooty friends. But the dog? Now that hurt because he wasn't hers to begin with. She didn't even like him. And the man gave it all away."

"You should have fought for what was yours, Max. After all, she was the cheater."

"It was much easier to give it all to her than to fight her powerful attorney and rich father. I was happy to stay on my high mountain until the flood receded. But she wasn't done with me until she had ran my name and my reputation through the mud. And the press? They loved printing their false stories because it drummed up readers. Who cared about the poor bastard they were helping slaughter?"

"I owe you an apology."

He shook his head. "Save it. We've both said enough. We've both come here for our own reasons. Mine is to find answers, not to create questions."

Ivy's sigh sounded heavy in the room.

He didn't want to speak to her and she didn't push. She said goodnight and left for her bedroom.

Max checked all of his equipment, situated his sleeping bag in front of the fire and lay down. He didn't even want to move upstairs to the bedroom.

He watched the monitor and his eyes grew heavy. He closed his lids, pondering his thoughts.

He wasn't sure what time it was or what had awakened him but when he brought his head up, lethargically scanning the room, he saw that he wasn't alone. Alarm brought him fully awake and into a sitting position.

At first he thought he was dreaming. He saw Ivy, her body sheathed in a thin satiny gown. Her long, silky hair hung in waves around her shoulders. By the golden glow of the light he could make out her glossy eyes, creamy skin and full lips. She was beautiful. Had he ever thought any differently?

It was dream. It had to be. It was all an erotic dream.

She moved closer. He blinked erratically, thinking her image would disappear. He opened his eyes wide. Nope, she was still there in all her splendid glory.

She lowered to her knees next him on the sleeping bag. Her scent surrounded him in an erotic cloud.

* * * *

Ivy felt the heated flames of the fire and her skin warmed. She drew in the masculine scent of Max through her nostrils. It teased her senses. She'd wanted to be near him, next to him, with him. She wanted to feel his touch, to taste him, to know him.

"What are you doing, Ivy?" Max's voice was low and thick. He started to get up but her hand on his arm kept him steady.

She allowed her eyes the enjoyment of roving over his finely toned body, taking in his rippled stomach and solid arms. His jeans were unbuttoned and partially unzipped. The tip of his erection was sticking out of the top. She sucked in a deep breath. She tossed her head back and looked at him through her lashes. "I'm here for you. I've come to you."

"I'm flattered, *oh damn am I flattered*." His words came out as a hiss. "But we shouldn't be here like this. I can't allow this to happen. If it were any other woman... But somehow it's not right, not with you."

"Why? We both want this, don't we?"

He remained quiet and turned his head, as if he feared she'd see the truth. She took his chin in her palm and gently brought his face to meet hers. "It's time to quit imagining what it'd be like being together. It's time to make it reality."

"You don't know what you're saying." His breath swept across her cheek.

She saw his fight diminishing as his face softened. His fire-lit eyes turned into red embers. His magnetism was so much more than she'd ever bargained for. He drew her to him, his soul called to her. She knew what she wanted. Ivy wondered if he could see her need in her eyes. Could he feel the burning desire in her body?

"You don't know what you're getting yourself into, Ivy. I'm not the white-picket-fence sort of guy. I'm a drifter and I like it this way. You're wanting more and deserve so much more than I can ever give. Don't you see? You want a man who will be there for you when you need him. That's not me."

"Don't lecture me, Max. I'm not asking you to marry me. I know fully well who you are. I'm not asking for anything more than your kiss, your touch and you inside of me." She rested her hand against his chest and swore she felt the thumping of his heart against her palm. "Neither of us will have regrets, I know."

He clenched his hand into a fist at his side as if the tension was too much. "Remember, I'm the cold-hearted bastard. You should take that into consideration."

"You know that I'm a journalist. I seek out the whole story for facts and truths. I'd like to research this circumstance a little further before I make a judgment. I'm a woman who goes for all she wants and 'no' is not an option here. You should take that into consideration." She leaned closer and placed butterfly kisses on his jaw. The prickly roughness of his beard scraped her lips, leaving them tingly.

"So, I'm basically a story?" She heard the jagged release of his breath when she lowered her lips to the pulse point in his neck.

"One story that I plan to investigate thoroughly from beginning, middle, all the way to the end." She continued to plant soft, light kisses on his collarbone. She popped her head up and asked, "Does this bother you?"

He hesitated a moment. "No expectations? No regrets?"

"No regrets. However, expectations, yes. I do expect this to be a mind-boggling, soul-tingling experience. How about you?"

He gently lifted her chin with his thumb and their eyes connected. "You are a tiger wearing a kitten's hide." He reached his arms around her and pulled her body down upon his. "I'm expecting you to give up that phony innocent expression you wear so well. It's completely misleading."

There was a mere second that lingered between them, eyes caressing one another, before his lips met hers.

His kiss was soft and tender, testing the water before jumping in with his entire body. Soon they were both caught up in the whirlwind of passion and intrigue.

Ivy moaned in pleasure as Max tugged one shoulder of her flimsy gown downward, sending it easily over the soft curves of her naked body. The cool air brought goosebumps to her skin but they disappeared with the heat wave created as he dropped moist kisses on her exposed skin. "You're so damn beautiful," he whispered against one nipple.

Ivy dropped her head back and reveled in the feel of his lips on her sensitive skin. She gave in completely to the flames licking at her skin. There was a throbbing at the apex of her thighs. It grew so sharp, so rapid, like a forest fire out of control. She dug her fingers into his shoulders and thrust her hips in a circle trying to ease the intensity. Arching deeper, she rubbed against him hungrily, and in a daze, she dipped her hips against the hardness behind his zipper, slowly and deliberately.

Chapter 12

Max wanted to take things slow, but Ivy was like sweet honey to his resistance. He was mesmerized by her femininity, her delicate skin. From her firm breasts to her slender waist--she was perfect. She was like a dream but hot reality to his senses. She reached out to him, fumbling awkwardly with the zipper of his jeans. He sucked in a breath and placed his hands upon hers. "Take it slow, sweetheart," he whispered next to her ear. Taking a leisure pace was not a possibility. The chemistry was intoxicating.

"Say that to me on our third or fourth time." She nuzzled her nose against his neck.

Max was lost. He buried his face into her scented hair as he threaded his fingers through the tangled length. Her skin was like satin against his fingertips as he slid them down along the feminine curve of her neck, the subtle dip of her collarbone and further downward to the low neckline of her gown. With the other hand, he found the hem and lifted it higher and higher until it was up and over her shoulders and lying in a silken heap on the floor. She wore nothing but a pleasured smile.

He dipped his head to nibble on one nipple, sampling her taste. The pert bud hardened against his tongue. He rubbed it until she moaned aloud. He smiled against her breasts. "Like that, baby?"

"Immensely."

Sliding his knee between hers, he gently parted them until her legs spread wide, enough to allow his hand access to her most sensitive part. She was wet and creamy smooth. He delved his middle finger between her folds, sliding the digit inside of her moist warmth. She groaned and gyrated her hips against his palm. "Yes, Max. Yes." She welcomed him with a seductive voice.

She tugged his jeans past his hips until his hard length was fully exposed. Her slender hand wrapped around him and glided along the sheath. He felt himself growing nearer to the brink. He didn't want to risk release before he had a chance to please her into insanity.

"I need you now." He forced the words from his mouth.

She lowered herself to the sleeping bag and he followed. Max removed his jeans the rest of the way in record speed. Grabbing a foil-wrapped package from his wallet, he made haste in sliding the rubber down his length. Tucking both hands under her, he cupped her ass. He lifted her hips, then thrust himself deep inside her. She molded around him like a leather glove. Every nerve cell in his body came alive.

They came together in a matrimonial explosion of bittersweet bliss.

* * * *

Ivy fluttered her eyelashes. She brought her fingertips to her temples and pressed, hoping to ease the headache. She caught a reflection of herself in the glass pane of the window. She was Elizabeth again. She had been lying in Max's arms one second and here the next. It left her cold.

She examined Elizabeth's image in the window. Her long dark hair was pulled up into a messy bun. Tendrils of hair had fallen lose and her cheeks were rosy. She reached up to push back a long strand when she noticed the paint splatters on her hands and green dress. She turned her attention to the canvas on the easel. It was only the beginning of a painting. There were only a few strokes of color on the stark white. The array of colors next to the painting reminded her of an abstract of a flower garden.

She dropped her hands into her lap. Her head felt better but her stomach was tense.

She moved, feeling a cool smoothness on her neck. She reached up and touched the necklace--a string of pearls. It was an exquisite necklace, the prettiest she'd ever laid eyes upon. She guessed it was a gift from Marcus.

Ivy felt an onslaught of explosions inside her brain, as if all of Elizabeth's thoughts were merging with her own. She was becoming Elizabeth, flesh and bone. It excited as well as frightened her. Before she was pulled out of her own life, she and Max had made love. She'd connected with him. She feared the outcome of staying here, in the past. What if she stayed in Elizabeth's life and couldn't find her pathway home?

Elizabeth loved Marcus. It was in her heart. Ivy felt it.

But Elizabeth's emotions were her emotions now, too.

Ivy wasn't sure how much time had passed while she was in the studio. She'd watched the sun move in the sky. She was in hiding. She stared at the unfinished painting in hopeless deliberation. She didn't have a lick of artistic ability and wouldn't dare touch Elizabeth's creation. A smile

Rhonda Lee Carver

curved Ivy's lips. What would poor Elizabeth think if she came back from wherever she was and saw a blotched version of her original?

Shrouded in her thoughts, a knock on the door caused Ivy to jump in alarm. Her sudden movement sent the paints onto the floor at her feet. The colors splattered onto her clothes and shoes. "Oh shit." She looked down at the mess. It was a disaster. She guessed Elizabeth wouldn't have been as flighty as to waste her paints.

Ivy did the best she could by fixing her messy bun and covering the paints with a drop cloth.

"Elizabeth?" Marcus called from the other side of the door. "Are you okay?"

Ivy glanced around the room. She'd have to concentrate on the paint later. Now she needed to focus on convincing Marcus that his wife hadn't flipped her lid.

"Elizabeth?" His voice raised in tone. "I'm beginning to worry."

"What...what is it?" she asked through the door.

"I'd like to speak to you." She heard the rustling of his clothes against the door.

"Go ahead." Ivy held her ear against the door. "I can hear you."

"I'd like to speak to you while I'm looking at you."

"I look a complete mess." If she could postpone conversation until later it would be better for both of them. Her nerves were frayed and she wasn't sure she could handle seeing him and not making an idiot of herself.

"Elizabeth, come out. Sally said you've been behind this door all day."

"Really?" She knew she'd been there awhile.

"Really. Now come out. I need to speak with you."

"Like I told you, I'm a mess."

"I won't look."

Ivy realized it was no use. He wouldn't go away without seeing her. With one last look at her skirt, she finally opened the door. He was standing in the hallway. His large frame leaned casually against the wall. His eyes whisked over her. She narrowed her eyes in dispute. "You said you wouldn't look."

"That would be impossible."

"What did you need to speak to me about?" she asked, eyes mechanically falling to the floor.

He pushed himself off the wall and walked the few steps closer to her. She brought her face up. "You were up quite early this morning."

His breath swept across her face and she could smell whiskey and freshly washed skin. "I'm an early riser." She fumbled for an answer.

His warm eyes caressed her. "I just assumed you were sneaking away into your hiding place." His mouth curved into a grin. He teased her.

Her bottom lip quivered, not just from the mention of her hiding place, but also from his close proximity. "Why would I sneak?"

"Why should you?" He lifted a thick brow.

"You're the one who insinuated that I was hiding so why don't you tell me why you think I would be," she demanded.

"You're dodging my question. Now, am I wrong?"

"About dodging your question?"

"No, about sneaking." His brows snapped together.

"Of course. But, you did say I could have this room as my own. Are you suggesting that I do not deserve my own privacy?"

"No, my lady, I am not. You're free to have secrets. I am, though, a husband who is interested in his wife's pastimes."

"Being a wife doesn't mean I shall share all of my confidences, does it?" The words were out before Ivy had a chance to speculate what Elizabeth would say in the same position. From Marcus's glare, he appeared surprised.

"My darling, you can have all the secrets and confidences you wish. I'm only hoping that in time," he reached out and gently swiped his finger along her jaw line, as if to wipe something away, "you'll come to trust me and open up to me. I'm not such a bad man, am I?"

She trembled under his touch. To her bewilderment, she wanted his touch to linger. She remained silent as he withdrew his handkerchief from his pocket and gently wiped her cheek. "There you are, all clean." He returned the handkerchief to his pocket.

With shaky fingers, she touched the spot where he'd wiped. "Thank you."

He remained close to her, quiet. She thought for a moment that he'd kiss her but instead he moved away. "Will you come to lunch with me?" he asked.

"Is it lunch time already?"

"Yes. I hope you will say yes because I've already asked Sally to prepare something for us."

She smiled. Presumptuous as he was, wrong he was not. She enjoyed the thought of spending time with him. "Can I freshen up first?"

"If you wish, my dear. But in my opinion, you look refreshing enough. However, it is best if you put on your riding clothes." He smiled deliberately as he walked away from her and headed down the hallway.

"Riding clothes?" Ivy involuntarily stiffened.

He stopped and turned back to her. "You've been cooped up long enough. It's time you got out and had the chance to admire this beautiful property as I have for so long."

Ivy had never been on a horse, or petted one, for that matter, in all her life. She had no clue how one even climbed upon one's back. Her mind searched for an excuse. If she told him the truth, he would suspect something wasn't right. She nibbled the corner of her mouth until a thought came to her. "But, Marcus, I don't have any riding clothes."

"I was aware of that, my darling. I hope the size fits." And he was gone.

Ivy went to her bedroom and found the beautiful riding gown laid out for her on her bed. On top of the elegant skirt was a yellow rose with a note encircling the stem. She gulped back her trepidation as she unrolled the paper and began to read Marcus's immaculate handwriting.

Elizabeth,

I hope you like my choice of riding attire. It is the style of fancy in the finest boutiques. Green is your favorite color, I have noticed.

Marcus

The outfit was splendid and fit for a princess. She was tickled that he'd noticed that green was her favorite color. Not very many men, especially men from the future, paid attention to these things.

She plopped down on the end of the bed and fell back onto the soft mattress. Blowing out a frustrated breath through her tight lips, she wondered what she'd say to a shocked Marcus when she fell off the horse and landed on her face.

Quickly dressing, she left her room in search of her husband.

Marcus was outside waiting for her. Two horses were saddled and ready. When he looked up to see her coming toward him, Ivy could see by his expression that he appreciated her outfit as much as she did. He sauntered in her direction. Her heart began to beat wildly. His walk, his features, his eyes--it all reminded her of Max. The more she saw Marcus the more she felt the two men were linked.

A smile broke out over his face and his eyes shone brightly in the sunlight. "Elizabeth, you look beautiful. And, I see I'm a good judge of size." His eyes swept along her slender body. "We'll have the seamstress make you another." He wiggled his eyebrows.

"Thank you, Marcus. This is thoughtful and green is definitely my favorite color." She fluffed the skirt and admired the glossy fabric in the sun.

"For you, Mrs. Thornton, anything."

The man was a charmer. With his looks, she'd guess he could charm a bear into lying down. And she was a sucker for a man who treated his woman with courtesy. She felt special here with him. He had a way of making her feel like they were the only two people in the world. But this wasn't real. She wasn't Elizabeth.

"Are you okay?" He looked at her from where he checked the saddles. Concern filled his eyes.

"Marcus, I need to tell you something."

"Yes?" He filled one pouch with food.

"I'm not a very good rider." She minimized the truth, she knew. How could she tell him she'd never been close enough to a horse to touch it and that she found it a bit frightening?

"You can't ride?" He lifted a thick brow.

Ivy swallowed the thickness building in her throat. Before she could examine her words, she blurted, "When I was eleven I fell off a horse and I haven't ridden since." Her mouth remained open wide. She had no clue where those words erupted from, but it certainly wasn't the truth about her own life. Had Elizabeth experienced a traumatic event involving a horse?

Instead of ridicule, his face softened and his eyes warmed. "You have nothing to apologize for. We'll just move to Plan B."

"Plan B?" she inquired. As long as it didn't involve a horse she'd be much happier.

"Yes, everyone should have a Plan B."

"May I ask what Plan B is?"

He smiled and winked. "Have a little trust, sweetheart. Plan B is for you to ride with me on my stallion. That is if you have faith enough in my riding abilities."

She still hesitated. Ivy had no doubt that Marcus was more than capable of keeping her safe.

"What's wrong, my dear? Don't you have confidence in me?"

"I have confidence in you." She had no reason to doubt him.

"Great! So come meet my horse. His name is Robbins. Robbins, this is my wife, Elizabeth." Marcus gave the horse's beautiful black frame a firm pat. Robbins responded with what seemed to be an equestrian smile. "No funny business, you hear? She's mine."

She admired the sweet expression of emotion he showed his horse. She'd never have suspected that he was this tender, especially toward a horse. When she didn't make her way to the horse, he held out his hand, palm up. She laid her hand in his and he threaded his fingers through hers. There was something about his touch, so different yet familiar.

"Are we ready?" he asked, interrupting her thoughts.

"Ready as I'll ever be," she murmured.

Once Marcus was seated in the saddle he reached down, and in one swift movement he lifted her easily into the saddle behind him. She settled into the soft leather, her body easing against his. She shamelessly wrapped her arms around his waist. She could feel his heart beating on the palm of her hand. A faint notion skittered through her mind that Marcus wasn't her husband. He was Elizabeth's husband. The idea wasn't enough to take away the feeling that she belonged here. She wondered if her attraction for Marcus was merely because he reminded her of Max.

"You better hold on tighter unless you want to fall off," Marcus called to her over his shoulder.

She clung tighter, but realized that he was only teasing when he started to laugh. She stuck out her tongue. He laughed deeper, vibrating his chest. Instead of laughing at her, she thought he should be commending her for even getting on the horse.

Chapter 13

Ivy jumped up, breathing hard. In panic, she turned around and saw Max lying beside her. She was with Max. She was home.

Reaching down, she touched her inner thighs. The awkward feeling of her legs straddling a saddle lingered on her sensitive skin. The numbness of her fingers felt like she'd been clenching her hands into tight fists. The dream had seemed so real.

Max, still lying silently beside her, didn't stir. His breathing was smooth. She moved her eyes down his nudity. The man was remarkably sexy. The thought brought a smile to her lips. Making love--or having sex--with him had not been only great, but probably bordered on perfect. They had come together in such a magnitude that she believed she'd be ruined for all other men. He was a skilled and giving lover. He'd taken her to new heights and she still lingered there.

The morning sun was just beginning to rise over the west hillside. The room was starting to lighten with the new day's presence. She'd never felt so good. So satisfied. No feelings of guilt or shame lingered. No emotions of regret. Only desire.

She couldn't believe that Max would feel guilt either. He'd opened up to her. She'd felt like they'd known each other intimately for years. He had touched her with unselfish warmth. In return, she'd given herself. It was a connection like none other.

The rising sun cast more of its golden glow through the window, exposing Max's body in its graciousness. She examined him more closely. She wanted to know his ins and outs. No doubt that the man was toned and strong. From his broad chest, his slender hips and… She stopped. On his left hip was a birthmark the size of a half dollar. She studied it. The pigmentation was in the shape of a leaf with a pointed tip. She'd never seen anything like it. Someone could have easily painted the permanent mark on his skin because it was perfectly shaped. She reached over and ran the tip of her nail across the contour.

He stirred. Ivy slowly laid back onto the crook of his arm. She didn't want to get caught ogling his goods, although who could blame her? She stifled a laugh. With man parts like his, one would have to be blind not to admire. And a blind person would enjoy using touch to examine his body.

Max fluttered one eye open and then the other. He pressed his fingers over his eyes. He moved so that he was leaning on one elbow and looking at her. "Hi." His voice was husky.

She bit her bottom lip as desire ripped through her without mercy. "Hi."

He whispered into her ear, "So, this was not just a mind-blowing dream?"

"Mmm. If it is, then don't wake me." She nestled closer to his warmth. It seemed to seep through her skin and inside her bones.

He took a piece of hair and twisted it around his finger. His eyes were liquid as he looked deep into hers. "You're beautiful."

"So are you." She twisted around to face her body to his. His hardness pressed against her thigh. "You read my mind."

He kissed the tip of her nose. "How long have you been awake?" He tossed a glance toward the window. He moved away from her.

"Not too long." She felt the dreaded cold sweep across her. She'd hoped they could have *dreamed* again. But instead of reaching out and dragging him back, she said, "I had a very important matter solved last night."

"What was that?" he asked over his shoulder as he fumbled for his clothes that were scattered around the room.

"You don't snore. However, you do talk in your sleep."

"I do?" His laugh was gruff. "Did I answer any more questions for you?"

"Just one or two. But don't worry, I'll keep the secrets to myself." She wiggled her brows.

"That's good because I'd hate to get revenge by telling the world that *you* snore." He kept a very serious face.

She immediately stopped laughing. Was he joking? Maybe he wasn't. "Are you serious?"

He found his clothes but didn't pull them on. Instead, he slid back down next to her in the sleeping bag. She wasn't about to complain. He played with the skin of her collarbone. She shivered in delight. "Well, honestly, no you don't. I don't think you even moved."

If he only knew just how far she'd moved--a hundred years or so. "Would you still like me if I snored?" She looked up at him through the veil of her lashes.

He smiled. "Snoring is one thing I can tolerate."

"Only one thing?"

"Maybe two or three."

Curious, she wondered aloud, "Tell me something you can't tolerate." She ran her fingers along the triangle patch of crisp hair on his chest. She slid her hand further down, stopping at his flat stomach.

He continued to touch her in all the right places. His fingers were deliciously capable and gentle. "Cages and chains."

She pulled her hand back. "Are you talking figuratively or tangibly?" He planted butterfly kisses along her neckline and down onto her breasts. She arched her back and moaned as he suckled her nipples. She had no idea that a man could give her so much pleasure just with his mouth on her areolas. Breathless, she managed to ask, "Are you trying to dodge me?"

"No. But if I were would it be so wrong?" He continued to administer havoc on her senses.

"Well." She curved her body against his. His erection touched her thigh as his hand slid up her other leg. She opened to him. "I do think it's a subject we can let pass. In fact, I've already forgotten what we were discussing. Something about whips and chains…"

"Shh…" He touched the tip of his finger against her lips.

* * * *

Max touched the smooth skin between her thighs and slid into her. She was slippery wet and on fire. He glided his thumb into her smooth ridged opening until she bridged her body. He plunged two fingers in and out until she moaned.

Max couldn't take his eyes off her beauty. She fluttered her eyes open as he tasted her dew from his fingers. He pressed his iron hardness against her thigh, needing her attention. She took his shaft into her palm, folding her fingers around him. She squeezed him lightly, rubbing along the pulsating vein on his length. He caught his breath with a moan. "That's good."

She stroked him into pure ecstasy. He couldn't take it any longer. There was a point a man needed more to tame his lustful beast buried within. "Stop," he murmured against her neck. She continued to touch him. "You've got to stop." He was breathless as he reached down and gently grabbed her wrist with his fingers. She smiled as he pulled her arms high above her head. "You like having power over me, don't you?"

"Oh? I have power?" Mischief filled her eyes.

He stared down at her and heaved a tense sigh. "Vixen." He reached for the last condom packet and tore it open. He started to unroll it when she grabbed it from his fingers.

"Let me." She glided the sheath easily over him, then led him to the center of her. She was hot and moist in anticipation.

In one swift motion he plunged himself deep inside her. A profound whimper filled the silence--he realized it was him. Her tight body enclosed around him in delicious sensation. He paused within her, holding her close, sinking into the feeling of pure ecstasy. He wanted--*no, needed*--to take it slow. If he moved too fast he was bound to explode before he was ready.

When the urge to burst eased a bit he moved in and out of her. He lifted her knees in the crook of his elbows, which gave him deeper access inside her heated core. It was hot and heavenly, and even through the barrier she felt amazing.

Max closed his eyes, consumed with the feel of her. Ivy called out his name over and over and over again as the tension grew in the center of him and spread like sweet honey throughout his body. She clenched her inner muscles, reaching orgasm. The feel of her spasms around him sent him closer to the edge. His rhythm increased in pace until he was driving with the force of a reckless man.

As he reached the peak of explosion, he whispered, "Ivy."

And he too found release.

Chapter 14

A languid hour passed until Ivy and Max finally climbed out of their warm abode in the sleeping bag meant for one. Their stomachs growled, reminding them they hadn't eaten in awhile and they were in dire need of nourishment. Also, they weren't sure when Jimmy and Delilah would wake up.

Ivy wasn't embarrassed at what she'd shared with Max but she didn't want to be caught naked in his sleeping bag.

While she gathered up the blankets Max went to wash up before he started breakfast. She had offered to make breakfast, but he'd volunteered and she gladly accepted.

Folding the last blanket, she heard her cellphone ring. She hesitated, not sure if she wanted to answer it. She wanted to keep the outside world at bay for as long as possible. Caller ID told her it was Marshall. She rolled her eyes. He'd keep calling until she answered.

Clicking the phone on, she said, "What is it, Marshall?"

"Am I bothering you, Ivy?" Marshall asked.

"Yes, but would that deter you?" Ivy knew he was only being sarcastic.

"No, but isn't it nice that I asked? Isn't that an improvement on my usual tactless nature you're always complaining about?"

"Sarcasm stinks, Marshall." Ivy gripped the phone. "It's only an improvement if you aren't being acerbic."

"A man set in his ways will never change. No use in trying." He had no shame.

"At least you're honest about your faults."

"Enough small talk. Got a story yet?"

"You wouldn't believe the story and treasures we've encountered and dredged up since we arrived. It's unbelievable."

"Are you serious?" he asked in a breathless voice.

"No. I don't feel like being serious this morning. I've told you, Marshall. There isn't a story." Her dreams weren't front page news.

"Oh, there's something there. It's right in front of your eyes."

"What's that? Dust and cobwebs?"

"Max Shepard, my dear. The mysterious man who manages to elude all publicity and interviews. An exclusive would be--"

"You stop right there." She checked over her shoulder to see if she were still alone.

"You're a journalist, Ivy, and a journalist doesn't have any morals or values. You know the thought has been tossed around your mind a couple of times. He's a man of interest, especially since he has come back from wherever the hell he's been hibernating. You said yourself you're looking for a real story, something worth biting into. Isn't the journalist in you taking mental notes on this Shepard?"

"You're unbelievable." She heaved a sigh.

"But think of the money involved. Wouldn't it be nice to set your mother up with a home nurse, someone who could stay with her while you're at work? Wouldn't it be nice to have someone reliable?"

"Okay, that would be nice, but what about your problem?" she asked.

"What problem is that?"

"Your cunning, ruthless way of walking all over people."

"If I didn't know you any better, Ivy, I'd take offense to that." His laugh rang through the phone.

"The only story the public wants with Max--" she lowered her voice to a mere whisper. "--is lies. The real story is how the media ran his name through the mud by portraying him as a two-timing, scheming creep. That just isn't true. He's a nice guy. Disconnected, but a good guy."

"Well, well. What do we have here?" Marshall's laughter grew deeper, grating against her nerves. "Do I sense romance in the air?"

"Your senses are all screwed up. Are you sure it isn't infidelity you're sensing? Or did Jasmine finally keep her legs glued shut?"

"The only infidelity in the works is with your boyfriend Max. Oh, excuse me, I forgot. The media portrayed him wrongly."

"There is no story with him. I'll stay and check out the house. I'll even stay up all night with video camera if I have to, but I'm not digging into Max's past."

Marshall sighed. His voice took on a different tone. "Ivy, you're getting too close. You're letting your feelings get in the way of your job."

She thought he actually sounded slightly concerned. "I'm fine."

"Come on, Ivy. I'm not asking you to smear the man's character all over the front page. That's been done. I'm asking you to get a personal interview. You'll be the first in print in years. Maybe he'll even agree to let you write his biography. You say the tabloids blasted him unfairly. Well then, you get a story that tells the truth. Give the public the truth. How can the man get angry if you do him right?"

"He'd never agree to a biographical."

"Then at least an interview."

"If I could see you now I bet your pupils are in the shape of dollar signs."

"I'm not going to play games here, Ivy. You betcha I think you have a story. I see money for you and I see money for the Tribune. I think there's more to this man than him wanting pictures of a dump. So we need to delve deeper into this."

"We?" She groaned.

"The public only gets his professional side and now, you can give them the inside scoop. This could start your career boiling."

Hearing a creak in the flooring she turned to find Max standing behind her, watching her. She turned her phone off, beginning to explain the conversation to him because she had no idea how long he'd been standing there and what he'd heard. Before she could find the words to explain, he asked, "Did I interrupt?"

Uncomfortable, she said, "No, not at all." Ivy had a feeling that anxiety was written all over her face.

"Sounds like you were having an argument with a lover?"

"Now that's funny. You couldn't be further from the truth, trust me. That was Marshall, my boss. He was just checking to see if all was going as planned."

His eyes fell over her. At first she thought he would ask her more about the call, but he didn't. "I was just coming to let you know breakfast is ready."

Ivy took a deep breath and dropped her phone back into her purse. She felt hypocritical believing that some of Marshall's points made sense. She didn't want to write a story about the bad parts of Max's existence, but the good parts. The parts that made him such a huge success at ghost hunting.

There was so much to this man that he kept hidden away.

She gathered that Max wouldn't care to have a story written about him in a good light because, basically, he didn't care what people thought.

He deserved the chance to tell his side of his unsavory past. His ex-wife had been given the opportunity so why shouldn't he?

The media had slandered him mercilessly through his separation and later divorce. They had accused him, or rather his ex had, of adultery and withholding of marital needs, like sex. They had depicted him as an emotionless husband who never provided his wife with love or support for her hard work as a fashion model.

Ivy remembered seeing a picture of Max standing beside his ex at a social gathering. The woman had been gorgeous. Tall, tanned and hot body all in one package.

A sliver of jealousy sliced through Ivy. She nibbled the corner of her mouth in thought. She had no right to have those emotions that were meant for partners. She was not Max's partner. She never would be. He'd made his beliefs regarding commitment evident.

She didn't want to be just another victory on Max's scorecard.

No doubt last night had been wonderful. Nothing that good came without punishment, though. She had to keep her emotions in check.

During breakfast, Max said, "You've been quiet since the call."

Ivy had a slight suspicion that Max had heard a part of her conversation. Taking a bite of bacon, she chewed the crisp meat but it wouldn't seem to go down her throat. She flushed it down with a sip of coffee.

"Is the bacon that bad?"

She smiled nervously. Why not just tell him the truth? "Marshall believes there's a story here." She had to be careful. She was afraid he would close himself off completely. She was skilled at asking questions and being clever in conversation, but with Max it was different. She was different.

"He's a man who believes in ghosts, is he?" He looked at her over the rim of his cup. The intensity of his eyes spoke a silent book.

"Not necessarily." Seeing his inquiry, she elaborated. "He sees that you're here, so, there's a story. That's enough for him."

"I'm the story." He relaxed back into the wooden chair and it popped and cracked under his weight.

Ivy kept her eyes steady on him. Only hours ago they had made passionate love, held each other close, and now she was feeling a wall of reservation surfacing between them. "You're an important man, Max. People love your work. It makes them believe in the unbelievable."

His laugh had the intensity of a tornado siren. "So what is it you're wanting, Ivy?"

"Wanting? Nothing."

"Everyone wants something."

She squinted at the harsh tone to his words. "I guess you're right."

"Take it from someone who knows--let your guard down for a second and you'll allow the sharks in."

"You're not as cold-hearted as you'd wish for people to believe," she said.

"And how do you know? It's not as if you and I have known each other long. Sleeping together doesn't make us confidants."

He was a scorned man. "I believe in you, Max."

His expression changed. He seemed to debate his next words. "You're too trusting, Ivy. I can't remember the last time someone actually believed in me or supported me without wanting anything in return."

She reached across the table and laid her hand on his. "I'm sorry. Everyone needs to have someone they can trust."

"I've done pretty well alone." He moved his hand and she wondered if the intimacy of her touch bothered him. "How about you? You got anyone who fits the bill?"

She nodded and drew her hand back into her lap. She felt isolated by the way he had pulled away. "My mother."

"What does your mother do?"

"I'm sad to say, but not much anymore."

His eyes softened. "Why?"

She lowered her eyes to stare into the empty cup. "She taught at the local university. I was away in my senior year of college when I received a call that she had collapsed during class. By the time I got here they'd realized she'd had a stroke. We didn't know then what devastation it had left her physically and mentally, or even if she would live." She took in a deep breath just to continue. "Fortunately, she has a fighting spirit and it carried her through. After long physical therapy sessions she did regain most of her functioning, except for movement on her right side."

"You stayed to take care of her."

She shrugged a shoulder. "I had a job waiting for me in New York and I gave it up. It's not so bad, though. I took a job at the Tribune and that's where I've been ever since."

He scrubbed his chin. "It's never fair to give up dreams."

"Moving is an option. My mom loves this town, though. I'd have to find a job making enough to support us and cover the cost for a nurse. Not to mention Mom drives away anyone who comes in to help her, except for the neighbors. She thinks she can manage all alone."

"There are competent nursing homes."

Her mouth dropped open and she threw up her hands to stop him. "If you knew me then you'd know a nursing home is not an option. Things are fine the way they are."

"You're not getting any younger, Ivy."

"Wow, you're on a roll. Keep the charm coming," she snapped.

He didn't even flinch. "You know as well as I do that it gets harder to get your foot in the door. The older we get the narrower our frame gets."

Ivy shook her head. "Do you enjoy being painfully honest?"

"I'm sorry." He sighed.

"I'm not sorry. She has taught me more about becoming a writer than any job could. Not only that, she taught me ethics."

"I bet she has."

Feeling vulnerable, she needed to get the attention off her and onto something less personal. "And how about you, Max? Where did you grow up?"

"Chicago. Born and raised."

"Any brothers or sisters?"

"No."

"Mom and dad still live in Chicago?" she asked.

"Divorced when I was ten. Dad moved to San Francisco after marrying his mistress. He seemed glad to leave everything behind for his twenty-something girl."

"Including you?"

"Including me." She saw the flash of disappointment in his eyes. Her heart sank. "Having a child wasn't tacked into his social plans."

"How sad."

"No, not at all. Mom provided me with all I needed. That is, when she was home. She's retired now."

"She was gone a lot?" Ivy kept the communication going.

"She was an attorney. A damn good one. She was always on the fast track of proving herself in a career monopolized by men. That meant working long, stressful hours." He pushed himself away from the table and took the dishes to the sink.

Ivy knew that meant the end of the conversation. He'd shared enough of himself for the time being. She liked that he'd allowed her a glimpse into his life. She sympathized with his family life, but understood the absent parent trauma. They both had fatherless homes--hers dead, his a deserter. Their mothers were ambitious in fields dominated by men.

She also knew that Max didn't want her sympathy.

She watched as he emptied a kettle of warm water into the old basin sink and dropped the dishes easily in. What if she told him about her dreams? Would he believe her? Especially if she told him she believed there was a connection between him and Marcus.

She got up and approached him. "You know what?"

"What?" He shot her a glance over his shoulder.

"How about we explore--together?" When he didn't respond immediately, she asked, "Aren't you curious, Max? Isn't curiosity what led you here?"

"I came to investigate the ghosts. So far I've gotten some great snapshots of the original woodwork and tons of cobwebs."

She laughed and tugged her hair behind her ear. "So now you're doing photos for decorating magazines, huh?" Her smile faded and she looked at him in all seriousness. "Why don't you just tell me what brought you here, to this house? It's a magnet drawing you in, isn't it? Why?"

"Even men like me search out neglected gems to polish until they shine. This house is said to be haunted and if it is, I'll find out. You're the one looking for the storyline. I'm just looking for the extraordinary."

"Peculiar," she mumbled in irritation. He was playing it down. Facts and answers of Thornton House meant little to outsiders. It was not a tourist attraction. It was not written about in books that romanticized haunted houses. It was only idealized by the people who lived in Morgan Sites.

Personally, her interest was growing stronger. Her dreams were becoming more and more lucid. Her instincts told her that there were hidden answers inside the house…somewhere.

Strangely, she'd lived in the town for almost her entire life and had never given the house more than the time that it had taken to write a short column about it years ago.

She heard heavy footsteps coming toward the kitchen and glanced up in time to see a sleepy-eyed, tousle-headed Jimmy amble into the kitchen. He was wiping his eyes and yawning. "Please tell me there's coffee."

Max grabbed the pot, poured a large paper cup of the brew and handed it to the younger man. "Nice and strong."

"Thank goodness." Jimmy took the cup and sat down where Max had been sitting earlier. Jimmy looked at Ivy and smirked. She smiled. Jimmy said, "Well don't you look like the cat who ate the canary."

Ivy snorted. "You look like the canary that was eaten by the cat. You look like hell."

He jabbed his fingers into his thick curls and pressed his palm against his forehead. "This is what a man looks like when he's had no sleep."

"If I was a man who'd lost sleep because he'd been kept up by a woman I don't think I'd be complaining," Max said. His eyes connected with Ivy's in silent acknowledgement.

Ivy's heart took on a fast rhythm and her toes curled. He could do that to her with one look. Before Jimmy read into their look, she pulled away and sat back down at the table. "Is poor Delilah okay?"

He peered at Ivy through the cracks of his fingers. "*Is Delilah okay*? I wouldn't know the answer. She left during the night. She couldn't sleep because of all the noises in this place."

"It's an old house. Old houses have old wood that settles and creaks." Max laughed.

Jimmy shot him a look of exasperation. "Creaks and settling? Nope. More like banging on the walls, wind whistling through the cracks and rattling windows. Not to mention that it was ice cold in here. How did you two keep warm?"

Ivy knew her cheeks flushed pink while Max appeared as expressionless as a statue. She knew Jimmy was completely unaware of what was going through her mind at that moment.

Jimmy looked from her to Max then back to her with a smile. "Well, hells bells. At least someone scored last night."

Her mouth dropped open and she quickly snapped it shut. Was it that obvious what she and Max had shared? Her cheeks became hot and it oozed throughout her body. If Jimmy thought she'd talk about her personal life then he was an egg short of a dozen. She was painfully aware that Max was leaning casually against the counter watching her. She slid back her chair and got up. "I'm going to go and explore the house." The heat was unbearable.

"You won't find anything." Max's voice stalled her in the doorway.

She turned and looked at him. "Really?"

"Really."

"Well, I'm going to go upstairs, change, then I'm exploring. If you're interested in helping, you know where to find me."

Max smiled. "I'll keep that in mind."

Chapter 15

Ivy was exploring and ended up outside. By any means there could be hundreds of hiding places for hidden treasures. It was like missing pieces that were right in front of her face. As Ivy sat outside in the morning sun she languished in its warmth. It was quiet and peaceful but her mind was anything but tranquil.

Marshall's words swept through her mind. She couldn't deny that Max Shepard was a story within a story. Writing about the history of the man, the man he wanted to be, and the man he saw himself to be in the future would be intriguing.

She only knew tidbits of information about him. His work became popular in his early twenties, after he left the military. He had covered stories of the Gulf War, suicide bombings, genocide and poverty-stricken countries. His resume was rich and full of experience in the field of photojournalism and investigative journalism. His stories were published in periodicals all over the nation.

And then he had quit. And interestingly, begun investigating the paranormal. She could have understood him leaving journalism during his divorce, but he'd changed the path of his career before the divorce.

He had lived a diverse life.

What had this man not done?

Was she bad to want to get his story now? She did care about a story.

On cue, she caught a glimpse of Max coming toward her. He was carrying his camera in one hand and had a mischievous expression on his face. She eyed him curiously, wondering what he was up to, until he stopped a few feet from her and snapped several shots of her.

Self-conscious, Ivy turned away.

"Come on, Ivy. You're not shy in front of the camera, are you?" he teased. "All journalists like the spotlight."

She refused the temptation to flip him the middle finger. "Yes. That's why I knew early on I'd never make it in television broadcasting," she admitted.

Max idled over and took a seat beside her. She dared a peek at his profile and couldn't peel her gaze away. It took a lot of self-control to resist falling against him and allowing nature to take its inevitable course. If he would turn and look at her with those amazing eyes of his she would've been putty in his magical hands.

She tore her revealing stare away and looked out over the fields of tall grass, using the calming scene to steady her breathing. What in the world was Max doing to her? Ivy realized she was losing her head, but she wouldn't dare lose more than that.

Ivy reminded herself that she'd already broken all the rules. No crossing the professional line. No close contact. No sexual thoughts. And the biggie, no sex.

She would enjoy breaking every single one of them again and again. Why deny it? Why fight it? She inwardly cringed. She was a goner.

"Done exploring?" Max leaned his back against the tree.

Ivy sighed in her dismay. "I know there is something. I just can't seem to find it." Did she want to tell him about the dreams? She wasn't sure. She slid him an unwavering look.

A corner of his mouth lifted as he caught her with a heart-melting gaze. "Hanging out with you would have been my choice."

"Choice?" Her throat became dry.

"Over Jimmy. He finally left. Said he had some work to do. If I'd known your buddy would have talked my ear off about everything from hot girls gone wild to expensive leather shoes I would have gladly helped. Does that boy talk that much around the office?"

She laughed. "If he did, Marshall would have his lips sewn together. I believe you make him nervous. He looks up to you."

"Do I make you nervous too?" he asked in a low, rich voice.

She shook her head, sending pieces of hair around her face. "No, not at all. Why would you think that?"

"Well, you did invite the schoolboy along."

"He's here to help," she said. She guessed he could see straight through her to the truth.

"To help?" He popped up a dark eyebrow.

* * * *

Max couldn't help smiling. Ivy twisted around to face him with her telltale expression of denial. Her bright blue eyes were like jewels in the sunlight. Her pale skin was slightly rosy from the warmth. Her lips were a bit pouty and moist from a lick of her tongue. She looked absolutely beautiful. How could he ever resist the strong urge to kiss her? He wanted to move in but his concentration broke when she started to talk.

"Jimmy sure has a male crush on you," she teased.

"That boy could deter a horny toad from chasing a frog." He laughed but was serious in his remark.

"Is that right? Are you the toad in that comparison?" she asked.

"If I'm the toad, you'd be the frog. And some things just can't be doused." She didn't seem at all flattered by his flirting. "You seem preoccupied."

She turned her gaze away. "Let's just say this house has a hold on me, Max. I never would've thought I'd get here and feel so--" She smiled. Her lips trembled. "--at home."

Was she holding back something? He didn't want to push her. "It's a shame that it's been left to deteriorate like this."

He followed her glance toward the house. "People don't want large houses these days, especially in small towns. It takes a lot to heat, to keep clean, and this place would cost a fortune to renovate. I guess it's possible that someone could buy it, make the renovations and turn a profit. But it would be risky. A person may or may not get his or her money back."

Max believed he could almost see the wheels turning in her mind. "The owner isn't asking a lot, is he?"

"He's not asking the appraised price."

She plucked a piece of grass and spun it between her fingers. "It'd make a fabulous bed and breakfast, or a banquet hall for weddings."

"Sounds like you've put some thought into this." Crossing his ankles, he sat back, listening.

"Not really. I just hope someone sees the potential and gives it the TLC that Marcus and Elizabeth would have wished for their dream house."

Max scratched his jaw. The more he got to know Ivy the more he was mesmerized. She wasn't the plain and simple woman she saw herself as. "You're a romantic at heart, aren't you?"

Her bright blues came to land upon him in bewilderment. "A romantic at heart?" She shrugged. "I would call it passion. It's like in my work. If I get wind of a good story I get a craving to unveil each detail, no matter how small or big."

Excitement turned her features child-like, expectant. Max couldn't resist the need to touch her any longer. She made no move to refute his touch as he reached up and twirled a silken tendril of her hair around his finger. Subtly, he let his knuckles glide over the smooth skin of her neck. It was a slight touch but he could tell it was a very effective one by the way she shuddered. He watched her throat as she swallowed. He found it seductive.

"Max, you have a natural magnetism about you. I can see why women like you. But with that comes your reputation of being a womanizer. I can't allow myself to believe that I am any different from the others."

"You make me sound like a male version of Cleopatra." He laughed.

"Nonetheless, when you look at me with those warm eyes, I feel like I am the only woman in the world."

Max thought it was refreshing to find someone willing to sacrifice every ounce of their pride to be honest and open. He admired her. His fingers slipped to her collarbone, enchanted by the feel of her.

Without warning, she stood up from her spot next to him and swiped her bottom. "I'm going in. I'll see you later, right? Of course." She seemed different somehow. She wouldn't even look at him. "I mean, after all, the house is only so big."

Max was dumbstruck as he watched her walk toward the house. He was confused because he had been cock deep in need. Now he was dumbstruck by the slight swaying of her hips, as if she were a human pendulum hypnotizing him. He knew how those thighs felt wrapped around his hips, and the feel of her tight ass molded in his palms. He grew harder and cursed his manly betrayal. There was nothing worse than getting a hard-on with every slight shift in the breeze. It wasn't good for a woman to have that much power over a man's libido. Dangerous, in fact. A man's erection caused him loss of all ability to function with clear thought, and Max knew he was no different.

Ivy disappeared inside the house but his solid length remained proudly in his pants. He smirked. He had a feeling she knew exactly how she had left him--horny and hard. His cell vibrated in his pocket and he grabbed it. "Max Shepard here."

"Hello there, handsome." The soft voice oozed seduction even through the cold phone line. "I've missed you."

Renee. What in the hell did she want? Did the woman have a sixth sense? He didn't doubt that all women had a built-in radar. "Renee, I'm working," he said.

"Didn't you hear me? I said I've missed you." He'd never known that sulking had a sound until he'd met Renee, who had it down perfectly. "Doesn't that mean anything?"

He sighed and tightened his grip on the cell. "I made it clear when I called you on my way here, Renee. It's not going to work. We're through." His mind rambled back to the phone conversation. He'd bluntly told her that he no longer wanted to see her. He'd felt a tinge of guilt when she'd sniffled and blew her nose, but there was no room for guilt, not when they both understood the casual basis of their association. They were both in it for a good time, and it had nothing to do with love. Not once in the last year had either said they wanted anything more than an informal fling.

Her hiss vibrated his ear. "You didn't mean a word of that silliness, Maxy. You were just stressed."

He laughed. "Renee, that shows how much you know me. When has stress ever influenced any decision I've made? Never."

"You can't mean this."

"I meant every word."

"Let me get this straight." Her voice rose in pitch. He could almost see her heaving large breasts and narrowed eyes. He'd seen her temper tantrums one too many times over the months and he'd grown impatient with her immaturity and princess attitude. "*You* are breaking up with me?"

"That about sums it up."

"You'll regret this, Max Shepard. Do you know how many men would kill to take your place?"

"Yes, Renee, I do. And I wish the next poor bastard luck." Before she could say another word he clicked off the phone. He reminded himself that he couldn't feel sorry for her. He knew he hadn't been the only man she'd pleasured since they'd met. It'd never bothered him before so he sure as hell wouldn't allow it to bother him now that it was over.

His eyes mechanically went to the door where Ivy had disappeared. He knew he wasn't Ivy's type, but what sort of man was? Did she have many men pursuing her? An icy sensation tore through his abdomen. Damn... He wondered if what he felt was jealousy. No way. No freaking way.

He was growing too close. What was wrong with him? It was the house. He suspected it had an allure, a power that was turning his ice barrier into a melted puddle. He spread his fingers through his hair. He'd forget everything once he left this godforsaken place.

At least he hoped.

Chapter 16

Ivy dropped to her knees beside the trunk and opened the heavy lid. Pieces of the worn leather fell to the floor but she paid them little attention. She was consumed in looking through the contents. Her eyes took in the once-lavish, hand-embroidered green gown and her breathing became ragged. Carefully, as if it were a rare diamond, she removed the gown and set it onto her lap. It was rarer than a diamond. It was history. It was a part of the past that had become so important to her.

Ivy's mind conjured up images of Elizabeth in the gown. How beautiful she must have been wearing the green velvet. Had she felt like a queen? She most certainly would have looked like one with her long black hair hanging in tight curls down her back and the eyes of innocence.

Gently laying the dress aside, Ivy stuck her hand into the empty inner recesses of the trunk. She found it odd that the gown was the only thing that had been stored in the large chest. Instinct told her there was more here than met the eye. She just couldn't find it.

Giving it one last perusal, she sighed in disappointment.

And then she saw it.

A raised area inside the chest. She bent half her body over the side and peered closer. Smiling at her find, she pulled at the section of leather and lifted it from its position. Pieces broke off into her hand. Her mouth fell open when she realized it was a carved-out area of the material and there was something shoved inside.

With a tender touch, she pulled out what appeared to be a folded piece of paper, yellowed with time. Although it was old and crumpled, she was able to smooth the wrinkles from the paper. Ivy stared down at the charcoal sketch in complete amazement. It was a picture of Marcus standing by the window holding an infant in his arms. His head was slightly bent and his eyes were on the baby. There was a faint curve of his upper lip. His hand rested upon the tiny head of the child in an admiring nature. Elizabeth's initials were scrawled in the lower corner.

Ivy's eyes misted with tears.

Elizabeth had drawn a picture of father and child while in a weak and ill state of health--during her *last* moments, considering it was documented that she'd died within twenty-fours of delivering. Ivy believed Elizabeth had wanted to leave a token of proof of her two loved ones forever in memory.

The baby, which history had assumed dead, was alive in the picture. The baby's hand was clenched in a fist high in the air, loosened from the blanket it was wrapped in. Marcus appeared happy.

Ivy wondered how hard it must have been for Elizabeth to be full of love as a wife and mother and to know that she'd only have this wonderful joy for a short time. Elizabeth had shown her strong emotions with her hand and pencil. The drawing embodied love and admiration.

Interest at a high, Ivy wondered about the life of the infant child. Had he died soon after or before Elizabeth? If Marcus held his sickly infant, suspecting death loomed for mother and child, then why did the sketch portray him partially smiling?

Ivy couldn't understand why there was no record of the newborn child living or dying.

Her eyes glazed over and the picture became fuzzy. Ivy sadly traced the stained outline of Marcus, puzzled over the tenderness and kindness portrayed in the simple drawing. Her mind ached for answers. Her dreams were like a portal into time. Were their spirits reaching out to her from the depths of death, asking for her help? Why did she feel there was a story she needed to solve? A mystery that needed unveiling?

Instead of answers, she'd uncovered more questions. Ivy was even more dumbfounded by the history of the Thornton family.

With a frustrated sigh, she folded the dress and started to place it back into the trunk when she had a second thought and decided to put it in the antique wardrobe where it belonged. She carefully folded the drawing and slid it into her back pocket.

Starting toward the door in hunt for more clues, a sound made her pause, steadying her at the threshold. She held her breath and listened closer--a scratching sound. She waited and it continued to grow louder. Slowly turning, she glanced around the room. Her muscles relaxed and her breathing returned to normal when she realized the clatter was only a tree branch scraping the glass.

She laughed. "Get a grip, Ivy girl," she whispered.

Going back into the room, to the window, she laid her forehead against the cool glass. What was she doing to herself?

She closed her eyes, then popped them open when a thought occurred to her. Awareness and exhilaration flowed through her veins as she rushed from the room in search of Max. He of all people would be interested in her speculation.

She found him downstairs rummaging through a kitchen cabinet. Ivy stopped in the doorway and watched him curiously. She enjoyed watching him. His muscles bulged underneath his black t-shirt as he moved and searched. An expression of concentration was on his face.

"How long you plan on standing there staring?" Max asked.

She swallowed. The man had honed senses. "Is Jimmy back?" Ivy walked farther into the room.

"No." Max carried his attention back to the cabinet he was rummaging through.

Sitting down at the rickety table, she laid her palms in front of her on the cold wood. "Max, I have a thought."

He stopped what he was doing and gave her his complete attention. "Did you find something?"

"I did." She couldn't keep the excitement out of her voice. She lifted the piece of paper out of her pocket, unfolded it and held it up for him to see. "You see who this is?" She pointed at the man in the picture.

"I see what appears to be a deteriorated image of--" He peered closer. "--a water spot."

She rolled her eyes. "Not that. This." She stabbed the paper with her nail. "Don't you see Marcus? He's holding a baby, *his* baby."

Max shrugged. "I guess that could be him with a baby."

"And you call yourself an investigator? If you can't see the resemblance between this man and Marcus then it's time you got glasses"

He eyed her with slight displeasure. He took the drawing from her and surveyed it closer. "This is old, beyond old. It's deteriorated almost beyond recognition. However--" He held it up to the light flowing through the window. "--I do see a man and a baby and Elizabeth's initials in the corner."

"Thank you. It's finally nice to hear you admit for once that I'm right."

"Hold up, Ivy. I agree that is a sketch drawn by Elizabeth of a man holding a baby, but I didn't say you were right."

"Oh, give yourself time, my handsome friend. You'll eventually come to your senses and see all things my way." She twisted in the chair and took the drawing back.

"Why do I not like the implication in that?"

"Because you're afraid of the truth."

"Just like I'm afraid we could go on forever discussing this subject and that is why I'm choosing to end it. Now, you said you had a thought." He reminded her.

She thrummed her fingernails on the table as she shuffled and straightened her thoughts. "Documents state that Elizabeth died soon after giving birth to a son. However, where is it written that the baby died too? People have just assumed that's what happened. Everything surrounding the birth is vague."

"Elizabeth was ill. Back then childbirth was different than it is now."

"Yes, but sometimes children did survive even when the mother passed away. Wet nurses could be hired to provide milk for the newborn. And, look at the smile on this man's face. Would he be smiling if his child were dying? Elizabeth drew this picture for a reason. She wanted to show the love she had for Marcus and her son. She wanted to leave something behind."

"It's a sketch, Ivy. Elizabeth could have drawn it however she perceived it. Maybe at the time she didn't know her son wasn't going to live. Maybe she didn't even know that she was dying."

"Always the cynical one, aren't you?" She sighed. "I don't think a woman who had just spent hours giving birth would be feeling so rewarding as to pencil in a false expression on her husband's face. History says that she died some time after birth. It was a difficult labor and she bled out. I believe the only thing that was keeping Marcus from falling apart was the knowledge that he had a healthy son. I'd say her intention was to make the moment last forever when time was unforgiving. She picked up the handiest material and began drawing. This isn't drawing paper so it wouldn't have been her material of choice. To an artist a drawing is a true way of documenting their emotions everlasting."

"You're a romantic." He snorted. "Not everything has a Hollywood ending and not everyone finds gold at the end of a rainbow."

"You have a right to your opinion, sourpuss, but if you will, entertain my thoughts for just a moment. If you owned hundreds of acres of land, where would you bury your loved ones?"

There was no hesitation. "I'd bury them on my land, as most rich property owners did back then. Especially the wealthy because the rich people's graves were known to be excavated by robbers looking for jewels that may have been buried with the body. These days, funeral homes go to great lengths to ensure that graves are safe from scavengers. This is beautiful land and this is exactly where he would have buried Elizabeth."

"I haven't read anything that cites where Marcus and Elizabeth were buried. I'm sure it's just an accidental void. It happens all the time when a story is written or historians are documenting information. If we find the grave sites then we'll see if their son was buried and when."

Max nodded. "Good thought, but the graves could be anywhere. The Thornton property stretches for acres."

"A lot of the land has been sold off over the years. If a person bought the land and the graves were on their property that would have become town knowledge. This town likes to talk." She buried her forehead in her palm and searched her brain for the missing link. "If I remember correctly, there is a clause in the land contract that ensures that a certain number of acres with the house can't be divided. So much of the land must remain with the house."

"What if someone wanted to tear the house down?"

"The court would have to rule against the original contract. People in this town are protective of this place. To them it's a historical gold mine, a part of this town's history that no one wants disrupted."

Max smirked. "A real estate disaster is what that is. You can only imagine how many land developers would love to get their paws on this prime land for a large housing project. I'm surprised the current owner hasn't gotten some killer lawyer to find a loophole in the original contract so that they can sell pieces of the property apart from the house. Anyone with any sense knows the land is valued more than the buildings. No wonder it can't sell. And there haven't been any rumors about the grave sites?" he asked.

She shrugged. "Not that I've heard. My thought is there must be a piece of land somewhere around here they enjoyed above everywhere else. That's where they are buried."

"Once again, on acres like this, it could be anywhere."

"In times like this research is the only choice for finding information." Ivy was still talking as she left the room, with Max following. "I'll give Jimmy a call and have him talk to the current owner. Maybe he knows something we don't. Jimmy is good at research."

"Hopefully better than you."

She shot him a bothered expression.

"Well, didn't you say you did research on this place? Not to mention the informative research you uncovered about me."

She realized he was teasing her. "I'll act like you didn't say that since we're way past that." She grabbed her phone from her purse and rang Jimmy's number.

* * * *

Max only partially listened to the conversation as she talked to Jimmy. From Ivy's side of the discussion, it was evident Jimmy was more than ready to take on the task. Max went to the French doors that overlooked the overgrown garden. He looked out but didn't see anything except for his thoughts. The path of discovery was growing fuzzier while something else was increasingly becoming brighter. He didn't want to ponder what it was.

"Earth to Max?"

He brought his head around and saw Ivy eyeing him curiously. He wondered at times if she could see straight through him--or directly into his thoughts. He'd never had a woman affect him in a way that left him wanting her every minute. "Say again?"

She smiled. "I was just saying, Jimmy is on the case." She came up beside him. He could smell her. Jasmine. He knew now what the scent was. "You seem miles away. Anything you wish to share?" she urged with a flash of a whimsical smile and a batting of eyelashes.

Oh, she was good at manipulation. If he knew this, he wondered why he wasn't immune. While he pleasured his eyes with following the contours of every curve, every feminine angle of her lovely face. Max imagined if he let his guard down for a mere second she'd have him blabbing about everything from his fears to his favorite food. Her inquisitive nature was like a rushing river and his dam was weak. "You're still trying to break down my restraint, aren't you?"

"I'm just asking questions. I call that conversation."

"A man needs a place to hide his secrets," he said. "You have your place. I have mine."

"Secrets, huh?" She kept her eyes on him, drilling him. "You're definitely a man of mystery, Max. Wouldn't it be refreshing to have at least one person to trust, one person to share with?"

"Are you suggesting that you're the one person for me?"

"Ooh! I felt the acrimony in those words. Should I be offended? Or should I be flattered, because I sensed a bit of panic."

"Is it possible it's your own panic you're detecting?"

"Me? Panicked? For whatever reason would I be?" He could see right through her and decipher her thoughts. How could they have such a connection? How could he want nothing more than to take her into his arms and kiss the sassiness right out of her? Damn. He was panicked.

Swallowing the apprehension growing in his throat, he managed to say, "Because you are searching for any opening, any break, so you can burst through to the *real* me. What are you after, Ivy? What if this *is* the real me? Are you hoping that you'll unmask a man who is kind and loving? Do you dare deceive yourself into believing I'll fall madly in love with you and we'll live happily ever after? Haven't I forewarned you enough? Don't you understand the facts? I'm not that man. Don't waste your time." He saw a flicker of a deep emotion flit across her features. He felt a tinge of regret but he knew he was doing the right thing. He couldn't change, not even for her.

She opened her mouth but no words came. He knew she wanted to say something. He could see it in her eyes and feel the burn of expectation. But her mouth snapped shut as she dropped her arms to her sides, turned on her heel and marched out of the room.

Well hell, he thought. Just when you think you know someone they up and give you a completely different opinion. He'd never guessed that Ivy would keep her thoughts secret. In fact, he couldn't deny he was somewhat disappointed. Was he beginning to enjoy her verbal thrashings?

"Fuck." The word tore from him on a ragged breath. A man had a good idea when his balls were in a woman's grasp, and damn, Ivy had her grip right where she wanted. He had to get control back. But what if he didn't want control?

He stood there at the doors for the longest time, long after Ivy had gone.

He'd hurt her. He knew. He'd seen it in her eyes. He wished now he could take the words back, but history couldn't erase itself. He'd treated her coldly.

Truth was, it had been his intention to be cruel. He'd wanted her to see that it wouldn't work between them. They were from two different worlds.

His raw inner emotions seeped out like jagged blades, cutting anyone near. He knew the facts. The more he felt trapped by his feelings, the more he pushed and lashed out. He knew the process well because he'd lived that way for years.

He'd grown numb in all aspects of his life. He spent most of his time working or traveling. Work had become his salve. Home had become a reminder of what he didn't have, not that he missed anything. Loneliness did him good. It seemed to fit like a hand and glove.

He had a few good friends. Ones he could trust with his life, but he didn't get to see them nearly enough. Friends had been lost in the past due to his insensitivity. Chances for a new life had been lost because of his stupidity. But why didn't he have the desire to change?

Or, was it change that he was feeling?

It scared the hell out of him.

He wasn't ready for love and a relationship. Ivy was younger than he was, but of course she wasn't immature. He could see she was innocent in many ways and wanton in others. Her deep passion for life exuded from her every pore. Last night, in his arms, she had been wild and carefree.

Ivy wanted to find the missing good guy within him, like it was lost and only needed found. She deserved a man who could give her the white picket fence, nice house in the suburbs and a couple of kids. All that sounded indulgent to the ears; however, nothing ever happened as planned. She deserved stability and romance in her world. He wasn't sure he could offer any of that. At least not in the way she wanted.

And yet knowing this, she touched a chord in him that he'd thought lost. The feelings he had for his ex-wife had been nothing more than a hopeful man's obsession over a beautiful, untamed, affluent woman. He was a grown man now with a grown man's emotions.

Why couldn't the past just be the past? It bothered him to think that a scorned marriage could sour his future with another woman.

His eyes lifted to where Ivy had disappeared. Ivy Kennedy was a woman a man could give his all to. And making love with her had been an experience that had left him wanting more.

Max sighed and rubbed his gritty eyes.

Maybe Ivy deserved to know the truth. He should tell her why he came here. He could trust her.

Chapter 17

Ivy wanted--*needed* to cry. She was a bundle of tender emotions.

She refused herself the benefits of releasing those emotions. No tears should ever be wasted on a man who didn't have the passion to appreciate it. How dare he believe she wanted his love? They had slept together, not shared wedding vows.

What had she expected? A man like Max lashed out when he felt his comfort threatened. He wished to remain closed off from everyone because that's how he stayed safe. She felt sorry for him. He was destined to a life of sadness and bitterness.

Ivy hadn't realized that she'd walked outside until she came to the huge oak. The spot brought her much peace. She sat down and breathed easy.

She enjoyed the sound of nothing but nature at its purest. The soft rustling of the wind's kiss as it touched the leaves. The high-pitched chirping of the birds as they swooped down to catch rations for their foundlings. The whizzing of bees as they buzzed merrily by on their way to find nectar. Everything in the environment was at harmony, and gave her balance internally. She believed there could be no other place on earth she'd rather be at that moment.

She stared up into the blue depth of the sky and watched as a billowy cloud moseyed by. She lifted her hand, as if she could touch it. It seemed to shift and take on form. It looked like a dog. It changed again, this time it altered into the shape of a heart.

Ivy sighed lethargically. She shouldn't let Max get her so angry. What good could come of it being emotionally disheveled? Fact was, she was hurt. What they had shared last night meant something to her. That was fine, as long as she didn't expect the same feelings to be mirrored by Max.

She wanted to believe the worst of him, but even now she couldn't deny that she was drawn to him. Ivy didn't understand why, but there was a reason they were at the house together. Was the ambience of the house tugging them together? Or something more? An inner connection?

Could they have lived a past life together? Their souls could have now found one another after years of searching…

Ivy moaned and closed her eyes. She was behaving like a romantic fool. Max was right. But she was right also. He was a pompous, arrogant ass. Unfortunately, she was developing feelings for that pompous, arrogant ass and that slanted the facts a bit.

She didn't want to give up on Max. At the same time, she knew she would need to find a way to break through his wall of resistance once and for all. He may hate her, but he would be grateful when he realized what kind of life was available to him.

She was certain she could forgive Max for his demented behavior, but first he would have to prove he deserved it. She definitely wouldn't make it easy for him.

All of that later, though.

Her body seemed to float on the cloud above her.

Ivy wanted to allow the serenity to drift over her body and release her of any bad thoughts. She shut herself off…only for a moment.

* * * *

"Elizabeth! You are the most beautiful lady I've had the pleasure of laying my eyes on." Ivy snapped her eyes open and saw Marcus. She was sitting across from him on a blanket on the grass.

"Marcus?" She had returned. She held her breath.

He laughed. "You choose not to hear compliments of your beauty. Is the rosiness in your cheeks a tribute to the sun's kiss? Or, are you embarrassed that I'm gushing over my wife's loveliness?"

Ivy swallowed. Everything seemed to come to her at once. "Both." She laid her shaking hands in her fluffy velvet skirt. She lowered her eyes to the food before them. "The picnic is lovely. It's exquisite here." She brought her gaze across the land in a sweeping movement. It was a lovely day. Ivy wondered where they were on the property. From where she sat she couldn't see the house.

"I'm glad you like the place. I had feared you would want to live in Boston." He picked a blade of glass and twirled it.

"Boston?"

"It is an exciting place to be, I suppose. Lots of festivities and banquets among the most prosperous and elite. Do you find such socializing thrilling?" Marcus continued to watch her. "Should I have not turned down Rosalee Sinclaire's invitation to dinner? I heard it was the social event of the season."

"The Governor and his wife invited us to dinner?"

"Yes. I can send her a message right away and tell her we've changed our minds, if you'd like?"

"Attending parties isn't my thing." At least she didn't think so. She'd never had the privilege of attending a ball or a dinner hosted by a nineteenth century socialite. She reminded herself that at the current time she wasn't Ivy the journalist; she was Elizabeth, Marcus's wife. She needed to answer accordingly. "Have you forgotten where I came from, Marcus? My family is not privileged, such as yours. I wouldn't fit in."

He smiled at her as if she was a cute child asking him why the sky was blue. "You may never have rubbed elbows with the wealthy but I do believe you must have dreamt. Do you wish you could be in another place? Do you wish you could be doing something different? Many times you seem like drift off to another world."

Ivy snapped her face around. His question hit close to the truth. She calmed her nerves, not wanting to show any sign of her inner turmoil. "I suppose I do. I suppose everyone has hopes and dreams. I guess I understand that some dreams are not meant to come true no matter how hard you wish them."

He curved one thick brow. "Really, my dear? How sad. Dreams give us hope, and once we lose hope we lose our way." His eyes bored into her and Ivy felt as if she were on the receiving end of one of Max's looks. "Maybe you would share your hopes with me?"

Uncomfortable, she twisted away. Her mind was blurring as thoughts rushed through her. If this were all just a dream, why couldn't she wake up? Why couldn't she command her mind to function if this was her sleep-induced world?

"What are you thinking, Elizabeth?"

Ivy looked back at him. This was her opportunity to learn more, to find the truth that was hidden in the future. "It's so beautiful here, Marcus. Tell me about this place, about you. What was your childhood like?"

* * * *

Marcus eyed her profile. He wondered if she were serious. His first wife, in all the time they'd been married, had never shown any interest in his heritage and the ancestors who had lived here before them. In fact, Elizabeth herself had never inquired before.

For that very moment his heart expanded to the size of the sky. It shocked him to feel such deep love for a woman who did not reciprocate the same feelings. It was bittersweet.

Her eyes widened. "Should I not have asked?"

"No, I'm glad you did. I, well, it just took me by surprise."

She smiled and her entire face lit up. She seemed different somehow. He could have sworn he saw stars in her eyes. "Then we're even, because you are always surprising me."

"I do?" At times he thought he scared her, but never would he have guessed surprise.

She nodded, sending long tendrils of hair around her face. He wanted to reach out and sweep them behind her ear but he feared she'd pull away. "Just like now, with all of this." She made a sweeping motion with her hand. "And the gown. It's lovely."

"I'm afraid the dress was simply material until you put it on." She laughed, but he was happy to see that she didn't blush as usual. "I'll tell you the story. My parents lived here, and before them their parents, and several more generations of family. This land has been loved by many a Thornton. I had a wonderful childhood. It was pleasant and very satisfying. My grandfather Emilio taught me how to farm and ride a horse. He knew all there was to know about both. He could take the wildest horse and within days have it tame enough to ride. He had a connection with the animals that I've never seen in anyone. My father was also a great farmer but he worked his fingers to the bone day and night. He cultivated this land and it thrived under his touch like never before. He was a damn good businessman to boot. When grandfather died, my father inherited all this. The land produces cotton and wheat and beauty."

He jumped up from the blanket and pointed to an area north of them. "The fields." He stuck out a hand as an offering to her. She took it and he lifted her gently into a standing position. "Look as far as the eye can see and you'll notice the prospering crops growing."

Marcus watched her follow the thrust of his finger with her curious gaze. She looked out over the immaculate fields. They both gazed out to where they could see the tiny figures of farm hands as they plucked the fields in a precise pattern, while even tinier figures of children dashed about playing.

He saw a smile erupt over her features. "My grandmother worked alongside my grandfather for many years until finally the day came when the farm flourished enough that she could retire from the fields to take care of her two sons who were still in diapers."

Her smile disappeared. "Two sons?"

He thought he'd told her but it wasn't as though they'd had long conversations since they'd married. "My uncle died when he was still a boy. He was swimming in the pond and drowned. He and my father were very close. My grandmother was a strong woman who found the strength to carry on with life, for my father and grandfather's sake. It was after she'd died that we had found the letters she'd written, describing years and years of agony and tears that were shed over losing her son. She had written her sorrow on paper as a means of enduring."

He left her side and went to the edge of the knoll, scanning the grounds proudly. "My mother--" He hesitated. "My mother died while giving birth to my sister. They both passed that horrible wintry day in January."

"I'm sorry, Marcus. It must have been difficult."

"I was seven and my anguish was dulled by a child's capacity to move on. When I look back I understand now why Father would sit for hours in silence staring out onto the fields. His lust for life seemed to have vanished and he moved through life numbly and without passion. He was still a good father, but I missed the way he had laughed and joked before her death."

"He must have been devastated at losing so many loved ones in such a short lifetime. You have lost too, Marcus. When you lost your daughter you understood devastation."

He turned toward her when she laid a hand on his arm. It was the first time she'd initiated touching him. The brisk wind swept her long, sweet-scented hair from the bun and across her face. His fingers ached to touch her velvety skin and spread through her silky tendrils. If he held her, he wondered, would his heart release its aching?

He held steady although it was hard. He didn't want to violate any trust he had gained. "Losing my daughter was a corruption to my soul. I had stayed here on this hill, begging for God to come and take me away from this miserable existence. Instead, I somehow managed to cope until one day turned into another and here I am standing next to you."

Her hand came up and touched his cheek. Her eyes held a compassion he'd never witnessed before. He wanted to bring her happiness. It was as if she buried herself within him and woke every nerve ending, every blood vessel.

"I'm sorry." Her voice was soft.

"Don't apologize. Can you see the torment I'm feeling inside? I want to touch you. You have me going crazy and I don't know what to do. I've made a promise to you that I won't break, but I must confess that the more I'm with you, the more I'm losing control."

She brought her eyes to his and her virtue shown in their blue depths. "How can it be that I'm so lucky to have you caring for me? You know so little about me."

"I know you well, sweetheart. I look into your eyes and I seem to fall helplessly. My lifeblood is connected to you. I know it must sound ludicrous, but trust me when I say I've never felt so kindled by anything in my entire life."

He heard her deep inhalation, as if he had caught her off guard. "I don't think it's ludicrous, Marcus. You make me feel things that I never knew existed. Right here." She palmed her lower belly. "There's a feeling here that burns. And here, too." She took his hand and placed it against her breasts, over her heart. He could feel the thumping. "Do you feel how my heart is racing?"

He smiled, feeling his own heart would explode. "Like mine." He gently guided her hand to his heart. Her slender fingers splayed across his broad chest. Through the opening of his shirt he could feel her fingers play with his chest hair. It sent a bolt of electricity through his body and he gasped. "It's all right to feel this way, Elizabeth. We are married and it is only right that we allow nature to take its course."

When she moved away, he felt his heart sink. He had done exactly what he hadn't wanted to do. He had pushed her away.

"You say this is right, but…" Her words faded.

"What, Elizabeth? Tell me," he pleaded.

"There's more to me than you understand."

He stormed across the yard, but didn't touch her. "Then help me understand, sweetheart."

She shook her head violently. "I won't. I can't."

He sucked in a breath. "But you can tell me anything, Elizabeth."

"I'm not sure why but when I'm with you I feel like I'm suffocating and losing control." There was a catch in her tone.

"I see that I have moved too swiftly. I should apologize," he said. He wasn't sure what he had said that was wrong but he could see the pain in her eyes.

She swiveled on her heel and moistened her lips. "But how will I know when it's right? How does love feel?"

He hesitated, pondering her question. "I remember sitting in front of the fire when I was a wee one. I watched my mother knit a sweater for my father for his upcoming birthday. I remember asking her why she married my father. Instead of reprimanding me, she deposited her work to have me sit on her lap. She said she had married my father because he was the only man who had snatched the stars right out of the sky and placed them in her heart. I now know what she meant."

When she didn't say anything he moved away and began to pack up their belongings. She joined him in the task. Silence lingered between them as they headed back to the house. When he did finally speak it was to warn her, "There's a storm brewing. It's going to be a big one."

She checked the sky. "How do you know? The sky looks perfectly clear."

"Trust me," he said. The wind blew across them. He looked up and felt the top button of his shirt open.

"What is that?" Ivy asked, pointing to his chest.

Marcus looked down at the area of his skin revealed by the open collar of his shirt. "That's a birthmark. Interesting shape, huh?"

"It's a leaf…" She turned pale.

"Elizabeth, are you well?" He supported her by the elbow.

"I…I…" she stuttered. "I've seen one exactly like that." And then she collapsed into his arms.

Chapter 18

"Wake up, Ivy."

She moaned. She nudged a troublesome arm off hers. When she realized the unpleasant feeling wasn't going away, she fluttered her eyes open to find Max hovering over her. A smile curved his mouth. She jolted upright against the tree. "What do you want?" she asked in sleepy irritation.

"You've been out here for two hours. I was beginning to think you had gotten lost. A storm is coming."

Ivy looked up at the gray sky. She scooted away from him so she could get up. When she was on steady feet she swept the dirt off her legs.

"You're still mad," he said.

"Good observation." She scanned the area around the tree, looking for her phone.

"Want this?" He held her cell out for her to take.

"I brought it out didn't I?" she sneered.

"Testy, testy." He clicked his tongue.

She heaved a sigh and then another, but the tension wasn't releasing. She was not only mad at him because of his earlier rude comments, but also because he woke her. She hadn't been dreaming. It had been real. And what she'd seen on Marcus's chest had helped her understand why Max was here. Marcus had the same birthmark--the discolored leaf--on him that Max had on his hip. That was the last thing she remembered.

Max shrugged. "I should have left you alone."

"You keep on heckling me and you'll see what happens."

"Has anyone ever told you you're beautiful when you're angry?"

"Get used to the look because it's what you'll be seeing for a while." As she swiveled around to walk away her toe caught in the root of the tree. She lost her footing. Max quickly caught her. Gratitude wasn't on her mind. She thrust his arm away. When he let go completely, instead of gaining her balance, she fell hard against his chest. She brought her hand up and palmed her forehead as a bout of dizziness washed over her.

"Are you okay?" His tone was sincere.

Ivy looked up at him and his warm gaze melted her. She didn't want his concern, but she also didn't not want it. A bit of embarrassment, mingled with a lot of displeasure, made her step back from him in a huff. "Why are you out here, Max? Did you come out here to rub it in my nose that you'd never fall in love with me? Or were you hoping I'd spread my legs for another roll in the sack? Were you thinking I may fall into your arms begging and pleading that big, bad Max Shepard make love to me? If a good time is what you're wanting then a good time is what you'll get." She moved forward. She reached out and grasped the back of his neck, pulling his large frame against her smaller one. She brought her hand up and cupped his erection that was prevalent even through his jeans. "Just as I thought."

Anyone watching the scene would think she'd gone mad. She knew her actions were a bit on the wild and crazy side, but she chose not to think about that. She pulled his cotton tee up and over his head and splayed her fingers across his smooth, massive chest before sliding them downward and wrapping them around his lean waist.

Max shook his head. "Ivy..." His breath was warm against her cheek.

She let her head roll back so she could look at him. His eyes were like molten lava and his body was tense. "What's the matter, Max? Got no words of wisdom now?"

"You're a beautiful and very seductive woman, sweetheart. I do feel the heat, but not in my loins, not right now."

"Oh? Is that right?" She stood on tiptoe and pressed quick, supple kisses along his jaw line. She only wished her body didn't betray her. She wished she wasn't overcome with the moistness between her legs and the sudden burst of emotion in her chest. "Remember, we had an agreement." She peeked up at him through her lashes. "Sex, but no feeling. Are you breaking that agreement?" She lifted an eyebrow, challenging him.

"Stop it, Ivy." He grabbed both her wrists and tugged her arms against his chest. She wouldn't have been able to go anywhere even if she'd wanted to.

A flash of lightening lit the sky followed by a loud crack of thunder, then the rain started. At first it was only a few drips, then the sky opened up. Fat raindrops the size of marbles pelted their skin. Neither Ivy nor Max made a move to seek shelter from the downpour.

Ivy stood there gazing up at him. She knew her tears mingled with the wetness from the sky. "I'm a big enough girl to handle the truth, Max. When you say you don't care about me, I know it's the truth. But what'll break my heart is if you don't quit looking at me like I'm some poor dumb chick."

"You're seeing something completely different than the truth." His lips were tight.

"And you tell me only what you want me to hear. You see a safety net available so you're planning your escape route. What I'd like to know is, do you really want to turn me down? How about staying for awhile and enjoying what I'm so willing to give?" She tossed her wet hair over her shoulder. The strands stuck to her face.

"Because you're asking too much of me." His words sounded strained. She knew it took a lot for him to say that much.

"Do you really know what I'm asking for?"

"You want to suck the life from me." His eyes radiated a fire directly through her.

"I'm not your ex-wife, Max. Can't you see I'm not a harmful person ready to take everything from you and then leave you? Can't you see that I'm not your mother and father who abandoned you?"

* * * *

A cold chill spun through his warm blood and Max shivered in response. He was fighting a furious turmoil, one that had kept him prisoner for years. He was afraid to allow himself to feel any emotion.

"You want me to stay within the boundaries of what you've laid out for me." Ivy's bottom lip quivered as she spoke.

They were both soaked to the bone and Ivy was starting to shiver. Her thin shirt melted against her body, her red bra visible and her nipples hard. The sight of her kept Max warm. He shook his head, sending water beads flying. "Ivy, you don't remind me of my ex. She never pushed me to the point where I felt like I would explode. It seems from the moment we walked into this place you've made it your agenda to strike at everything I want to keep secluded. It may not be what's best, and someday I may die a lonely man. You know what, Ivy, it's what I choose. You ask why I don't give into these emotions and desires I'm feeling. You can't be content with what I have to offer. It's not enough for you."

Standing on tiptoes, she reached her arms around his neck. "Yes Max, it will be enough. If we have each other for only a short time then that's okay." She lifted her face to look up at him. "I'm a pushy person. It's my

Rhonda Lee Carver

character. I just know I want you, Max Shepard, like I've never wanted anything in my life."

Her hair was plastered to her head and she was covered in rain and goose bumps, but she was the sexiest woman he'd ever laid eyes upon. She looked at him and his insides melted. He couldn't resist her. Max dropped his mouth to hers and dipped his tongue in to taste her warm sweetness. There was a charge between them as powerful as the lightning that lit the darkened sky. "We better go in."

She tucked her hand into his and together they raced for the front door of the house. Once inside she turned to him. She wrapped her arms around his neck, pressing her wet body against his. She lowered her hand, toying with the bulge behind his zipper again. Ecstasy spread through his body.

He knew that she wasn't the type to sleep around. She didn't have an ulterior motive. He liked her, a helluva lot. Too much for his own good. Max opened his mouth to tell her how sorry he was for what he'd said earlier but she stopped him with a finger against his lips.

She popped the button of his jeans. She slid her hand inside, past the elastic waist of his boxers. He sucked in a deep breath when she touched his sensitive head. She teased his tip, stroking the hardness until he thought he'd let loose right there in her hand.

Max didn't want it to end so soon and that's why he took her by the wrists and gently pulled her hand away. "You little vixen, if you want this to go nice and slow then you've got to stop that." He'd never had a woman drive him so close with only her hand. He felt like he was back in his early twenties, when he'd had no self-control and no idea how to please a woman. It mattered more now that she was satisfied.

He pushed her body against the wall. He lifted her arms high above her head, making sure not to hurt her. Bending his head, Max kissed the v-neck opening of her shirt. He slid his tongue along the edge, taking his free hand and dragging the material away from her breasts.

He suckled one nipple until she let out a deep, needy moan. He lifted his head to look at her. "What is it, baby? What do you want?"

"You, Max. You." She wriggled her hips as he dipped his fingers into her shorts, past her lace panties, and buried them within her damp folds. She rolled her thighs against his touch, taking his fingers deeper. She rode him like a cowgirl, frenzied and passionate. Her muscles tightened as dew covered his fingers.

She dropped her head to his shoulder and he released her wrists. She pulled and tugged at his shirt. When she spoke he detected her desperate need. "Max ...please."

"I know, baby. I feel it, too." He pushed her pants along her hips and down slender legs until they were at her feet. She gave them a toss with her foot. Her panties quickly followed.

He stepped back only as far as he needed to rid himself of his jeans and boxers. She took his cock into her hand and gently led him between her thighs. Max placed his hands on her bottom and easily lifted her and pressed her against the wall. "You're so hot, Ivy. I think you'll burn me alive."

"Hot for you, Max Shepard. Take me, please."

And he wasted no time. He slid himself into her wetness and plunged deeply, filling her. She fit around him snugly, the perfect taut silken warmth. With each thrust he soared closer and closer to the magical abyss of satisfaction. It took all of his control to wait until she had reached her own release. When he felt her body pulsate around his erection he knew she was there and he quickly followed. When the spasms left each of their bodies she relaxed against him, letting her hands fall at her hips.

Later, in the master bed, Ivy lay in the crook of Max's arm. They were discussing the advantages of sex outside of the bed.

Max sighed. "Your mother would beat me over the head if she knew what I was doing to her daughter."

"Whatever for?" She sounded sleepy.

"Because she would think that I'm a well-seasoned man who knows better than to be sleeping with a twenty-nine-year-old who has barely experienced life." He knew he'd just admitted one of his issues.

Lifting herself on elbow, she looked at him in absurdity. "My mother would be telling me to go for it. Not that she believes sex before marriage is the best thing for me, but she does think that I deserve to be happy. And another thing, Max Shepard." She tapped him playfully on the chest. "I'm twenty-nine, not nineteen. I'm more experienced than you give me credit for."

He rubbed his tired eyes. "Are you happy?" If she said "yes" he wouldn't believe her. So when she shook her head he felt relieved. He didn't want her to lie about her feelings. "I didn't think so."

"Not that I didn't just experience the most thrilling sex I've ever had, but a part of me feels sad because I wish you could feel as wonderful as I do."

"Trust me, I feel wonderful if not ecstatic." And it was the truth. She made him feel great.

"You're talking sex, Max. I'm referring to something much deeper than that. I'm experiencing all that we share with all the feelings and emotions I have. You allow your body to experience the pleasure, but you don't allow your mind and heart to feel it too."

He sighed again. "There's that romantic side rearing its head." He moved his arm. He felt guilty. He'd never felt guilty before, not after sleeping with a woman who literally threw herself at him. Dammit, he was getting soft. "Look, I've got something to tell you." He knew it was high time to change the subject.

She rolled her eyes. "Oh no, you're not going to lecture me again on the shallow man that you are. That you'll never love me so give up any thought--"

He swatted her playfully on the bottom but came back with a sweet kiss on the tip of her cute nose. "No, I wasn't going to preach to you. I've got something I want you to see."

Chapter 19

Ivy watched Max climb from bed. Without any consciousness to his nude body, he walked the length of the room. She gazed at his tight buns until he disappeared through the door. He had the body of an athlete and an intelligent mind. If there ever were a perfect man, he would be it. From his beautiful face to his toned upper body down to his long lean legs. He was all male. She could stare at him forever.

He came back. "Take a look at this." He handed her a sheet of paper.

Ivy looked down at the paper, brown with age. Her mouth fell open in shock. It was a colored sketch of Thornton House. Not as it was today, rundown and in need of repair, but years ago when it was lived in and loved. "It's this house, years ago."

"Turn it over." He sat down next to her on the bed.

She flipped the paper over and read the words, "Elizabeth Thornton, 1897." She gazed up at him. "Elizabeth sketched this. Where did you get it?" Her heart took on a wild beat as anticipation rushed through her. She noticed his hesitation. "You don't want to tell me?"

"When my grandfather, mom's dad, was dying, he gave me this and told me to find the meaning of the mystery behind Thornton House. When I asked mom what mystery he referred to, she had no clue. Grandfather had always been vague about his childhood, except that he'd been adopted as a baby. When we'd ask him questions he'd shrug off our curiosity by telling us he didn't know a thing about his birthparents and didn't want to know." He laid his head back on the headboard. "I did research on Elizabeth Thornton. I didn't find a lot of information about her and this house, not anything that you don't already know. I figured the sketch came from an antique shop. He loved going to all of the shops and finding treasures. I had pushed his words aside because he was senile during his last few months so I couldn't be sure what was fact or fiction."

"But do you think there was more to his request than asking you to investigate a picture he found?"

"Not sure." He shrugged. "It was eerie, standing in the driveway and looking at the real house, not the image of it in a drawing."

"And that's why you're here?"

He nodded. "I've felt linked to this place. I don't understand why. I wasn't sure what the connection was to my grandfather."

"Do you think your grandfather had a connection to Marcus and Elizabeth? Could he have been blood related?" She knew it sounded far-fetched but anything was possible. Why else would Max's grandfather have Elizabeth's drawing of the house? It was all a mystery, one she wanted the answers to and she was certain Max did, too.

He shrugged. "I don't know, but it seems almost unlikely."

"But not impossible," she said. She ran her fingers through her hair as her mind wandered. "How old would your grandfather be today if he were still alive?"

The ringing of her cell phone broke through the silence. It was in her purse across the room. "I think I can make it." She jumped out of the bed and struggled with the sheet, trying to drag it across her nudity.

"You'll never make it."

The last ring rang just as she grabbed her cell. "It's Jimmy. He left me a message." She clicked the button and listened, smiling.

"What did he say?" Max asked.

"Let's just say, I think we're in luck. Let me call him back."

Fifteen minutes later, Max and Ivy were in his Jeep and heading up the hill behind the house. "Jimmy said the owner told him that the new property line reached to the hill."

Although the hill was visible from the house, it was farther than it appeared and Ivy was glad they had decided to take his vehicle instead of walking. As soon as they had pulled away from the house the downpour had started again.

The ride was bumpy. They reached the top of the hill in one piece. He shut down the engine and turned to her. "Did I scare you?"

"Hold on before I answer so that I may pry my fingers from their death grip," she stated.

"Come on, sweetheart. Haven't you ever been mud-running?" His eyes gleamed.

"Mud-running?" She eyed him. "Is that a nice, leisurely jog on a muddy day?" she asked, only partly teasing.

"Haven't you ever driven on sand dunes?"

She shook her head sharply. "No."

"Then you haven't lived. You're missing out on tons of adventure."

"You bet I am. Nothing like a bruised rump."

"You know you loved it. You just don't want to admit that something you did with me felt so good."

"That's not true." She nibbled on the corner of her mouth. "I can tell you, without a doubt, that everything that I do with you feels good."

"I meant with clothes on." Bending over, he gave her a quick kiss on the lips. He opened his door and said, "Let's check this place out."

"The graves must be here." Anticipation boiled through her veins.

"Let's see."

Twenty minutes later they were both disappointed. They hadn't found the grave sites, at least not those of Marcus and Elizabeth or an infant son. They had, however, found the graves of the grandparents of Marcus. The stones were weathered and the names etched into them were almost indecipherable.

A few feet away was the young son they'd lost. This was the family's first tragedy. She read the inscription aloud. "Teddy Thornton. Son. Brother." Such a short and simple epitaph. "He died in a swimming accident, you know."

Max had shrugged. "No, I guess I didn't. I didn't know there was another son besides Marcus. How did you know?"

She waved a hand through the air. How ridiculous he would think she was if she told him that Marcus and Elizabeth were living in her dreams? He would probably say she'd read about the accident involving Teddy but just didn't remember.

She took a step through the wet grass. Footprints from her shoes were left in the soggy ground.

"And this little one here," she pointed at the site, "is Marcus's first child, Sarah. She died at five years old." Her voice shivered uncontrollably from sadness. She continued down the row, as if in a trance. "Marcus's parents, Justine and Martin."

"There are no dates on the stones except for the words mother and father," Max replied, following behind her.

"Marcus's father died in the 1800s. His mother died before him, during childbirth." Ivy was encased in her thoughts and didn't hear the thunder in the distance or feel the drops of rain splashing upon her skin.

Max came up behind her and his warmth was the only thing that she felt. "Documents say that?"

"No," she admitted.

"Then how do you know she died during childbirth?"

"I guess I don't really know." She touched a broken slab of stone with the toe of her shoe. Ivy turned and stared into the distance at the house, which looked like an image in a painting surrounded by overgrown weeds. Max came to stand next to her. "I thought they would be here."

Ivy wrapped her arms around her shoulders as a chill brushed her skin. "It's a perfect place, with the view and all of their relatives placed here."

"Maybe their headstones were here but were destroyed over the years. It was so long ago and the property has exchanged so many hands."

She didn't want to believe that Marcus and Elizabeth's graves could have been ruined. It made her sick to her stomach. But another thought lingered in her mind. "They are buried somewhere on this land. I feel it in my bones."

Silence enveloped them for the longest time as they stared down at the house, waiting for answers. Finally, Max broke the stillness with his words. "Didn't you say that Elizabeth loved her garden?"

Ivy looked up at his profile. "Yes."

"If I were in Marcus's shoes, and I had just lost my one true love, I would bury her right where she would be at peace."

"Yes," Ivy whispered, gazing at the garden. It was barely visible through the fog rolling in, only a speck of land visible from where they stood. "But someone could have dug it up, even by accident. Wouldn't he think of that possibility?"

"Was he thinking clearly? I'd say his future seemed pretty dismal."

"Let's go and check out the garden." She pulled her damp hair away from her face.

"You're soaked, Ivy." Max's voice was husky.

"I can't wait."

The ground in the yard was moist and it was hard to walk through with the dense weeds. They could have easily overlooked the slabs of rock buried deep within the soil if the ground had been hard. But the mud had washed away, making it visible. Although they had a shovel they had found in one of the barns, once they started using it the dry, rotted wooden handle snapped and it was useless. Ivy found that using her fingers worked just as well. She may have minor cuts and stains for a few days but it didn't faze her.

The yard was a mess and the downpour made it worse to contend with. Her clothes were like a second skin, making it difficult to move, and her hair hung in ringlets around her face. Max had told her several times they should wait until the rain cleared as he dug beside her. Ivy couldn't stop.

She didn't care that she was wet and cold. She didn't care that her hands hurt. She needed answers.

Max prodded through the muck until he freed their find.

The two stones were worse for wear. They were flat instead of the usual upright tombstones. Pieces were broken from the thin blocks but the engraved names of Marcus and Elizabeth were still visible in the chipped rock. They had been buried side by side in the garden Elizabeth had tended with care. It had become a shrine to a couple who loved each other dearly. Together in life and in death.

"We found them." Ivy felt the tingle of tears as the wetness filled her eyes.

"Yes, we did." She heard the breathless tone to his voice. It could have been due to the digging, or something else. She guessed he was as unnerved at seeing the tiny plots left unkempt and forgotten. It was humbling.

"It feels as if we've passed through a doorway of time." She took in a deep breath, filling her lungs with the fresh air.

She felt his eyes on her profile. "What do you mean?"

"Well, it's just that--" She swallowed her words. It took her a long moment before she could continue. "We're intruding on a piece of land that must have meant a lot to this family. A private world." She felt like an intruder and yet a part of it in an uncanny way.

There were no words of memory written in the stone. No mention of a loving wife, a kind husband, or a mother or a father. There was suddenly an icy chill in the air that came so quickly that it sent an unexplainable bite through her. She wrapped her dirty arms around her waist, stiffly clinging to herself, but the bitter cold was relentless.

Max removed his lightweight jacket and swung it over her shoulders. The shivering abated, but the chill remained. "You'll get cold, Max."

"I'll be fine." The wind shook the limbs of the trees around them and the sky lit up with lightening. "The wind is picking up. Are you okay to stay out here a bit longer?"

"I can." Ivy was touched by his concern. She pulled his jacket closer to her body and took in the clean fresh scent of him. The smell made her tingle and her heart race. The thought of what they had shared earlier made her smile.

"You're smiling."

Ivy looked at him. Their gazes met and connected.

* * * *

Max couldn't turn away from Ivy. For the life of him, he wasn't sure why, but he was bound to her. She was as much a necessity in his life as his next breath. Her cheeks were rosy, her eyes bright, and wayward hair whipped around her face. She looked like a maiden standing on a ship as they sailed through the raging sea. For that moment all that he could feel was infinite desire for her. She was a magnet and his heart was steel. She pulled him closer with each breath.

He swallowed the cotton-like tightness building in his throat. "We didn't find a baby," he said.

That opened a whole new subject involving the Thornton family.

There was a missing link and it could easily be Max's grandfather. "If Elizabeth died in 1897, the baby would be one hundred and twelve years old. That means he's dead." Max pinched the bridge of his nose.

"But what about his children? Did he leave behind descendants?"

"Are you a Thornton descendent, Max? Are you a successor to the Thorntons' fortune?"

"Ivy, that sounds crazy. It's not possible." Or was it?

"It's not crazy, Max."

When he didn't answer, she sighed, got up and went into the house.

Max tossed the unanswered thoughts around his mind. His grandfather had been almost ninety-nine when he died. That was thirteen years ago. His head was aching.

Max went inside and grabbed a bottle of water.

"I think we have a problem."

"What's that?" Max asked Ivy at the same time he stepped in a puddle of water. He looked up at the ceiling and saw the wet spot. Another large droplet fell to splatter onto his cheek.

"What room is directly above us?" Ivy asked.

With a brief pause, he said, "The master bathroom."

"Did you leave the water running?"

"No." Max put his bottle down on the table and took off toward the stairs.

"Then what is it?" she said as she followed him up the staircase.

In quick strides, he scaled the stairs, through the bedroom, and into the bathroom. As Ivy came up behind him, he heard her gasp.

Water was running from the bath faucet, the excess spilling over the rim. Max inspected the bathroom. The water had been running for some time. There was a good two-inch puddle. It was slowly seeping under the door and was spreading into the bedroom.

Condensation covered the mirror above the sink and the full length one hanging on the wall. Steam floated upward from the hot water in the tub.

"It's freezing in here." Ivy's breath formed a mist.

Max waded through the water and twisted the faucet. It wouldn't turn. "It's already turned off. It must just be a leak in these old pipes."

Max felt Ivy behind him. She slipped her hand into the water and then pulled it back. "It's burning hot. How could there be hot water for this long?"

"It wasn't leaking when I was in here earlier." He still fidgeted with the faucet. "We've used the water more here in the last few days than it has been utilized in years. It was a chink waiting to happen."

Ivy pushed his hand away and tried turning the knob of the faucet herself. With what seemed like little effort, it closed and the water dwindled to a small drip. "Now what's your reasoning?" She lifted in a brow in third degree interrogation.

"Then one of us has left the knob turned on to the hot water."

"Okay." She nodded in compromise. "But why is this room so cold?"

"Someone also forgot to close the window." He went to shut it. "It's getting chilly outside. This is an old house, it's drafty and it takes a lot more than a tub full of hot water to heat a room that has no insulation."

"You've got an answer for everything, don't you?"

"Sure do, thanks for noticing."

"People don't like geniuses who are pompous to boot."

He'd almost take her words as sarcasm if she hadn't been smiling. "Did you leave the window open?"

She crossed her arms over her chest in defiance. "So you're saying that the *someone* who left the faucet turned on and the window open is *me*?"

"Well, was it?"

Her eyes narrowed. "Yes, I did. It was warm in here this morning and I lifted the window. I guess it's possible that I didn't shut off the hot water knob all the way."

He grinned. Truth was, he felt it was a little uncanny to come into the house to find the hot water overflowing onto the floor. The room was at least twenty degrees cooler than the weather outside. On the other hand, eerie things could and did happen. And maybe a deep part of him wished he could believe that Marcus and Elizabeth were reaching out beyond the grave in an attempt to connect, but there were reasonable explanations for everything odd that had happened since he'd been here.

"Why are you snarling at me, Max?"

"I'll admit, this is strange," he said. "But not unimaginable."

"What would it take for you to accept the fact that Marcus and Elizabeth's spirits still linger in this house?" Ivy's tone rose a notch. A tendril of her hair sprung out to touch her cheek and she blew it off her face.

"Something more noteworthy than strange noises at night, leaky faucets and cold rooms." Max shoved his hands into his pockets. "My equipment hasn't even twitched."

"What if I told you that Marcus and Elizabeth are trying to reach us? I know it for a fact." She tilted her chin.

Max hesitated. He'd known she'd been hiding something. "What have you been keeping to yourself?"

"Maybe something. Maybe nothing." She simply shrugged.

Max started to open his mouth but a smashing sound, followed by a loud *thwap,* ricocheted into the room like a gun shot. When the plug popped up from the drain it caused a huge air bubble explosion, sending the water into a shooting spray across the room.

Ivy jumped and started for the door. The water had made the floor slippery, causing her to lose her footing. She slid, arms flailing. She thrashed about, trying to gain control but her legs parted, one went one way while the other the opposite direction. She landed on her backside with a loud thud and splash. But she didn't stop there. Her body slid and landed smack dab against Max's legs. She looked up at him with an expression of embarrassment and shock.

Max reached down to help her but he knew immediately by her strained features that she was hurt.

Chapter 20

Ivy couldn't have been more humiliated by the event, or at least she thought she couldn't until she started to push herself off the floor and realized she'd strained a muscle in her calf. A tight cramp caused her to clench her teeth.

Max bent to her side. She wanted to shoo him away and drown herself in mortification, but once she saw the sudden concern etched into his features, she couldn't bring herself to tell him to leave her alone. In fact, she was glad to have him there with her. For many women, being the damsel in distress was a little old-fashioned, but at that moment she enjoyed feeling like she had a hero at her side rescuing her from the mishap. And to have a hero as appealing as Max was just too good to be true.

"Let me check this leg out." He ran his hand down along her calf and ankle. "I don't feel a break so I'm going to carry you into the bedroom."

"I can probably walk."

"Don't even think about it until we get an idea how serious the injury is." In one swift, easy movement she was in his arms and he was carrying her gingerly into her temporary bedroom. Steadily and carefully he eased her down onto the mattress. "We'll need to look at this leg closer."

She eyed him. "And what are you waiting for?"

"I'm going to need to take your pants off."

"Boy, you'll try anything to get my pants off won't you?" She looked up at him through her lashes.

"I'll be on my best behavior." His eyes melted into hers.

"Is that a threat or a promise?" she teased.

"You're an imp, you know that?"

With a melodramatic exhale, she asked, "Can you at least turn your head?"

"Are you afraid I'll see something I haven't seen, or touched, before?"

As much as they had shared their bodies during lovemaking she still had a sliver of coyness that remained intact. "Just turn around."

And he did.

She slid her wet jeans off, for the second time that day, and tossed them to the bottom of the bed. She even dragged off her wet thong. She covered her body, except for the injured leg, with a sheet. "You can look now."

He examined her leg and she watched his profile. "There's not much swelling. Is it very tender?" he asked as he gently pushed at places on her leg.

"No, it feels better now. I think my ego is bruised more than my leg." His hands on her flesh did help her forget a bit.

"It's definitely not broken and it doesn't appear to be sprained, so I'm guessing you just pulled a muscle. It'll be sore for a few days but you'll be fine."

She laughed. "Doesn't this seem like serendipity?"

"And you thought you would not be punished for socking me." He smiled. "It's probably best you keep off the leg for a few hours."

"You can't mean that I'm stranded in this room, in this bed?" She rolled her eyes and planted her palms over her eyes.

"Look at it this way. If there are truly spirits roaming around this place you'll definitely have time to investigate."

"You love this, don't you? You'll have me sequestered in this room and you'll be free to meander around as you please."

"Well..." He seemed to actually contemplate her words. "Yes." He situated the pillows under her leg. "Don't worry, I'll come and check on you every now and then."

"If I didn't know you any better I'd say you were joking with me."

"Stay here in bed and I'll be back in a flash."

"I've heard of men running out for milk and never returning. Is that your plan?" she yelled to his back.

He stopped at the door and tossed her a smile. "First, I'm not vacating the premises to go get milk. I'm going downstairs to get something that I think we both could put to good use. Second, men only feel the need to disappear when they are married."

"And that's right, we're merely friends, aren't we? We're just having an uncomplicated, casual affair, right?"

"That sounds sexy coming from your lips"

"You would think so."

After he'd gone, she buried her head back into the pillow and closed her eyes. She wondered what she had done in her lifetime to deserve torment like she was experiencing. How could Max drive her so crazy?

She wasn't sure if Max had only been teasing her about being stuck in the bed, but she refused to stay there. She couldn't imagine staying. She was too restless.

And very dirty from digging in the dirt.

She dug into one of her suitcases, grabbed a pair of sweats and an Ohio State sweatshirt and headed partially naked, and with a slight limp, to the bathroom down the hall. It was much smaller than the master bathroom, and not nearly as nice, but all she needed was running water and a mirror.

She used a wet washcloth to clean her skin. Chilled, she quickly dressed in the clean clothes, brushed her hair back into a ponytail, and applied a dab of lip tint to her lips and a healthy dose of mascara to her tired-looking eyes. She hadn't slept much last night, but what she had lost in sleep she had gained in other ways. *In heavenly, body-satisfying ways.*

Why was it that when she was almost convinced that Max wasn't a sweet, gentle man, he turned around and did something completely and utterly sweet and gentle? When she had fallen in the bathroom, more humiliated than hurt, he had done the gentlemanly thing by lifting her up into his capable arms. He'd taken her off to bed, and then followed with a tender inspection of her limbs.

Wasn't that what fairytales were made of?

She had almost divulged to him that she had been plagued with compelling dreams of Marcus and Elizabeth.

She respected Max, and in fact, she liked him a lot. It was one thing to like him and sleep with him as a means of satiating her animalistic needs, but she didn't want to fall in love with him. In the end she would get her heart broken.

Going back into the bedroom, Ivy sat on the edge of the bed, feeling as if she had fallen into a new territory. Could she be in love with Max?

She closed her eyes and held back the tears.

She heard Max's heavy footsteps in the hall, and opened her eyes just as he came in carrying a bottle of water and a bottle of something else.

She saw the familiar label. "Is that aspirin?"

"Yes." He handed her the water and the two pills, then watched her swallow them. "Now, are you hungry?"

"You don't have to fix me anything."

"And you really do need to stay off that leg awhile." He glanced over her changed clothes and clean hands. "I'll run down to that corner market up the road."

"That's fine."

He left the room again and time seemed to sputter by in year-long minutes of boredom. Ivy lay back into the pillow and said in a whisper, "Elizabeth, I need your help. I need to understand the mystery surrounding this house and Max." She laughed. Was she losing her marbles? Was she asking a dead woman for answers?

"Ugh." She rolled over and pressed her face into the pillow.

She was so tired. It felt so good to lie there with her eyes closed and her body relaxed.

On the verge of drifting off, she heard something. She resentfully opened one eye, then the other. It took her a long moment to realize that she wasn't in the same room, at least not the way that she remembered. It was different, in a pretty and clean sort of way.

Alarm brought her up in the bed as she darted her gaze around. Where was she? Why was there a blue gown laying across the bottom of the bed? Why was the comforter bright pink and scented with lilacs? The room was the same room but the flowered wallpaper was pristine. The headboard was dark and free of the dents and scrapes. There was a black-and-white picture of an older man on the nightstand and a fresh vase of purple flowers.

The sun filtering through the window warmed her skin. The bed was now against the wall by the window instead of situated in the middle of the room.

She was back in time again.

A sound to her right brought her head around in that direction. She almost jumped from the bed at what she saw: the most beautiful woman with strikingly silken, black hair. Ivy recognized Elizabeth. She covered her mouth and didn't move a muscle from fear.

Elizabeth stopped suddenly, brush suspended mid-air. She narrowed her eyes questioningly. She turned on her heel and scanned the room. Ivy waited in expectation. Could Elizabeth see her?

Elizabeth stared right at her, but looked through her. Ivy waited with bated breath, in anticipation of how Elizabeth would react. Would she scream? Would she pass out?

A few long seconds passed before Elizabeth shrugged and continued brushing her long hair. Piling it high on her head, Elizabeth secured it with a shell clip. She stared into the mirror, as if she could see more than just her reflection. "Who are you?"

Shaking, Ivy withdrew her hand from her mouth. Was Elizabeth talking to her? Ivy whispered, "Elizabeth?"

Elizabeth didn't respond.

Ivy blinked her eyes. Her head became fuzzy as Elizabeth's figure blurred. Elizabeth dropped the brush as Ivy saw a flash of bright light.

* * * *

Ivy rubbed her eyes as she turned and checked herself in the mirror. She was Elizabeth. She twisted and looked at the empty bed. Her limbs grew weak. Ivy was confused. How had she taken over Elizabeth's body?

A sharp rap at the door broke through the silence, a reminder that she wasn't alone. She grabbed the calico dress from the bed and slipped it over her head. Giving herself a quick glance in the mirror, she went to the door and opened it to find Marcus. "I was just on my way down." she told him, guessing he was tired of waiting for her.

"Elizabeth." There was an urgency in his voice and in his expression.

Alarmed, Ivy raised her palm to her chest. "What is it, Marcus?" Her stomach dropped.

"I rode as quickly as my horse would carry me. It's your father. He's fallen seriously ill," he said through heavy breathing.

His words fell upon her like a ton of bricks. Ivy shouldn't be here for this, she knew. Why was she here and not Elizabeth? She felt her knees grow weak and she swayed. Marcus reached out and steadied her.

"It's okay, Elizabeth. We'll go there now."

Ivy knew that Elizabeth's father had been ill for quite some time, but nothing could have prepared her for what she saw when she got to the small, shabby cottage where Elizabeth had grown up.

Elizabeth's sisters were waiting for her when she stepped into the front room. Ivy stopped and awkwardly greeted each of them with a quick kiss and hug. They didn't seem to suspect anything.

"How bad is he?" Ivy asked.

The one Ivy remembered as Molly, the middle child with her bouncy curls and big green eyes, stepped forward to answer, her grief evident in her pale features. "He's dying. The doc just left a few hours ago."

Ivy clasped her hands together and twisted them in distress. The other sister, Lila, laid her hand on Ivy's shoulder. "Lizzy, he's been asking for you."

Her throat became tight and her breathing ragged. "I… I, uhh--"

"What are you waiting for? Go." Molly gave Ivy a little shove toward a door to her right.

Ivy had no choice but to do as she was requested.

She entered the tiny room located in the back of the house, where there was only one candle lit. The room was cast in shadows. She blinked as her eyes adjusted. She found the man lying in the narrow cot, his body indiscernible under the thick blankets. His face, pale and thin, turned toward her. His eyes were slits as he stared at her. He slid a weakened hand out from under the covers, palm up, reaching out to her. "Elizabeth."

Ivy had a feeling if anyone would know she wasn't Elizabeth, it would be a parent. She stayed by the door.

"Elizabeth…" he called again to her in a feeble voice.

Ivy crossed the room, wishing she'd zap back home. It didn't happen. She made it to the bed. She hesitated before taking his frail fingers into her palm, giving them a gentle squeeze. "I'm sorry." The words floated on her heavy breath.

"Nothing to be sorry for, Elizabeth." His tongue darted out to moisten his bottom lip. "I'm an old man. We expect our time will come. And so it is mine."

Movement in the corner caught Ivy's attention. A woman sat in a rocking chair, the glow of the candle flickering off her stoic features. Ivy believed it was Elizabeth's mother. The older woman had pretty features, smooth skin and delicate bones, but worry had apparently aged her. Her eyes were rimmed with shadows and her frown etched lines around her mouth.

"When did he worsen?" Ivy asked.

"This morning. As the sun began to rise."

"I've been waiting for you, my dearest." His voice was barely audible, softened by illness.

"I came as fast as I could, Father. Marcus rode all the way from town to get me when he heard."

"How is my Elizabeth? Are you happy?"

She knew exactly what he wanted to know and she wouldn't disappoint him. "Oh, Father. Yes. Marcus makes me very happy."

"Will you ever forgive my stupidity? I shouldn't have allowed your talent at painting to be hidden in embarrassment. See there." He pointed up to a small framed painting of a deer grazing in a field. "It was your first. Remember? I've been staring at it the entire time I've been stuck in this bed."

"Father, there is nothing to forgive. You've always done your best for me." Ivy didn't know this man but she could see he was kind. She had no doubt that he had been a loving father to Elizabeth. Her eyes misted with tears. Ivy felt Elizabeth's loss.

His dull gray eyes scanned her features as he managed a weak smile. "You look different. You're glowing. I guess that's what love does for a woman."

Her cheeks turned pink under his perceptive scrutiny. She had the strongest urge to confess her soul to him. "Marcus makes me feel like my heart is about to explode out of my chest. I hope that is normal."

"Beyond normal." He winked. "You're in love." His eyes passed her forehead to something above her. "And how are you, young man?"

Ivy realized Marcus had been standing behind her all that time. She heard him step closer to the bed, first greeting his mother-in-law with a hello then his father-in law. "Fine, sir."

Ivy looked up at him from where she knelt at the bedside. Marcus's large frame filled the room. Having him close made her feel better-- secure. A jerk at her hand brought her face around in concern. "Father?" She saw his chest rise sharply and then slowly fall as a deep hollow breath left his mouth.

"Samuel!" Elizabeth's mother jumped up from the chair, sending it hard against the wall. The woman came rushing to the bedside, tears streaming down her swollen cheeks.

A coldness overcame Ivy as she watched in despair as the older woman buried her face into her dead husband's chest, sobbing painfully. Ivy wanted to say something, do something, but fear held her steady. She swiped at her own tears and felt Marcus's hand fall to her shoulder in support.

She allowed him to help her to her feet. He led her out of the bedroom and into the kitchen. Her sisters watched with questioning eyes. They knew the answer without Ivy saying a word. They turned to each other and began to cry. Ivy walked out of the cottage and into the cool morning air. She was numb to the bitter cold air sweeping across her moist face and whipping its icy fingers around her body. Neither did she care that her hair had fallen from her bun and was in wild waves around her face.

Elizabeth's father was gone.

Marcus came behind her and covered her with her cloak. "You'll catch cold."

"When you lost your father, Marcus, how did you feel?" she asked with unusual bluntness.

He faltered momentarily. "I felt like I had been kicked in the stomach. I had lost one of my favorite people."

"Why do I feel frozen? I feel as if I am stuck in a daydream."

"You're in shock, Elizabeth. It's okay to feel deadened."

"Once upon a time I dreamt of adventure and the happiness I would accomplish in my life. I visualized visiting abroad. I fantasized having tea in a castle with a prince."

"We all have fantasies and dreams, Elizabeth. I used to dream that I would sail the ocean in my ship to find treasures. That's one dream I'm glad that didn't come true. Not all dreams are meant to befall upon us." He sighed. "Don't you believe that our paths are drawn for us the moment we come into this world?"

"I'm not sure what I believe anymore." She wrapped the cloak tightly around her shoulders. "I want to go home, *our* home." She didn't belong here. Elizabeth belonged here. What could Ivy do here but make things worse for Elizabeth?

Ivy was happy when they finally made it back home. She was drained of energy and wanted only to rest, but Marcus wouldn't hear of it. He told her he knew that she was cold from the ride back. He insisted she take a hot bath. She didn't resist. Sally fixed the water for her in the luxurious tub and she almost melted when she sank into the warmth. She stayed there for a long time, hoping she'd disappear.

A light rap came at the door and Ivy self-consciously covered herself. "Yes? Who's there?"

"It is Marcus. I have come to check on you. You've been in here for some time. You will catch your death," Marcus said through the door.

Ivy's heart beat faster while her stomach did a topsy-turvy. To have him near, standing so close, and although he could not see her nudity, it made her cognizant that she was naked. She continued to cover her exposed parts. "I... I'm almost finished."

* * * *

Marcus anxiously pushed his hands further into his pockets. He wanted to say the right thing, to do the right thing, to make Elizabeth feel better. "I'll wait out here for you."

The door came open and Marcus felt his heart drop into his gut. Elizabeth was dressed in a thin cotton gown, and without undergarments the material gave an exposed view of her firm breasts, slender hips and the dark pinnacle of her inner thighs. He dared not alert her for fear that she'd slap him for peeping. He was, however, a man, and she was a woman. He could not be expected to turn away from such beauty without first admiring its grandeur. Nonetheless, he did not take advantage of the situation and kept his eyes locked on her flushed face. "Are you warm?" he asked.

"I'm getting chilled."

Marcus pulled his hands from his pockets. "I'm sorry. I... You should go and put something on. I wanted to talk." He spewed his words. "We can go into the sitting room if you'd like."

"We can stay here."

Marcus paused before answering. Not once since she had arrived had he entered her bedroom and now here he was. He felt as giddy as a schoolboy, even knowing that it was an invitation given in all modesty. "Sure." He silently warned himself to behave properly. There were certain things a man had no control over, and being in the same room with his wife when he ached to have her was his gravest weakness. *How strange,* he thought. He was chastising himself for desiring his wife. It was definitely not one's normal marriage.

She sat down on the bed, still not aware that her body was visible under the gown. Marcus studied the room with underlying interest. "Can I get you a cup of tea?"

"You don't have to. I'll ask Sally."

"I let Sally leave for the day."

"Oh…"

"I hope that was okay." He saw her downturned expression.

"It's fine. Don't you have work to do?" She played with the wrist of the gown, her bottom lip slightly puckered. She was a woman of many different expressions.

"No. Work can wait." He shoved his hands into his pockets as his body grew rigid with need. The shadow of her nipples pulled his gaze.

"I apologize."

Jerking one hand from his pants, he swept it stiffly through his thick hair. "Don't apologize. For heaven's sake!" He paced the room in exaggeration. "This is ridiculous!" He heaved a sigh of frustration.

She worked her eyes into him. "What is it?"

Marcus paced the floor a few more times before stopping at the bottom of the bed, eyes lifting to her face. "I'm your husband and here I'm treading the room like a mad stripling. It should not be natural that we are trampling around each other afraid to act and say what we feel. Don't you think it would be a foolish thing if I left my wife to tend to work when she has lost her father? What kind of man do you take me for?"

She sighed and lifted her palms up in confusion. "I'm sorry, I didn't mean--"

"*I* should be here with you, not the hired hand. I know you and Sally have grown close, but I am your husband. I want to console you when you are sad, for heaven's sake. I feel like I'm trespassing here with you." Irritation made his mind spin. It was long overdue that they had this conversation.

"I asked you to stay," she reminded him.

He buried his face in his palms. When he tore his hands away, he gazed at her, not worrying to cover up his emotions. "I know, but I'm here for a completely different reason than yours."

Her eyes lowered. He wondered what was in her mind. Why couldn't she share with him?

"I heard your words to your father." This brought her face up. "I want you to know how much hearing that meant to me."

"I can't deny that my feelings have grown strong for you. My father deserved to know how happy I am, how happy you've made me."

"Were the words said for his benefit to ease his grief?" He held his breath.

She shook her head in disbelief, as if she couldn't believe he'd ask such a thing. "I would not lie to my father, not even to appease him on his deathbed. It's true. Eliza--I am happy."

"I'm glad to hear that I've risen in your scale a notch or two. You must understand that I find you beautiful, and I want you, but I feel guilty for feeling so needy. I feel I could burst. I can't control these feelings. My heart aches when you're close to me and it aches even deeper when I'm away. Your sweet scent lingers in my senses all day long and through the night. For the first time since I can remember I've anticipated coming home. I cannot endure the mere thought of leaving here, not for a week, not for a day, not for a moment for fear that I cannot see your lovely face. I'm becoming a crazed man."

Her eyes were innocent. "I'm frightened."

He went to the edge of the bed and sat down next to her. "Why, my love?" he asked. "Do I frighten you?"

She shook her head. "Not you, exactly. You don't understand. These feelings and the thoughts, well, of consummating our marriage vows. You're my husband, yes, but..." She stopped. She bit her bottom lip. "You may be disappointed."

"My dear, sweet Elizabeth. Being together is not something to fear. It's something that two people share to become closer. It is a natural experience for two people to make love when they are committed to one another. You have no reason to feel that you are inadequate because I know that when the time comes neither of us will be left feeling disappointed." His eyes were sincere.

"Can we take things slowly, just a bit longer?"

"For as long as it takes." He got up from the bed only to have her take his hand. He looked down at her.

"Where are you going?" she asked. Her gaze fell to the bulge behind his zipper.

As if he realized what she saw, he turned slightly away. "I guess I'm in need of a cold splash of water."

* * * *

Ivy bit back a chuckle. She almost felt sorry for the poor guy because his wife wasn't putting out. The man had patience of steel. She wondered if men in the future would be as patient and understanding. Six months into a marriage and both parties expected a sexual relationship…man or woman.

He must have taken her long silence as her embarrassment or shame for his apparent arousal. He sighed heavily and crossed his arms over his chest. "I'm sorry, Elizabeth, but I'm a red blooded man and you're, well, a beautiful woman who is as enticing as a drink of water to a thirsty man."

"Marcus, you don't need to apologize. I understand."

His arms dropped to his sides. One thick brow shot up. "You do?"

She nodded, tucking a strand of hair behind her ear. "That--" She pointed with her gaze. "--is not only normal but expected." She wondered if that was relief or shock that crossed his features. Either way, she knew she'd overstepped her boundaries. "Now I'm the one who should be apologizing."

His eyes narrowed. "Whatever for?"

"Speaking so bluntly."

He laughed. "I find it refreshing--different."

She moistened her lips. She reminded herself to be careful. She didn't want to spoil anything for Elizabeth.

His intense eyes swept over the large bed. "Elizabeth, if I promise to be a pure gentleman, do you think it's possible I could sleep here, with you, tonight?"

Ivy hesitated. She'd never slept with a man before. That is, just slept. She looked up at Marcus and knew she could trust him. "I think that would be fine, Marcus."

Rhonda Lee Carver

Without hesitation, Marcus joined her in bed. He didn't touch her, nor did he ask for anything more. He made no move to take things further. Ivy knew, without a doubt, that Marcus was a true and wonderful gentleman.

Her mind drifted to Max. If he woke her from her sleep, would she travel back into *her* time? The dreams were becoming more vivid, and it scared her. What if she got stuck here, with Marcus? She dared a glimpse of Marcus and his eyes were closed. He appeared to be asleep. Could she love Marcus?

She swallowed. Her heart was with Max. Even if he didn't feel the same.

Moments after Marcus's even breathing was heard, Ivy felt herself drifting into a heavy slumber.

Chapter 21

Ivy shot up in the bed and gasped for breath. Her body ached and her heart beat wildly. With a trembling hand she reached up and pulled her hair away from her damp skin. She scanned the room. She was alone and back in her own world.

It took a long moment but her breathing calmed.

She had smelled Elizabeth's fragrance, lilacs... Or was it lavender?

Ivy questioned her sanity. She was beginning to wonder whether these were actual dreams or if somehow, some way, she was being tugged back in time. The more she was surrounded in the dreams, the stronger they felt.

She fell back onto the pillow with a weighty moan. The house and its history were pulling her in. She was more certain than ever that Marcus and Elizabeth were sending messages to her from the grave. It was up to her and Max to solve the mystery. But first, she needed to disclose to Max what had occurred and find out his thoughts.

"You're finally awake?" Max asked as he came into the room. While she had slept he had changed into a different polo and jeans and had gotten rid of any evidence that he had been digging in the dirt. His hair was damp and he smelled clean. She wondered how long she'd been asleep.

With a strained sigh, she lifted herself up in bed. "Yes," she answered.

"Feeling better?" He came to sit down beside her and handed her a plastic-wrapped sandwich.

"Some." Ivy's stomach gurgled and growled as the delicious smell of the roasted turkey and cheese drifted under her nose. She was starving. She had the appetite of a marathon runner. She immediately attacked the sandwich.

"Hungry?"

She nodded because she couldn't talk through the mouthful of turkey.

Rhonda Lee Carver

"I can tell." He smiled. "I wanted you to know that I called a friend in Chicago. He owes me a big favor and I'm calling it in," Max said through a smile. "I don't think I've ever seen a girl enjoy food so damn much."

Swallowing, she finally answered, "We've been through this Max. I'm obviously not like your other women. I enjoy eating. I may not be a size one, but I'm fine with that."

"*My* other women?" Max cocked a brow. "And I thought we had settled the fact that you can't believe everything a tabloid tells you."

She shrugged and stuffed her mouth with the last bite, sweeping her hands down her legs. She wouldn't go there again, to the tabloids. "Now, back to the mystery of the Thorntons. What favor are you talking about?"

"A man who owes me a great deal. I called him and--" He stopped. "Okay, you're not listening. You look like you have something on your mind."

She sighed. "Can we talk?"

                          * * * *

Max never liked those words, 'Can we talk.' Nothing good ever followed. And by Ivy's pale expression, this was no different. "Sure." Following impulse, he took her hand into his. "Why are you trembling?"

"I had a dream, if that's what you could call it."

He smiled. "Okay, a dream. Was I in it?" But he knew it was more serious.

"Remember, we talked about my dreams? In these dreams...or visions, I'm not sure what to call them, I've been seeing Elizabeth and Marcus. Not just seeing Elizabeth, but I've taken over her body." She shifted and seemed uncomfortable once the words were out.

Max could see the alarm in her eyes. "Describe 'taking over her body.'"

"After you'd gone from the room, I fell asleep, or fell into an abyss, that took me through time. I was here...in this room, but not now. Elizabeth's and Marcus's time. I was there when Elizabeth's father died."

"Ivy, no offense, but we all have dreams. You've been consumed by this house and its history, we both are, and I believe it could be very easy to let our subconscious minds be influenced." He saw disappointment sweep across her features. What mattered was, she was convinced. That's what he needed to know. "Next time you sleep, I'll be here watching you. Do you have any objections to me taping you and having the equipment set up?"

She shook her head, sending wild tangles across her face. "Not at all. I think they're trying to send a message."

"Wouldn't be the first time the dead have spoken. Tell me more, Ivy."

"They've communicated with me through my dreams." She seemed to grope for an explanation as she spoke. "There is no logical justification. But the feeling, the sensation of being there, is getting stronger."

He knew her concern without asking. "There would be no reason to believe that you'll disappear from here and stay there. They're dreams--"

She placed her face into her palms and heaved a long sob. "Please, Max." Her words were muffled by her hands. She brought her eyes up to look at him with beseeching expression. "Do you think I'm the type of person who goes around saying uncomfortable statements like this? Don't you think I understand that it sounds ludicrous? It has taken me a lot to tell you. You of all people should stay open-minded for just a moment and listen, really listen, to what I'm telling you. Because if you believe in me, just even the slightest, and trust in my lucidity, then you'll know what I'm telling you is much deeper than a dream or two. Let me go over the events, and help me figure out what they mean."

Seeing her determination, he listened.

Realizing that he got her point, she continued, "Even I, at first, thought it the ambiance of the place making my dreams feel so real, but somehow this out-reaches any dream. Marcus and Elizabeth are searching me out in my sleep and answering questions. Just now--" She moved a shoulder toward the pillow. "I was there." She looked to a place in the middle of the room. "I could have touched her but I was frozen in place. I called out her name and then something strange happened."

"What?"

"I faded into her body."

He remained quiet. He hadn't dreamed, or had visions, but he felt an intensity here that was far greater than any invisible force he had known.

"Her father died," she blurted. She looked at him with sad eyes.

"That's a good possibility." As sarcastic as his words sounded, he meant them without ridicule. "Of course her father had died."

"Yes, but... No, just now in my dreams, he died. Marcus came to Elizabeth right away and took her to her father. He died of something, a disease that was incurable."

"Ivy, most things were incurable back then. Even a common cold could kill a person." He had to state the facts.

His cell rang before she could answer. He looked at her, as if to ask if it were okay that he answer it. He hesitated before pulling it out of his pocket. "Max Shepard."

The conversation was short. He hung up. "That was a man by the name of Gary Whiting. He is one of the best field reporters I know."

"I've heard of him. Who hasn't? I must say I'm impressed with your circle of friends."

"Admit it, you're just impressed that I have a friend." He gave her a wink.

"Okay, you're right. I am fascinated, though."

"Gary left field reporting and is now a huge success in his weekly, live television investigative news program."

"I haven't watched the show much, but doesn't Gary himself go undercover with a hidden camera, leaving no stone unturned?"

"Yes, he demands that he does all the investigating himself."

"Is it real?"

"Huh?" She'd lost him.

"Rumors say that he wears a wig."

Max laughed. "Just between us, Gary is as bald as a cue ball. But he has connections in the right places and I've asked him to use those to dig up the information about my grandfather's adoption." Max scrubbed his jaw in thought.

"Didn't your grandfather ever ask about his birth parents? Wasn't he curious about his lineage?"

He shrugged. "I guess not, and if he did, he never mentioned it to anyone. My mom has very little information regarding her family on my father's side. My grandfather grew up in Chicago, his parents were wealthy, and he didn't talk much about his childhood. He was always reserved and I don't remember seeing him much while I was growing up. He was an attorney, and before his retirement, he worked all the time. After retirement, he holed himself up in his townhouse and kept to himself. I visited him when I was in town and he was always happy to see me, but he never talked about his personal life. I respected that so I didn't pry."

"Maybe your friend will have some luck finding the answers. He certainly can wrangle information from everyone else. His show is a hit on cable."

Max agreed. The man had found his alcove in television investigation. "Bad news is he's leaving for out of state tomorrow, but he'll hand over the information to his assistant to check into further. He did dig up something interesting, though, just in the short time that I left him a message an hour ago."

"Really?"

"Elizabeth's middle sister, the middle child, Molly, was a published writer." Seeing her surprised expression, he continued, "She married at eighteen to a college professor. They moved to New York, had a couple of kids, and she wrote mysteries."

Ivy squinted in thought. "I've never heard of her."

"She took a pen name, Amelia Christen."

"Amelia... She wrote youth novels about haunted houses and mysteries, didn't she? I read a few of her stories when I was younger. I'm impressed, once again."

"We both should be. Gary gave his assistant my number and she'll call as soon as she uncovers anything. The family may have been popular here in Ohio, but to outsiders, they were just another family."

"Maybe, but their lives were full of ups and downs."

He looked at her uneasily. He had his doubts that anything would be uncovered. "There's not much for us to do but to wait it out." He got up and started for the door.

"Max?" She caught him before he walked out the door. "What if you are a descendant of Marcus?"

He looked at her and without hesitation, he said, "If." He shrugged. "It won't change anything."

"But this house would rightfully be yours," she said.

"It's not my house, Ivy. I wouldn't want it." He sighed heavily. "I travel all the time and I wouldn't be the owner it needs."

"We're not talking a pet here, Max. We're talking about a house. Imagine the possibilities. The house has enough rooms to do wonders with. All of this space needs filled with laughter, joy, and possibly the pitter-patter of small feet. It would take a good amount of money to do all of the repairs to make it more livable and modern but I have no doubt it would be worth it to the right person."

"Ivy, that sounds like a pipe dream."

"But Max. You and Marcus are identical."

"Ivy, there are no 'buts.'" He sighed.

"There is when I'm sure you're related to Marcus."

He crossed his arms over his chest. Where was this heading? "Okay, Ivy. Tell me."

"The birthmark on your hip… Marcus has the exact one."

* * * *

Max left the room in need of alone time. He'd never had the answers about his past, and although he'd like to, he wasn't sure he'd find them here, at an old house in some unknown town in southern Ohio. But whatever was happening to Ivy, she was in a metamorphism.

And what about the birthmark Ivy spoke of? His grandfather had the same mark on his back. Max felt his control spiraling.

"Marcus…"

Max heard the name. "I'm not Marcus, Ivy. Drop it." He turned, expecting to find Ivy standing down the hall, but it was empty. He tensed. He was certain he'd heard a voice call out Marcus's name. A cold breeze swept over him and he caught a scent of something--lavender maybe?

He stood there as seconds turned into minutes. Waiting for something. Nothing but silence greeted him.

"Damn house," he murmured. Frustration made him edgy. Ivy's connection was affecting him--that's all.

Chapter 22

Night had come and the bedroom grew dark. Ivy started for the lamp, but instead reached for candles. She was in the mood for a calm environment. She lit two pillars and the room took on a perfect glow. The dirty walls and marked flooring somehow seemed less evasive with the candlelight.

The mellow lighting didn't help her relax as she'd hoped though. Her exasperation grew.

After she'd mentioned the birthmark, Max had stomped out of the room. Why was he denying the facts? She guessed he needed real proof. He was a man who believed in spirit connections--unless it dealt with him personally.

She'd find the answers. She knew it. They were here somewhere.

But where?

These days people kept security boxes or safes to keep their cherished items in. In fact, she had a safe at home. Not that she had valuables to fill it with, but she kept pictures and the few pieces of jewelry she had in it for safekeeping.

She wondered where people kept their valuables before safes and security boxes. Under the mattress? Under the flooring? Or perhaps in the walls?

Getting out of bed, she stepped vigilantly on her tender foot. She examined the walls with a careful eye. A hidden panel in the wall would be the perfect place for something precious. But Ivy guessed in a house this big a secret place could be well hidden.

Still pondering her ideas, she didn't hear Max come up the hall and stand next to her until he said, "Yeah, that is an interesting stain on the wall."

Turning, she saw that he had a bottle of wine tucked under his arm and two paper cups in his hand. He held one out for her.

"I recognize the label," she offered.

"You should. It's grown, bottled and labeled in a native vineyard. I passed it on my way out here and I thought I'd stop and see what they have. The owner told me the red is the best seller. I bought a case. If you'll just excuse the fancy cups."

"Well, I think I see a touch of admiration in your eyes for our little town's value. And here you thought all we do is milk cows and have spitting contests," Ivy teased.

He shrugged indifferently. "I never said that I didn't appreciate small towns. After all, it's very handy to have a cow in the backyard. That cuts the middleman out completely. Just think of the possibilities if more people would cultivate their own food. As a kid, I had a fascination for growing vegetables. Of course, the townhouse where I grew up didn't have much space but I did grow tomatoes one year, and the next year I attempted cucumbers. They didn't turn out so great."

"So, should I assume then that you weren't the jock who had all the girls?" She lifted a brow.

"Oh, I was a jock and had the girls, but I was intelligent to boot." She watched as he took an opener from his pocket and removed the cork on the bottle. It made a loud popping sound that reverberated off the walls. "That should wake the dead."

She wrinkled her nose at his loaded words. "I must say, Max, the more that I get to know you the more I see that you are full of different ideas and knowledge."

He eyed her as he poured each of them a small amount of wine. "Is that right?"

"In many ways you are more--" She carefully selected her words. "--extraordinary than I could have ever imagined." Seeing his questioning expression, she explained, "I mean that as a compliment. You've got to admit, when we first met you didn't leave a whole lot of room for a generous first impression."

"I realize I only allow people to see a few layers of my character, and those layers aren't exactly the most indulging. Once upon a time, believe it or not, I was known for charm and tolerance, if I say so myself. It's easy to lose the charm."

He handed her a cup, then sampled his. "Nice flavor." He poured himself a smidgen more. "My mother had a wine cellar. When she had her huge, high-society parties she would ask me to make the wine selection. Once, I asked her how she could trust me to make the right choice at a young age of ten. She told me that she didn't doubt my instincts one minute because she knew I would always make the right decisions, in wine and in life." He shrugged.

"Your mother sounds like she was encouraging."

He laughed, which sounded more like a scoff. "She was, I guess, until I married Marie. She got all pissed off. Not sure why, really."

"You know what they say, Mother always knows best."

"If that were true then I believe my mother would have chosen different paths for her own her life instead of living in regret." He knocked back the rest of the wine in his cup.

"Do you mean her marriage to your father?" she asked. If he was willing to share, she was more than willing to listen.

He nodded. "She still loved him even after he divorced her and married another woman. She eventually did remarry, but I don't think it was because it was a match made in heaven--rather a match made financially. Today, my mom and stepfather are retired and living in Florida. I don't get to see her much, but she understands." He poured himself another cup. "You'd like my mom, though."

"What's she like?" She took a sip from her cup, enjoying the combination of sweet and tart.

"She's very independent, outspoken and delightful."

"And you think I'd like her?" She lifted a brow. "Which characteristic do we have in common?"

He shook his head. "Not because you're alike, but because you're very far apart on the scale of likeness. You both give me turmoil about the same things in my life. You two could have a field day discussing and dissecting my life. That's a scary thought."

"You're her son, her only child. It's natural that she wants more for you and your future."

"Really? What more do you think she could possibly want for my life?"

"For one, working all the time isn't enjoying life, no matter how much you enjoy your job. Everyone needs a break. Second, all mothers want grandchildren." She paused to take another sip of the wine. It warmed her insides as it slid down. "Mothers need to be mothers-in-law. They need daughters-in-law to pick on."

"Why do you think that?" He laughed.

"Let's face it, Max, even though a woman may be the right one for her son, a mom still doesn't want to admit it. Intruding on their marriage is the only way she can always feel like she's number one."

"My mother isn't that type. She hated Marie, and told me that many times, but she never intruded on our marriage. She stuck by her old verse,

'You know what's best.'" He shook his head in thought. "Is your mother intrusive when it comes to your personal life?"

Ivy glanced up from her cup. "Well... I think mother feels that I'd be happier with a partner, someone to share my thoughts, my dreams and my stories with. However, she realizes that I'm very particular and finding a husband may not come in the near future."

He relaxed against the bedpost. His eyes were steady on her. "Are you that tough on all men?"

"Are you surprised?"

"I must say, yes. More wine?"

She nodded and let him fill her cup to the brim. "Why would you think I would be any less vigilant about finding a partner than I am with writing my stories?"

"Where do I stand in all this? Am I an exception to the rule?"

"Don't sell yourself short, Max."

His gaze held hers. "Is it possible that your opinion of me isn't as low as I thought it was?"

"Possibly. Let's just say, I'm awaiting a final conviction." She sighed, wanting to ease into a different path of conversation. "Max, we've become lovers and I'm not regretting that. We both went into this knowing that it's casual, nothing more." Saying the words allowed cut through her like a dull knife. She knew she was falling for Max but she would never tell him, not with the knowledge that he wasn't the type of man that made relationships.

"I think we should change this subject before it leads into an argument," Max said.

She didn't respond.

"Are you happy in this town, Ivy?"

"No matter your opinion, this town isn't so bad."

"I never once said it's bad, but you can't deny that the storylines here are dim."

She went to the bed, sat down, and leaned against the headboard. She was far from drunk but she felt good. "No, I won't deny that. But a storyline isn't the only thing I need to consider."

"You should think of your mother too." He filled in the meaning to her words.

"She's the biggest factor. She loves this town and the people. She needs twenty-four-hour care. Hiring a nurse full time is not an option."

"Because of the expense or the guilt?"

She shot him a serious look. "No expense is too much for my mother's well-being."

"Then it's the guilt. Just as I suspected."

She ran her finger around the rim of the cup. "Your attitude tells me you don't understand what it's like to be obligated or connected to someone. I don't feel guilty for taking care of my mother. I just know it's what I wish to do. You just wouldn't appreciate that because you don't have the capability to."

"Same ole' same ole.' You're always pointing out my flaws."

"That's right. You need someone telling you that you're cold-hearted and have no association with anyone, not even yourself," she snapped. The wine was working.

"You're sensitive when it comes to someone questioning your reasoning but you sure don't mind dishing it out. Is it so hard for you to believe that I may understand the need to please our parents?"

"I have no need to prove anything to my mother. She is proud, and will be proud of me, no matter what I do. I do what I do because I love her and want the best for her," she said with determination.

"I don't think love holds you caged in where you don't want to be. My definition of love is freedom to follow one's dreams. To make the most of this short, complex life we've been allowed to live. I think you stay here because you want to. Otherwise, you would have found a way to do both, follow your career while taking care of your mother."

She laughed while really wanting to scream at the top of her lungs. "You're a good one to be giving advice. You may have a huge bank account and have been to every corner of the world, but what peace and happiness has it brought you? I think you traipse all over the place because you don't want to be home. And that bothers you. You aren't quite sure where it is that you belong, do you?"

Her words didn't seem to bother him. "Whatever you say."

"This isn't about me, Max. This has come full circle back to you and how you are unhappy. When are you going to allow yourself some happiness? You can't see the truth through all the pain that's obstructing your view."

"This is who I am. I enjoy my job. I don't need a place to call home or feel like I belong." Not a muscle tensed in his body.

"I don't believe that. I can't believe that."

"Why can't you?" His words were low and husky and seemed to touch her skin, erupting goose bumps over her body.

Ivy heard a moan and realized it was her. She felt her cheeks grow warm and turned her eyes away from him. "Because I've seen the sweet side of you, the giving man. The little time that we've spent together I've witnessed bits and pieces of a man who wants to love, and be loved. When you're not protecting that barricade of yours, your eyes soften when you look at me. I try to ignore the way it makes me feel inside but I can't. You want to take the safe route but you must admit that it's not the best route." Her words were pleading, but not just for him; for herself as well. She wanted to reach him. She couldn't bear the thought that in a little more than a week they would be leaving Thornton House and they may never see one another again.

Her throat tightened. How had she fallen in love with him?

She couldn't deny it any longer. It was obvious as a bullet to the head. It exploded every logical thought.

* * * *

Max felt himself being pulled toward Ivy reluctantly, like a man savoring his last meal on death row. The inmate knows it's the last enjoyment he'll have before the end. She had the ability to reach him like no other did, but it'd fizzle like everything else. "What do you want, Ivy?" His voice was rich with taut emotion. "Do you want me to say that I am a changed man? Why can't you see that you deserve so much better than me?"

"Instead of allowing yourself to use your words as an excuse, I want you to be responsible for giving me solid reasons why you can't change."

His breath caught in his lungs. "We've been through this, Ivy. No emotions, remember?"

"I've already invested emotions in this relationship, Max. It's too late for me to back away and forget what has occurred between us. My only alternative is an honest attempt to figure out why you want to be left alone to wallow in your own pity." She clasped her hands tightly in her lap. "Maybe what we have, and all that we can ever have, is a two week fling in a run-down, haunted house, but if you respect me, you'll stop with the measly excuse that I deserve better. Is that too much to ask?"

She seemed to bury her eyes in his skin and see straight into his soul. He smiled. Maybe it wasn't the appropriate response under the circumstances but he couldn't help himself. What did this woman do to him? "When I'm around you I get an uncontrollable urge to draw you into my arms and kiss you until you are mindless." Hell, he didn't think it would hurt to be honest--at least a tiny bit. He was glad to see her smile, too.

"All it takes is one look, Max. One glance and I'm mindless."

"I've wondered if that's possible. You always seem to have an intelligent observation about everything, especially where I'm concerned."

"You know, I'd say you should follow your urge, the kissing one." Her eyes twinkled. Her voice was as smooth and silky as velvet, making it hard for him to resist.

"So, you want to be kissed into mindless passion?" He pushed away from the bed.

"Do I need to ask again?"

"I don't want to feel like I've taken advantage of you in this situation, Ivy." He was serious. "You can't change me. You take me as I am, without promise and devotion."

He watched in quiet anticipation as Ivy lifted herself onto her hands and knees on the mattress. The form alone was enough to cause his cock to jerk alive, but when she started a slow crawl toward him, her eyes warm and steady on him, not only did his zipper stretch to mammoth proportions but he felt every muscle in his body come awake in need. He smelled her jasmine scent long before she reached him. And it tickled his senses. Mixed with a womanly scent, it almost drove him over the edge right in his jeans.

She stopped in front of him, still on hands and knees--he assumed for his carnal pleasure. She moved closer, enough so that their noses touched. Her hair fell around her face and he got a whiff of coconut shampoo as the tresses framed her vixen expression and heated, needful eyes.

"And you must take me as I am. I'm a sensitive, giving person. I find it only normal to care for people, and even love some. I challenge you to hold up against that." Her voice was as satiny as the expensive bed sheets he liked so well. "Give in to me."

He was close to doing two things. One, he could bolt out the door and run for his life. Or two, he could let himself, for the first time in a long time, allow someone into his heart. He wasn't sure that she hadn't already found her way there. She was driving him mad. Wasn't this emotion what men wanted to feel? Wasn't it a man's desire to be seduced beyond control?

Damn, he was losing himself. Losing his control. As he started to reach out to touch her soft, silky hair, she unexpectedly pulled back, not far, but just enough to tease him longer. He could see her naughty enjoyment at his anguish. Hell, it was a turn-on for him. "You're testing my will."

"Maybe. But, if you're a strong man like you say you are, you can handle it, right?"

Rhonda Lee Carver

Her breath was laced with the sweet wine and he wanted to drink it from her mouth. "I won't deny that I want you, sweetheart. Denying it would only be futile." His heart pounded like a mallet inside his chest and his body grew hard. The crotch of his jeans became uncomfortable as his blood pounded into every inch of him. He couldn't remember ever feeling so turned on that he wanted to pull his cock out right then and there and jack himself off. What he wanted more, though, was what rested between her beautiful inner thighs. He knew her taste and he wanted to slide his tongue over her silken core until she bucked like a harnessed horse.

A slow smile spread over her face. Damn, this woman was poison to his senses. Sliding a hand toward him, she touched his cheek with the tip of one finger, softly and lightly, gliding it along his jaw, onto his neck until she reached the opening of his cotton shirt. She teasingly dipped her finger inside, as if she was drawing upon his warmth.

"Shall I remain aloof, Max? After all, you can't just expect to have me without some sort of commitment. I know you need me. I know you want me. I believe you're more like most of the human population than you think. You're in need of some companionship." She pressed her lips against his neck. "You smell good."

"You do too." His voice was throaty. He wanted to move to touch her, but he knew she would back away. She wanted to take the torment a step further.

Her lips fell lower. She reached the hem of his shirt and lifted it over his head, discarding it to the floor. "You're beautiful in every way, Max. You're finely chiseled. Your muscles are rigid and toned. This triangle patch of crisp hair, sexy." She kissed the spot, as if in proof. "Everything about you is an invitation for my touch." She lowered her other hand to the waist of his jeans.

He was fixated on the lovely lines of her face and the way her tongue swept out and licked her lips as she concentrated on the exploration of his body. "Do you know what you're getting yourself into?" His voice was bursting with need.

"Haven't you asked me this before?" She looked up at him through a veil of fringed lashes. Her bottom lip was puckered.

"And I believe you've felt regret," Max said.

She brought her mouth to his ear and whispered, "Are you having second thoughts?"

In a hurried tone, he asked, "Second thoughts about what?'

"I'm breaking down that barrier and you're enjoying every second, aren't you?"

DREAMING IVY 185

"The only thing that's breaking is the zipper in my pants, sweetheart." He groaned. "And I am enjoying it immensely."

She closed the meager distance between their bodies and pressed against him, then kissed him slowly. At first it was a searching kiss, then it turned into a spiraling of deep hunger. When everything was becoming a whirlwind of intensity, she must have sensed his weakened level of control because she pulled back.

He watched her with confusion. If he had to guess he'd say she was pleasuring herself in the control that she had over him. He didn't mind her teasing, but there was only so much he could stand.

In one quick motion, he slipped his arm around her waist and eased her back onto the bed. A shriek slipped from her lips but was lost when he covered her mouth his. There was no objection from her, even her palm pushing against his chest dropped away in abandonment.

He broke the kiss and buried his face in her hair. He loved the feel of it against his skin. He dropped his lips along her collarbone, tasting her. With an agitated moan he pushed her shirt off her body.

He explored her beauty, especially her creamy soft skin and full breasts straining against her lacy bra. He reached around and loosened the clasp and let the delicate material fall away. When he cupped her breasts in his hot palms she pushed against him, as if in invitation, eager to have him touch her. Pressing a hand between their bodies, he undid the button of his own jeans. She helped in sliding them down his hips and off his long, muscular legs. He savored the feeling of her naked body so close to his. She took his male hardness into her hand and stroked him until he moaned from her touch.

He gazed down at her. She was smiling up at him. That smile that could knock him off his feet. When his hand fell to the pinnacle of her thighs her smile faded into a look of complete arousal.

"I want to taste you," he said in a low growl as he slid down her body. Max tucked his head between her waiting, parted legs. He moved his tongue over her moist pink folds and she bucked her hips off the mattress. He eased his hands around her hips to steady her. Slipping his tongue deeper into her velvet smoothness, he suckled the softness until she rolled her hips. He plunged his tongue in and out in gentle rhythm. It wasn't but seconds until he tasted the release of her body succumbing to orgasm.

He moved away. She smiled mischievously. "My turn."

Ivy took his hardness in her mouth, and he felt the sensation of her lips wrapping around his full erection. Max could bet there wasn't a man who didn't like a blow job. Even when it was bad, he could still find pleasure in it. This wasn't just good, but Ivy made him feel like he'd never felt before. He threaded his fingers through her hair and gently tugged her mouth lower onto his shaft.

She pulled away. He lifted his head in disappointment. Ivy reached for her cup from the nightstand and came back to him. He watched her turn it upside down. The shimmery red liquid trickled over his length. She licked it up with the tip of her tongue.

He moaned in delight. It became too much. He was going to come in her mouth if things didn't change. He pulled her upward until she straddled his hips.

She twisted her body slightly, still straddling over him, as she reached the nightstand to replace the cup and grabbed a condom from the box he'd placed there earlier. She quickly ripped it open and rolled it onto his shaft.

Neither could wait another second. The tip of his penis curved into her moist folds, and although purely done accidentally and caused by her movement, he almost lost all control. He wanted to bury himself into her sweet heat and explode.

She lifted her hips above him, and when their eyes connected, she lowered herself onto him. It took a moment for her tight opening to ease around him. As she settled onto him, pulling him deeper into her moistness, she made circling motions. He felt her pulsating muscles. He pulled her into his chest, kissing her face, then her closed eyelids. Then came his own release.

Too spent to move, they lay together.

Chapter 23

"Ivy..."

Ivy jolted awake, her body tense and clammy. Max was lying beside her, sound asleep, his profile shadowed in the gray light flowing through the window. The sun was starting to come up and the room was chilled.

She had been sleeping so soundly. What had awakened her, she wondered?

Propping herself upon her elbow, she glanced around the bedroom while listening closely. Only an occasional pop and crackle of old wood violated the silence. It was strange. She felt odd, as if someone had been watching her.

She swallowed a nervous lump in her throat as the feeling grew.

Ivy glanced over at Max again. He wasn't moving and she didn't want to disturb him, but she couldn't defy the strong urge to pee. She slid out from under the sheet, careful not to wake him.

With little attention to what she was grabbing, she threw on the first article of clothing she came to, which happened to be Max's shirt. Pulling it over her head, she caught the tantalizing scent of musk and soap. A tingle sparked through her. She loved his smell, his touch, and for heaven's sake, everything about him.

She glanced back at Max as she tiptoed across the room. He slept so peacefully. His head was buried into the softness of the pillow, his handsome face shadowed with stubble. She wanted to awake him just to have his company but she didn't want to be selfish.

She stopped as she reached the door, a thought overcoming her. What would become of them? She was making this relationship too easy for him. What was it that her grandmother used to tell her? *"Why buy the cow when the milk is free?"* She cringed at the thought. She was looking more and more like the poor cow.

She left the room with her thoughts heavy on her mind.

After using the restroom she padded barefoot back down the hallway, and instead of going back into the bedroom, she went downstairs. She stopped in front of the portraits of Marcus and Elizabeth in the sitting room. She stared up at them for the longest time, questioning the connection she felt to them. "Tell me something. Anything."

She ran a hand through her mass of tangled hair and sighed. This was all foolish, she knew it. She was only having dreams, not sightings of their ghosts. Who was she to believe that they were trying to tell her something?

Why was she doubting the truth when it was blaring right in front of her face? Elizabeth was sending messages through her paintings.

Elizabeth had been an artist, a good one, and would have painted many paintings. So where were they? Had they been sold? Had they been lost with the change of ownership of the house?

And what about the baby? Had he lived? Was Max the great grandson of Marcus and Elizabeth?

She was full of questions. Why were the answers hidden?

"Did I miss something?"

She jumped at the sound of Max's voice. She turned and gave him a smile. "You frightened me. I was just thinking."

"You keep staring at the walls." He lifted a thick brow. "Is there something new about this one?" he said in a teasing tone.

With hands on hips and nibbling at the corner of her mouth, she said, "Elizabeth was a skilled artist. So where are her paintings now?"

Max rubbed his eyes with his thumb and forefinger. His was shirtless and his jeans were frayed from years of wear. Just as his life, she thought sadly. His face hardened and he said a little too gruffly. "Maybe Marcus became distraught after she died and got rid of them."

She wasn't buying it. "Imagine if you were in love, so in love that one person made your world a happier place. Then picture having that person stripped from your life. Wouldn't you hold on to every memory and personal item? I would."

He just stared at her.

"What's wrong with you. Max? You look like you're angry."

He shrugged his shoulders. "I woke up in a hurry, I guess."

"Okay." His whole appearance seemed to change right before her eyes. The mere mention of relationships and love could always put him into a foul mood. It was a violation of his beliefs. She knew by now that he was damaged from his marriage and she couldn't hold out hope that he would eventually come around.

She was sick to death of his changing moods. One minute he was giving and passionate, then he'd crawl out of bed acting like a son-of-a-gun. She'd ask why but she knew the answer she'd get, and she was also damned tired of getting a cold-hearted-bastard excuse for an answer.

She would throw herself into getting a story. To work. To find answers. To hell with Max.

* * * *

Max twisted his mouth. He had woken up from a bad dream and found Ivy gone. His heart had dropped. He'd wondered if she'd finally come to her senses and realized he wasn't the man for her and taken off. The thought provoked his irritation.

He knew it wouldn't be safe to discuss emotions with her, especially now that he felt no matter what he said it wouldn't be the right thing. He couldn't deny that feeling, the one that was filling the void he had experienced most of his life.

Damn--she was wearing his shirt. It tore through his heart. So did the determined set of her jaw. She had a fervor for journalism in her blood and it shone in her eyes. He couldn't begin to explain the feeling in the pit of his stomach. It was a cross between arousal and...*shit!* No way could he allow himself to fall for Ivy.

He smirked. It wasn't love, but instead a really bad case of lust. That's all.

Her sudden silent temperament concerned him. In actuality, he had waited for her surge of words to rip into him, but surprisingly, it didn't come. The silence was similar to a loaded gun. When would it fire?

"Ivy, I think you're full of questions and it's important for you to realize you're not going to have them all answered."

"Are you referring to the house or our non-committal relationship? It doesn't matter," she said as she turned away from him and left the room. He heard her yell from the top of the stairs, "Your phone is ringing."

Leisurely, he made his way up to where his cell sat on the nightstand in the bedroom. He didn't want to speak to anyone at the moment.

He caught a glimpse of Ivy out of the corner of his eye and turned to watch her as she took off his shirt. She didn't seem to care that his eyes were on her as she dressed in her own clothes, brushed her hair and slid on a pair of her flip flops.

He hit talk. "Yeah?" It was Whiting's assistant on the other end of the phone. With frustration, he listened.

Hanging up the phone, Max turned to Ivy, who was standing in the middle of the room, watching him with laser-sharp eyes .Her arms were crossed over her chest. He believed she'd give a raging bull a run for his money. He wondered if he should even tell her what the woman on the phone had told him. He knew he should. "Well, my grandfather wasn't the child born of Marcus and Elizabeth."

Some of the anger eased from her features as she came over and sat down at the bottom of the bed. Instead, another emotion crossed her pretty face. Disappointment? "Oh Max, I thought for sure--"

Damn, he felt worse because of her discontent. He felt for himself, well, nothing. "It's okay, Ivy. You can't let this news bother you. I'm fine, you should be fine."

"Was she able to verify who his biological parents were?"

He rolled a shoulder and steadied his glare on a spot on the wall. "She couldn't give me a lot of information except that it was a couple who lived in Chicago."

"But why would your grandfather have kept the picture drawn by Elizabeth?"

"He bought antiques, Ivy. It's a good possibility he bought a piece of furniture that had the drawing tucked inside. It was of interest to him and he thought it would be of interest to me, also."

"I guess that's possible." She rested her chin on her fist. "You know, you're probably right. I'm trying to find answers to this mystery that are far-fetched."

He didn't like to see that spark in her eye fizzle. He wanted to say something but he didn't know the right words.

They heard the opening and closing of the front door and looked at each other curiously. "Must be your pal Jimmy." Max wouldn't have appreciated the intrusion any other time but at that moment.

* * * *

Max and Ivy made their way down the grand staircase. Ivy was first and she saw Jimmy passing through the foyer. "Hey Jimmy," she called out, but he didn't answer. Then she heard a female voice, followed by Jimmy's nervous laugh. Ivy looked back at Max in curiosity. "He must have brought Delilah with him."

Ivy stepped into the sitting room and saw that it wasn't Delilah. This woman, with her extreme good looks and elegance, probably wasn't Jimmy's type. She was very tall. Fashion-model tall. Her white-blonde hair was long and silky, and her bright blue eyes were a warning that she was a danger to men, not to mention that her low cut red sweater made her full breasts an immediate attraction. She was a beautiful woman. Ivy thought she looked very familiar, but she couldn't get a closer view because the bombshell turned to stare at the paintings of Elizabeth and Marcus.

Of the pair, it was Jimmy who first noticed Ivy, and he gave her a quick, uneasy wave of his hand. "Hey, Ivy."

Ivy narrowed her eyes at the young man. Did he have a cold? Or was he about to throw up? Either way, he looked like he was about to drop.

The woman's gaze came around. She made a quick sweep over Ivy and smirked, or at least Ivy thought it was a smirk. Buxom Blonde stuck out a finely manicured hand. Ivy didn't want to shake her hand, knowing fully well that her own chipped nails and rough hands from digging in the dirt wouldn't go unnoticed by the woman who was dressed in a stylish, white, skin-tight dress and expensive leather knee-high boots.

Before she could deny the woman a friendly handshake, the blonde snapped back her hand and passed Ivy without a simple "excuse me."

Ivy was caught off guard when the stranger passed her as if she were nothing but a puny ant that deserved to be squashed. The woman wasn't the least bit interested in Ivy when Max walked into the room.

Ivy noticed that Max, a man who exuded all forms of masculinity and confidence, looked a bit ruffled. Ivy felt Jimmy's hand on her shoulder as he whispered, "I'm sorry."

She glanced up at him, misunderstanding his apology. "It's okay, I guess. But who is she? Is she interested in buying the house?"

He looked as if he had swallowed a frog. "Don't worry, you'll know soon enough." His voice was still low.

"What are you talking about, Jimmy?" She mirrored his low voice. "And why are we whispering?"

"She's--" Jimmy stuck out a slender finger in the tall blonde's direction. "--Max's girlfriend."

Jimmy's words hadn't yet registered when the blonde laid a hand on Max's bare chest and said with the most sugary tone, one that had acting potential, "Maxy, you've been a bad boy."

Ivy was stunned. She felt woozy as the scene played out before her like a bad dream.

"Renee, what are you doing here?" Max asked. His voice was calm but his expression was loaded.

"After we talked on the phone I just couldn't shake the feeling that you were stressed and needed me by your side." The woman *Renee* placed her other hand on the other side of his chest as if to stake claim. "Chicago was getting real lonely without you."

Max slid his eyes past Renee and onto Ivy. Ivy narrowed her eyes. Boy, did he have some explaining to do.

"Renee King, this is Ivy Kennedy. Ivy, this is Renee." Her name spilled from his mouth like a bad tasting food. Even Ivy caught that.

With a coldness that dripped from her every beautiful pore, Renee turned to face Ivy, and once again, she extended a finely shaped hand. Ivy felt Ice Queen's stare beating down upon her until she finally had no choice but to give in to the not-so-friendly gesture. Ivy placed her hand in Renee's. *Torture, complete torture.*

When Ivy felt that it was safe for her to speak without making it headline news that she was in between breaking into tears and screaming obscenities, Ivy asked, "You've come all the way from Chicago?"

It didn't go unnoticed that Renee casually wiped her hand against her thigh before answering, "All the way."

"How did you meet up with Jimmy?" Ivy felt Max's gaze on her, but she dared not look at him. It was taking too much control not to pick up the crystal vase with the poor dying wildflowers and throw it straight at his head. Could he even begin to understand that a part of her was disappearing into sadness as she was forced to stand two feet from a woman who claimed to be his girlfriend?

Jimmy stepped forward, almost between Ivy and Renee. Ivy wondered if he sensed the tornado brewing. "She walked right into the Tribune and announced who she was."

Renee smiled, showing off a straight row of pearly white teeth. That smile must have cost a fortune, and so had her breasts. Ivy smirked. "He--" Renee used the generic "he" instead of "Jimmy," as if he weren't worthy of his name. "--started to call you, but I'm afraid I insisted that my arrival be a surprise. You know how much I enjoy surprises, right Max?" She slithered over and looped a possessive hand through his stiff arm.

"You should have asked first, Renee. I could have told you not to waste your time and trouble in coming all the way out here." Irritation grew on Max's face.

"No trouble whatsoever." She oozed seduction as she rubbed her in-the-next-county breasts against his arm. "Jimmy gave me a scenery tour on our way here. I've never seen so many barns and farm animals in my life." Her words were coated with a layer of sweetness but it was obvious she was being cynical.

Ivy watched in astonishment as the blonde touched Max's arm, his chest, and then his face with familiarity. Ivy wanted to hit her, to hit Max, but it wasn't worth it. She couldn't believe that all the times they had made love, the closeness they had shared, was being flushed down the drain. *He* was a liar!

Stepping away from Renee, Max said, "That's because you've never been outside of city limits before, Renee. There is a whole world outside of your boutiques and spas and studios."

If Renee caught the sarcasm in his tone, as Ivy did, it didn't seem to inconvenience her. "You've left me no choice. I've called and called and either you've ignored my calls because you've been busy--" She slid Ivy a knowing, and very nasty, momentary look. "--or your phone isn't working."

"My phone's working," Max answered without hesitation.

Ivy and Jimmy looked at one another in disbelief. The room was growing tense. Ivy knew it was the respectable thing to leave Max and Renee alone. She had been sucked into the middle of this drama and she forbade herself the option of bailing out like a scared mouse. Max had a lot of explaining to do and she was more than interested in hearing his excuse.

"I guess I should be--" Jimmy started toward the door, but Ivy's hand snaked out to grab his wrist.

"Why leave so soon, Jimmy? Let's get to know our guest and show her some Midwestern, farm-grown hospitality." Anyone who knew Ivy would know she was being defiant but to anyone else her words seemed natural.

Jimmy swallowed with difficulty as Ivy shot him a look of warning. She knew he valued his job, and every part of his anatomy, and she had no doubt that he was unwilling to take the chance that she would hunt him down and wring his neck if he dared escape.

"Fantastic." The word oozed from red painted lips. Ivy glanced up and over at Evil In Heels.

"I'm interested in knowing why he didn't answer or return your calls myself." Ivy's gaze met Max's. She silently screamed, *Why, Max, why?* "After all, he's just been hanging out here with an abundance of time on his hands."

Max kept his eyes hooked on Ivy as he explained, "I made myself clear during our conversation on the phone, Renee. We broke up, remember?" Ivy swallowed the tension in her throat. Broken up or not, why hadn't Max told her he had been seeing someone? What kind of crappy relationship did Max and Renee share that he was so brutal as to break up with her over the phone? Ivy couldn't deny that Renee was a woman whom men would fall to their knees to be with. Ivy didn't consider herself to be in the same league, and it didn't bother her. She had never been high maintenance and never would be.

"Max, dear, we've broken up before and you've changed your mind. This is your mode of operation. You get sidetracked," she shot Ivy another ice-tinged look, "then you decide we're good for one another and we get back together."

This struck Ivy straight through the heart. Had Max broken up with Renee to ease his conscience while he allowed himself to get "sidetracked" with her? Was that all Ivy was to him? A deviation from his beaten path? As hard as it was, she kept the pain from her eyes. She wouldn't give Max, nor his overpriced bimbo, the satisfaction.

Chapter 24

Max wanted and needed to speak to Ivy alone. No matter what he said in this situation he was bound to be the jerk. Renee, in her usual catty style, would make it seem as conspiratorial as possible because that was the type of person she was. She didn't want anyone to call it quits until she made the call that it was over.

He cursed himself for ever allowing himself to get involved with Renee.

"Ivy, may I speak to you alone?" he asked.

Ivy wouldn't even look at him. "You can speak to me here. I'm sure you don't have anything to say that your girlfriend and Jimmy can't hear."

Obviously offended that Max was attempting to exclude her, Renee's collagen-spiked brows furrowed only slightly. "Sure Max, what is it that you don't want me to hear?" she challenged.

Max shot Jimmy a look of advice, to get the hell out of the room. The young man looked from Ivy to Max and then left the room in a rush. Max was a far bigger threat.

Ivy shot daggers into Jimmy's back. Max looked at Renee and said sternly. "Renee, I need to talk to Ivy. You and I can talk after I'm finished."

Renee couldn't have appeared more appalled if she'd been slapped in the face. "Max, I've never been asked by anyone to step out of a room in my entire life."

"There's a first time for everything." Max still didn't look at Renee. He kept his eyes glued to the one woman who meant something to him. He felt her slipping away and he didn't like the feeling.

"Never mind. I'm leaving." Ivy brushed past them both on her way out the door. "I wouldn't dare have Little Miss Thing go out of her way. I don't want to hear what you have to say anyway, Max".

Max caught up to her and placed a hand on her elbow. "Stop, Ivy. I want to explain this to you."

Ivy whirled around. Her glare went from him to Renee and back to him. "Explain what, Max? That you have a girlfriend and you did the right thing by breaking up with her long enough to sleep with me? I'd like to hear the explanation for that. You can empty your lies and bull onto a woman with fake hair, fake breasts and fake nails because, more than likely, her feelings are fake too," she snapped.

Max gritted his teeth. "First of all, let's get the information straight. You seduced me, remember? You came to me and offered yourself on a silver platter, not the other way around." His voice was low but charged with tension.

"And that makes it all okay. As long as I made the first move." Ivy threw up her hands.

"That's not what I'm saying. When I broke up with Renee I had no idea that we, you and I, would make love. Our relationship was over the day I left Chicago to come here."

"Make love?" She shot up a brow. "Is that what we did? I always thought for two people to make love there had to be some sort of emotion of love involved. We were having sex. Satisfying our animalistic desires. Exploring new ground. Take your pick." She turned her gaze just for a moment, as if to gain her composure. "It's okay, Max, because I was in it for the casual fling, too. You're not my type. I like men who are kind and relationship-worthy. And by the look of things, I'd say it's pretty clear that I'm not your type, either. I'd have to get stupid real quick before I'd make your cut."

He felt like he'd been beaten and left for dead. Ivy was angry and it hurt like hell. "You're upset, Ivy. I know. My relationship with Renee has nothing to do with us."

She shook her head vehemently. "Max, it has everything to do with us." Her voice was calmer. "Take a look at her and then at me. We are two completely different people. I never realized how much of a dispassionate man you are until she walked in here with her snobbish attitude and plastic parts. It's clear that you are a man who wants a warm body in your bed and a disappearing act by morning. If it wasn't comprehensible to me before, it sure is now. You'll never change. You should go in that room and make amends with her because as far as I see things, you've got it made. I bet she's a real pleasure between the sheets."

Max didn't say a word. Ivy shook her head and stomped up the stairs. Max started to go after her but he stopped.

He needed to take care of things with Renee once and for all.

* * * *

Safely in the bedroom, away from prying eyes, Ivy started crying. Isolation penetrated every cell and her heart ached with a pain she'd never known. She sat down in front of the door, blocking it in case Max followed her, and cried and cried until all of the tears dried up and she was left exhausted.

Ivy didn't know if Max had gone, or what was happening downstairs, but she wondered how she could ever face him again. She had been the worst type of fool because the warning signs had all been laid out for her and she had ignored them. No, she hadn't ignored them. She'd believed Max would change. She'd wanted to reach though the barriers and find emotion.

She'd fooled herself.

Her legs were starting to cramp from sitting in a crouched position on the cold floor. She stretched them out. When she did, her shoe got caught on a rusty nail head sticking out of a wooden board. She got up onto her knees and examined the spot.

Looking closer, she saw something unusual. Marks marred the old board, as if someone had taken a hammer and forced the slab into place, or had removed it several times. She glanced around the room for something to use. She ran to her purse and grabbed the nail file.

With the wide end of the file she began pulling on the head of the nail until it freed from the cracked wood. Once the nail was completely out, she went to the task of tugging up the board. It was loose. There was dirt and grime wedged into the cracks and when she finally managed to lodge the file between the grooves to lift it up, the wafer-thin metal file broke in half.

"Shoot." She had almost given up until she caught a glance of something shiny on the table. "Yeah." Ivy went to the nightstand. The bottle opener was perfect. The corkscrew fit perfectly between the slabs and was strong enough to pry the wood up from its place.

Board removed, Ivy peered inside the dark hole. With the aid of her flashlight, she saw through years of cobwebs that there was something shiny. Digging through the grime, she reached for the item, a rusted old can with a lid. The tin had long since lost its color and was dented, but when she popped off the top, she was amazed. Inside was a treasure. She found a tattered journal and two envelopes. With shaky fingers she took her fortune to the bed.

The yellowed cover of the book had a thin layer of dust. Ivy swiped it clean with her palm and blew away the remaining particles. It cracked as she opened the cover. Inside the first page she read the name "Thornton." This was Marcus's grandmother's diary.

The pages were badly stained and molded. Much of the writing was too faded to read, but it was still a precious find. The two envelopes were in much the same discolored shape. They felt damp to the touch. Her heart sank. She was frightened to look inside for fear that the contents would be damaged.

With unsteady fingers, she lifted the flap of one envelope and carefully extracted a folded paper. She sucked in a deep breath when she grasped the deepness of the find. It was a letter addressed to Marcus from Elizabeth, dated August 1897. She threw the paper down. She couldn't read it. She wasn't ready.

Who was she kidding? This was what she had waited for.

Once the initial shock dissipated she reached for the letter again and began to read the scrawled words aloud…

My dearest husband, Marcus,

Our son is born and words cannot tell you how proud I am. The doctor says I am sick and there is nothing that can be done for me. Why is it I do not feel less than blessed in the life I have been given? We have loved a lifetime in a year. My gift to you is our son. When my body gives up its fight, remember my soul will remain.

Your wife forever,

Elizabeth

Tears fell down Ivy's cheeks. She wiped them but they kept coming. *How heart wrenching*, she thought. This woman Elizabeth, who had just given birth to a son, must have been devastated, joyful and brave all at the same time. Elizabeth knew she wouldn't be alive to watch his first word, his first step, his lifetime of firsts. Her husband, whom she had loved so deeply, would never smell her or feel her or taste her again. She wondered how they had shared those last moments. Was it hours, was it days?

Ivy swiped the moist trail from her cheek. She carefully unfolded the next envelope it as if it were precious gold. She flattened it out before her. As she had suspected, it was a letter from Marcus.

It was dated July 1898.

Dearest Samuel,

As we come upon your first birthday, I long for the right words to say to you, my son. My heart aches that my one true love shares her death with your birthday, yet I still find that she is with me each day. She would be proud of the little boy you are and the great man you will be. My heart fails me, my dear son. I find myself having so much to share with you but without the time to do as I want. I have found a perfect family for you when the time deems needed. They have longed for a child but have never been blessed. They will be kind and good. My wish is for your mother's memory to live on. I sold her paintings. Of course there were only a very few but they are worthy of others' admiration. Maybe one day you will find them and admire them as I have. The portraits she so lovingly created will remain with the house. They belong here. As I finish my life here, I know that soon I will join your mother and your sister in peace. In all my years I could not have imagined that I would be blessed with such joy and love. It is not a sad time, but a joyful time.

Your loving father,

Marcus Thornton

Ivy was in utter shock at what she had just read. She held the paper gently with her trembling fingers and reread the words until they were branded into her mind.

If she told anyone of the events she had witnessed and lived they would never believe her, but now she had proof that Marcus and Elizabeth's son had not died at birth and instead had been adopted by another family. Samuel was his name. A strong, beautiful name.

Ivy imagined she could close her eyes and see his physical appearance--dark hair, mesmerizing eyes, and prominent features life his father. A stubborn, creative, giving personality like his mother. One image popped up in her head. *Max Shepard.*

Yet Max had said he wasn't a Thornton descendant. It had only been a coincidence that his grandfather had come upon the drawing. But how could she dismiss the birthmark? The similar physical characteristics between Max and Marcus? Could that be just a mere fluke?

Knock! Knock!

Ivy almost jumped off the side of the bed. She hesitated. If it were Max, she had nothing to say. Who else could it be? She opened her mouth to let out a string of curse words--but Jimmy's voice stopped her.

"Ivy? Are you okay?" he asked.

As much as she hated to admit it, she felt a sliver of regret that it wasn't Max. She gritted her teeth. She'd venture a guess that Max had run as fast as his feet carried him.

Didn't Max think he owed her a bit of begging? Of course, she'd turn him down dead flat, but it'd make her feel a tad better to see him on his knees pleading for her forgiveness.

She began to tell Jimmy to hit the road when a thought crossed her mind. Why would she be angry with Jimmy? She finally got up, crossed the room to the door and opened it.

Jimmy's nose wrinkled and his mouth curved downward. "Girl, you look like--"

"Stop right there. If you've come to talk about my crappy appearance now is not a good time, especially after I find that I have been sleeping with a fashion model's lover." It hurt to even vocalize the words.

Jimmy nervously shifted from one booted foot to the other. "I won't, I promise. And here all these years I thought women with..." He gestured a full chest with his hands, but seeing Ivy's frown, he dropped his arms quickly to his sides. "I'm just trying to say that Renee isn't that pretty. Who'd want a woman with fake breasts, collagen lips and a pebble for a brain." Ivy burnt her way through him with her stare and he daringly confessed, "Okay, I admit she's beautiful, but really, Ivy, she has nothing on you. You're beautiful. You're a breath of fresh air and you're as smart as hell."

Ivy waited for his laugh, but it didn't come. She saw that he was being very serious and she thanked him. "But I'm not the type for Max. Tell me, have they gone?"

"Long gone," he said. "Let me just say with great pleasure, that witch of a woman was not happy." Jimmy shoved his fists into his pockets.

Ivy shrugged. "Well, she should be happy. She came to collect her man and she left with him."

"Nooo!" Jimmy shook his head eagerly. "They didn't leave together."

Those were not the words Ivy had expected to hear. She looked at him through fuzzy, tear-strained eyes. "What do you mean?"

"They didn't leave together. I watched the whole drama play out from the front row seat of my Volkswagen, and the tickets were cheap." He laughed, smacking his thigh for effect. "I've never seen a model's face look so unattractive. Her red lips looked like they'd been planted on a snowball, she was so pale. She was heaving so deeply that her breasts were jiggling. I didn't think fake breasts were supposed to move like that."

She touched his forearm to draw his attention back to the subject. "Jimmy, they didn't leave together?" She was stuck on the first part of his explanation.

"Once he was done with her I'd say she got the point. It's over, O-V-E-R."

"What happened between them?" She wanted every detail--every juicy detail.

"They argued, she stormed off calling him names, some I've never even heard, and he left a few minutes later with his bags. She couldn't get too far on foot, so she asked me if I'd drive her back into town. So, I did." He sighed heavily. "I hope no one tells Delilah I had another woman in the car. If she gets wind I'll be handed my walking papers, too."

Ivy felt her heart drop into her stomach. The whole situation was confusing. She was hurt, but why didn't she feel the slightest relief knowing she wouldn't have to see Max ever again?

"Hey, what's that?" Jimmy made a sweeping, pointed gesture from the uprooted board to the bed.

She followed his hand motion. "A clue. A huge clue. I've got a big job for you. Do you think you can handle it?"

A few minutes later, Jimmy left the house with a new bounce in his step. Ivy felt certain that he'd find the information she asked him to search for. She'd have gone herself but she wasn't quite ready to leave the house. If she left, she wasn't sure she'd ever be able to reach Marcus and Elizabeth again through her dreams.

She knew her time had come to an end at Thornton House but she wanted to stay at least one more night.

That night, the house was eerily quiet, yet she didn't feel uncomfortable. Ivy packed up her belongings in sadness. She took a break to read the letters again. Her cellphone rang and she almost jumped out of her jeans. Seeing the number on the screen, she frowned. It was Marshall. She didn't answer. She didn't want to speak to him. She knew he would hound her for a story, but there was none, at least no story that was any of his business.

Ivy felt numb.

The day's events had left her cold and lonely. It would take a good day or two before she would thaw. She had fallen in love with Max and she would miss him. She had every right to be angry with him, but she was angrier with herself for having allowed him to reach her emotionally. He had made no promises. Had he actually lied? No, he hadn't. He had made every attempt to tell her he was not the man for her but she had held out hope that her instincts weren't mistaken.

The last words she'd said to him had been laced with hatred and bitterness, charged by anger and hurt. But what would he have said to her? Would he have told her that she knew the price of sleeping with and falling for a man like him? Would he have rubbed her nose in the fact that she wasn't his type?

Rhonda Lee Carver

Maybe she wasn't his type, but she could not fathom that a woman like Renee was his type, either. It was a sexual thing, just like it had been between Ivy and him. But his touch had left her warm and satisfied. He had shown her that having sex wasn't an obligation but rather a form of art. They had certainly created masterpieces together.

Thinking about it now made her hands tremble and her insides ache. She would never find another man that would come close to making her feel the way Max had. She was broken for anyone else. Rather, she had been broken when she met him, and he had fixed her. He had shown her that she could love--deeper than imaginable.

Ivy walked through the empty rooms of the house, her mind conjuring up memories of the home it had once been. Her questions had not been answered, or had they? She had made memories, fallen in love, and felt more alive than she ever had in her life right there in that house. Maybe those were the answers.. She needed to be awakened on the inside.

It bothered her to think that she would be leaving tomorrow and the house would once again grow quiet and abandoned. It made no sense to her why the house hadn't sold. The options were amazing.

Pouring herself a cup of the wine from the bottle Max had brought, she relaxed in the sitting room, staring at the portraits of Elizabeth and Marcus. "What shall I do, Marcus?" she called out to him.

She sipped her wine and was caught with a sudden thought. It burst through her like pins and needles. An answer washed over her like a soft cloud. Ivy knew without a doubt what she needed to do. What her calling was.

Grabbing her phone, she pushed in a number, not caring that it was almost midnight. She didn't have a moment to spare.

Chapter 25

Elizabeth sat propped up in the huge master bed, framed on either side by a flowing white drape. The red silk sheets and expensive matching duvet covered her. Marcus had bought them especially for her from an Egyptian dealer. She looked amazingly beautiful with her dark hair brushed out along her shoulders and her cheeks rosy.

"You're not cold, are you?" Marcus asked.

"No, I'm fine." Her voice was soft.

"Are you feeling well?"

She twisted slightly and the covering fell away from the mound underneath her thin cotton gown. She placed a hand on her swollen belly with a soon-to-be-mother's kindness and anticipation. "I feel magnificent. The little one is kicking like it wants to come out." Her eyes brightened as she witnessed their baby's movements. "It's too early for that."

Marcus shifted and he sat next to her hip on the edge of the bed. He had rearranged his schedule so that he was very seldom gone, and when he did leave, he hurried home to be by her side. She had been on bed rest for a month now and since she was growing weaker as the baby grew larger inside her stomach, he worried more about her. She had only two months to go until their child would be born into the world. "Elizabeth, the doctor said you must stay in bed and rest. We cannot have you fainting and hurting yourself or the baby. You're too weak now to be doing anything without help."

Elizabeth peered at him with loving green eyes. "You look tired and distraught from the worry, Marcus." She reached up and ran a finger along the stubble on his chin. "You're not sleeping much, are you?"

He raked a hand through his hair. "More than you are," he replied with a lifted brow. "You must promise me, Elizabeth, that you will not leave this bed." He couldn't mask the fear in his voice.

She dropped her hand to her side. "I promise. I would never do anything to harm the baby. I just get so bored sitting here all day without a thing to occupy my time," she stated through a grim pout.

"I hope I can bring a little smile to that pretty mouth when I tell you that you will not have to endure this alone from this point on. I have hired someone to take care of my business dealings and I can stay here with you. If anything occurs it will be you growing tired of your husband."

* * * *

Elizabeth had known after her last fainting spell that Marcus would never leave her side. Guilt plagued her. It was sad enough that she was stuck inside the house and now he was imprisoning himself too. She had known better than to climb out of bed two nights ago in an attempt to go to the bathroom without the help of Sally. The younger woman had already been waiting on her hand and foot and Elizabeth hated to call for her to gain help to the lavatory. She'd no problem getting to her destination, but when she had started her trek back to bed, she had felt her body grow weak, and then everything had gone black. Sally found her later and had sent one of the farmhands to gather Marcus and the doctor.

She had awakened and found a petrified Marcus, a curious Doctor Jenson, and a scared Sally hovering over her like she were some type of alien specimen. She had told them she was fine, but the doctor hadn't been convinced. He had given her a gentle lecture on following his medical orders then taken his leave with plans to come again the next day.

"You'll grow tired of me, Marcus," she said.

"Not in a million years." He kissed the tip of her nose. "What is there to miss outside of this house? We have everything we need right here." He lovingly palmed her baby mound. He touched her stomach often. She smiled, remembering when he had felt the baby move for the first time and leaped into the air with a loud yelp of delight.

"Although I do love it here, I cannot lie. I miss our rides into town. It reminded me of the few times as a child my father would take me into town while he gathered farm goods. While he stopped at the mill I would walk down by the shops and admire the textiles and goods. Everything seemed so bright and shiny. Maybe that's normal for an eight-year-old who had nothing to play with. I remember looking through the window of a shop and seeing the prettiest rag doll. I mentioned to my father on our ride back home how lovely the doll was. I knew we could not afford such luxury items but it was fine to dream. The next day my father surprised me by bringing home that little doll." Her eyes filled with tears "I cherished that doll."

"Your father appreciated how special you are. Just as I knew how special you were the first day you came bouncing into this house, filling it with life and laughter. You would dance around in the garden in such faraway enjoyment. You seemed to be dreaming of a better place beyond this town."

She laughed. "I thought I was being helpful, cleaning, but apparently by your description I was playing all the time."

"Your mother appreciated having you here."

"I wouldn't be so sure." Since her father had died she had barely seen her mother or sisters. Her sister Molly had married a rich man and moved to Boston, and her younger sister had gone to help Molly.

She caught him watching her with tender eyes. "Your home was never dirty, Marcus. I wondered what my mother was cleaning while she was here."

"This big place gets dusty overnight, as you well know." He seemed to drift off for a second. "I liked having the noise. Noise always made the loneliness a little more bearable."

"I used to sit and watch you, you know," she confessed.

He looked at her funnily. "I never knew."

"You'd sit in your overstuffed chair in the study smoking your corn pipe, staring out the window as if you were expecting someone. I would tiptoe around the door, afraid to disturb you," she said.

"Why tiptoe?"

"So you wouldn't snap at me."

"I wouldn't have snapped." He sounded shocked that she would even voice such a thing. "I was wading in a pool of grief. When pain becomes so overwhelming it seems to overtake your world. I never knew I could be lucky to love again."

"You've been so patient and loving to me. You've tolerated so much."

"Yes, you have been such a pain."

He laughed and she tenderly slapped his arm. "You should not joke with a pregnant woman in such a way."

"Tell me, Elizabeth, what were your childhood dreams?"

"Something very different than marriage and babies. I've always been different." She sighed heavily. "When all the other little girls were playing house, I was daydreaming. Mother used to get so angry with me because I was resisting the plans she had for me. She wanted me to be normal."

"Normal? What does that mean? I do not believe I have ever had the pleasure of meeting someone who meets the definition."

"Mother's definition was very clear-cut. She wanted me to dress prettily and smile at the boys, the good boys, that is. She warned me if I ever planned to marry someone worth his weight in gold then I would need to give up all of my silly notions of doing something with my life other than becoming a wife."

"I'm assuming you didn't dress up prettily and smile at the boys?" He lifted his brow.

"No, I didn't. If anything, I did the complete opposite. That's when she saw the opportunity with you. She thought she had better not waste any time."

"So, you really never had dreams of a husband and children?" he asked.

She knew it sounded cruel to admit that point now that she was happily married with a baby on the way into the world. "I guess I didn't. Or, maybe I did." She shrugged at the thought. "I just knew I didn't want to give up my interest."

"Painting?"

She had allowed him into her 'secret' room where her paintings were hidden. He had immediately requested that she hang them proudly throughout the house, and she had. She could not imagine that anyone could have made her happier. Since then she had merrily painted a portrait of him and a self-portrait, both of which hung above the fireplace. Her favorite, and his too, was the painting of Thornton House structured in a gold frame that now hung above their bed.

"Yes, my painting," she admitted. She glanced over at the simple charcoal drawing she had been working on the last few days. It was of the house. She had wished she could pull out all of her paints. It would have been so lovely in color. That would come, eventually.

"I cannot believe you kept your talent hidden from me during the first part of our marriage. I was beginning to suspect that you were hiding a lover in that room of yours."

Her mouth fell open in shock. "You stop that this very minute. You know I would never do such a thing!"

"There are women who have lovers beside their husband."

"You're teasing me," she said. Her cheeks were red and she couldn't believe she could still get embarrassed around him after all they had shared.

"No, I am not teasing. In fact, ten years ago the barkeeper shot a young man because he was fooling with his wife."

"You'd never have a mistress, would you?" she asked, partly out of gesture.

"Never." He kissed her fully on the lips. "When you find the one there is no need to look any further."

Her interest dissipated as pain slashed through her abdomen. She slumped over instinctively. She felt Marcus's hands on her shoulders. He asked, "Are you okay?"

The pain subsided and she looked at him. "Marcus, I--" She reached up and grabbed his arm, leaning forward. Another pain wrapped her body in its vise-like, torturing grip. She moaned as the room swirled.

Elizabeth felt Marcus grow tense. She wanted to hide her pain, but something was wrong, she knew it. He moved back the covers, this action followed by his gasp of breath.

"What, Marcus?" She saw his panicked expression and she looked down at her lap. A stain of crimson covered her gown.

"Damn!" The word exploded from Marcus. He ran from the room. Elizabeth heard him yell down the stairs. "Sally!" His booming voice resounded off the walls.

Sally came bustling in, fear etching her dark skin. Her eyes were blinking wildly. "What is it, Mr. Thornton?" Sally looked past Marcus's shoulder and saw the bed. "Oh my Lord." Sally's hand went to her throat.

"Go get Doctor Jenson, Sally. Tell him she's bleeding." Marcus turned pale.

"Yes, sir, right away." Sally dashed out of the room and her heavy footsteps could be heard all the way down the stairs, through the foyer and out the door.

* * * *

Marcus stayed at Elizabeth's side, watching as wave after wave of pain assailed her body. His eyes were drawn to the bloodstain on the front of her gown. It was spreading and now covered the sheet. Time seemed to tick by at a turtle's pace until finally the doctor came scurrying into the bedroom, followed closely by a frightened Sally.

"Step back, Marcus." Doctor Jenson gently touched Marcus's shoulder. "I need room while I examine her."

Marcus stood behind the doctor, peering over his shoulder, his eyes glued to Elizabeth's face. She was now white and her hair was plastered to her forehead. She was drenched in sweat. He wanted to be by her side. It tore at him to watch her in pain. As the doctor examined her, Marcus waited with hands fisted and knuckles white.

The doctor stood up and Marcus knew by Jenson's somber expression that it wasn't good news.

"What is happening?" Marcus made no effort to hide the trembling in his voice. He had no one to prove his bravery to but Elizabeth. She lay sick. He was sick too.

Jenson hesitated, his thick gray brows furrowing. The older man seemed careful with his words as well as to mask his own uncertainty. "She is bleeding heavily. It appears the baby will be born tonight." Sweat appeared on Jenson's wrinkled brow as he turned to a frantic Sally and commanded, "I need you to get me clean sheets and a pot of hot water. Have you delivered a baby before?"

Sally nodded her head wearily. "I helped my two sisters come into the world."

"Good. I'll need an extra pair of hands." Jenson turned to Marcus in concern. "You may want to leave the room."

Protectiveness made every fiber of Marcus clench. "I will not leave her."

"Then grab hold of yourself, man. You must be strong," Doctor Jenson said in a whisper.

The doctor's words drove through Marcus's brain over and over again as the next hours passed in painful torment. Elizabeth's pain seemed to never cease in its intensity. Doctor Jenson offered small amounts of laudanum and it seemed to only take the edge off. He said he wanted to be careful to not harm the baby.

With each moment that passed, Elizabeth grew weaker and more tired until she fell to the pillow, looking up at Marcus with pleading eyes. She curved her thin lips into a smile. "It will be fine." And even as the words left her the truth was etched in Doctor Jenson's sad eyes.

The sheets had been changed and towels had been spread underneath Elizabeth. They too were immediately stained with her blood. Marcus sat at her side, conjuring up bravery he never knew existed. Bravery, or maybe he was numb with fear, he wasn't sure. All he wanted to do was sob like a baby.

Doctor Jenson laid a hand gently on Marcus's arm. Marcus had always believed Jenson a skilled doctor and a kind man. Now in his early sixties, Jenson had always been a friend to the Thornton family. He'd delivered both Marcus and Elizabeth, and his own sadness was evident in his wrinkled thin face. He nodded for Marcus to follow him into the hall.

Marcus went along with Jenson but didn't go any further than the doorway. He didn't want to leave Elizabeth alone. With a steady breath, Marcus carried his gaze to Jenson. "All right, Doc, tell me what's going on."

"Marcus, you know I have delivered many children, and it doesn't look good for Elizabeth or the baby. I didn't want to be too hasty in telling you this because I know Elizabeth is a fighter. But now I know the time has come."

"What are you saying? There's nothing we can do for Elizabeth?" Marcus choked on his words.

Doctor Jensen sighed and rubbed his chin. "I don't think so."

Marcus died that moment, although his heart still beat and his lungs still filled with air. He wished he could die too. There was no longer any reason for him to live.

"There is a way…maybe to save the baby." Jenson pushed his glasses further up his nose. The air grew stale. "You have to understand, though, that it's early. The baby's lungs may not function."

Marcus brought his gaze up. "And my wife?"

"She's lost a lot of blood. If we proceed to save the baby…"

Marcus felt a knife bury deep into his back. "What?"

There was a long pause and Jenson's face grew grim. "You have to make a choice."

"A choice?" The words fell from his lips like acid.

"If we don't do something soon, mother and child will both die. If we take the baby now, it may live. This may be the infant's only chance of survival. For Elizabeth, we may not be able to stop the blood."

If the house had crumbled down around him, Marcus wouldn't have known. He was absorbed in the pain he now faced. A part of him wanted to wring the man's neck for even suggesting such a horrid thing, but he couldn't take his emotions out on the doctor. As Jenson continued explaining, Marcus listened, but his head whirled.

His world had come to an end.

* * * *

Ivy woke with a start. Sweat soaked her body and clothes. Her heart was racing and her breathing was shallow.

She had fallen asleep, not in bed, but on the couch. Her cheeks were covered with tear tracks and she swiped the moistness away. She had dreamed of Elizabeth and Marcus again. Somehow she knew that she'd never dream of them again. She fell back onto the pillow and moaned.

Elizabeth and Marcus were long gone.

Chapter 26

Ivy sat down on the white rattan rocker on the newly finished outdoor stone patio. Her mother was busy planting flowers in the garden. The older woman's immobilized hand was steady at her side but she worked with a smile. This was the happiest Ivy had seen her in years.

Ivy looked out over the field of her backyard and sighed blissfully. She had done the right thing, buying Thornton House. She had talked the owner down to a price that she could afford. With the sale of her mother's home, they were able to start many much-needed repairs on the interior. She had gone to the library and borrowed loads of books on remodeling, and through trial and error, she had done much of the work herself. It amazed her that with her own two hands she had accomplished so much for her new home. What she had been unable do herself she had hired local workers for--fixing the roof, sanding the wooden floors. It helped that she was friends with skilled laborers and they had given her good deals.

She had hired a painter to start painting the rooms in bright colors, knowing that it would lighten up the old house. She was disappointed that she wasn't able to do the painting herself, and it would have saved her a good amount of money, but she had no choice.

She had big plans for the house and she trembled with excitement at the mere thought.

As she had suspected, she had never dreamed of Marcus and Elizabeth again. However, after reading Grandmother Thornton's story, Ivy had gotten much encouragement and motivation for life from the older woman's wise words. Ivy believed it had been her destiny to find the journal and the letters under the floorboard. She realized that although many of her questions had been left unanswered, the biggest issues in her life had been resolved.

It had been two months since Max had walked out of Thornton House, or rather, Ivy's house, and he was gone. She could not deny that she had secretly hoped he would call. She wasn't surprised that he hadn't.

She missed him. Especially at night when she lay in bed--the same bed where they had made love. She would always remember the love they'd shared. She would close her eyes and imagine he was beside her, touching her body with his magical hands. Then she would open her eyes and reality would slap her in the face. He was gone too.

Ivy's only solace was the house. It was slowly becoming a home as it once had been years ago. This was the home where she would raise her family.

After resting for another few minutes, she got up from the comfortable chair and called to her mother, "I'm going in to get a glass of tea. Would you like some?"

Elaine sent her a wave. "You go on ahead. I'll be in later."

Ivy doubted she'd be in before dark but that was okay. Working in the new garden pleased her mother.

Ivy smiled while looking over at the old garden by the house, Elizabeth's garden. Since Marcus and Elizabeth had been buried in that spot, Ivy had cleaned the weeds and foliage and set up a sanctuary of sorts. She had planted beautiful flowers and placed a stone monument with their names engraved on it. Although there would never be a garden in that area again, their burial spots would always be remembered appropriately. She would be forever grateful that they had reached her through her dreams and told her their story of true love.

The house was cool to her skin as she came in from the hot outdoors. It had been a steamy summer so far and she made herself a mental note that she would have to look into getting a heating and cooling system before long. In another month she would be sensitive to the hottest month of the year.

Entering the kitchen, she stopped, as she always did. She couldn't get over how different it looked since the remodeling. She'd had the cabinets painted a bright white. She put in new laminate countertops. She'd replaced the old, large white ceramic tiles. Simple touches like pretty curtains and rugs made it worthy of a kitchen straight out of *Better Homes and Gardens*, where she had had gotten many of her creative ideas.

She poured herself a glass of tea and sipped at its sweetness. She heard footsteps coming through the hall and she laughed. "So, you did decide to come in early from the garden, huh, Mom?" Ivy started to grab another glass when the voice behind her made her stiffen. Her heart fluttered.

"Ivy?"

She turned slowly, knowing who that voice belonged to and wondering if she were imagining things. There he was, the real-life, warm-blooded, sexier-than-ever Max Shepard. He was dressed in a red polo and dark jeans. His hair was longer by an inch or so and he looked amazing.

"Max."

* * * *

"Ivy," He said her name again. She was beautiful. Her hair was pulled back from her lovely face and her eyes shone like stars. She wore a loose fitting dress that stopped a few inches above her knees, showing off her lovely tanned legs. She was scrumptious from the top of her silky tendrils down to her cherry painted toenails, which were visible in her wispy sandals. It had been too long. He ached inside and hoped she wouldn't turn him away.

"Max, what are you doing here?" She clutched the edge of the counter.

"I stopped in town at the Tribune and Jimmy told me you quit." He remained still in the doorway. He wasn't sure yet how she'd respond to him being here.

"I did. There have been many changes, but I don't see how that's any business of yours."

He flinched. "I understand you're angry but--"

"Stop right there." She held up her hand as confirmation. "You left here two months ago--disappeared. Now you come here and tell me you *understand* that I am angry? How generous of you to understand my feelings and emotions, Max. Did you consider that I may have moved on with my life in these last two months?"

"You're beautiful." The words came out of their own accord.

Her eyes narrowed. There was the Ivy he knew. Sassy and challenging. "Do not try and sweet talk me, Max."

"The place looks nice. It suits you here." He took one subtle step closer to her.

"And you're a big fat liar, Max Shepard." She placed her fist on her hip.

"I'm sorry, Ivy. I wasn't ready--"

"Ready?" she said through gritted teeth. "Ready to tell me that you had a girlfriend?"

"To realize that I had connections here in Morgan Sites and to this house."

"Is that why you're here? To take this house from me?"

"No, Ivy. You should know me better than that."

"Didn't you think I would find out the truth, that you are Marcus and Elizabeth's grandchild? I think you knew before you left here but chose not to tell me."

He took a step closer. "Yes, I did know. Whiting's assistant called back and said she had overlooked something the first time she checked out the records of the adoption. I guess I needed to come to grips with the truth before I shared it with anyone. And then Renee came and we didn't get a chance to talk." Would she ever understand how he'd missed her? Every day he had picked up the phone and started to call her, only to stop himself.

"Max, this house... It belongs to you." She sniffled.

"The house is yours, Ivy." He took one more step closer. "You're meant to live here. Jimmy told me you're in the process of writing a book on the history of this house and Marcus and Elizabeth. He also said you have great plans for this place. A bed and breakfast. Wow."

She nodded. "It'll be years before this place is completely remodeled."

"Ivy, I've missed you." He needed to tell her.

She brought a hand to her forehead and as she started for the table he noticed that she wobbled. He quickly went to her side and wrapped an arm around her waist.

"Whoa, you okay, sweetheart?" Max lifted her up in his arms and carried her into the sitting room, which was now filled with antique furniture and bright red curtains pulled back to allow the sunlight to spill into the room.

He laid her down on the overstuffed couch.

Ivy sat up against the cushions and pulled her knees up to her chest, tucking her skirt around her thighs. He sat down at her feet.

"Ivy, I have a lot of explaining to do." When she remained quiet, staring out the window, he continued, "I was seeing Renee before I met you. My relationship with her was one of, well, mutual understanding. I decided, and had told her before I got here, that I was ending my contact with her."

She still kept her eyes diverted. "Even if you and Renee were in a relationship when we met I still would not have any right to be angry. You never made me any promises. I was hurt because I truly thought what we had shared together had been special. That was my fault that I allowed myself to fall for you."

Max wanted to touch her, to hold her, anything just to be near her. "Ivy, I was a jerk. I tried to tell myself that what we had wasn't special, but damn, I couldn't help myself. I knew the moment I saw you that I was in trouble. I left here, went back to Chicago. I tried to pick up the life I'd been living." He looked at her profile, silently wishing she would look at him. "It didn't work. It didn't take long for me to realize that I had to be near you."

"Not long, Max? You have been gone for two months. Do you understand how long that is when you love someone and you don't know if they are forever gone from your life? Do you know how hard it is to be... Oh, never mind." She started to get up but he caught her wrists.

"I know how it is to be in love with someone and want to be with them every waking moment. But I couldn't change overnight. I had to be sure that I could be the man you need, one that you deserve. I needed you to be sure that I was the man for you. All I could think of was never seeing you again."

"Max Shepard?"

Max and Ivy both turned to the short, gray-haired woman standing in the doorway. She held gardening gloves in one hand, a spike in the other and an expression that said that she wasn't happy.

He stood up. "Elaine. Right? Ivy's mother."

She sized him up with wise eyes. "I'm not sure if I should throttle you for putting my daughter through hell or congratulate you." She spoke with a lisp.

Ivy's gasp was loud and Max looked down at her. Ivy jumped up from the couch and stepped toward her mother.

Max was curious. "Congratulate me?"

Elaine looked at her daughter in amazement. "You haven't told him? You said you called him right after you found out."

Ivy buried her face into her hands as if she needed a moment to gather her thoughts. "Yes, Mother. I said I called him and I did, but I couldn't reach him."

Max was more confused than ever. "You tried to call me?" he asked Ivy. Then he turned to Elaine. "Found out what?"

"Mother, I need to speak to Max alone," Ivy said.

Elaine looked from Max to Ivy and back to Max. "You better behave yourself."

He lifted his hands in surrender. "I will. I promise." He wanted to smile but didn't. It wasn't often a woman Elaine's age and short stature stood up to a man with his large frame.

When Elaine was gone, Ivy turned to Max and said, "You should sit down."

"I don't want to sit down." He could see that worry marred her features and he was beginning to fret himself.

"Would you like a drink?" she asked.

He sent a hand through his hair. "No, Ivy. What's going on?"

"We used condoms when we made love, except once. And it's true that it only takes once." She could barely look at him.

He nodded. "Yes. I learned that in health class in the seventh grade."

"Well, I'd say we are among the rare cases." He still wasn't getting it. "It's true what they say, Max. It takes only once."

Thoughts quickly rushed through his head. He was certain he had no venereal diseases. Renee was the only woman he had slept with for years and he had always, *always,* used protection with Renee. For one, he had doubted Renee's fidelity and two, he'd never have risked getting her pregnant. Renee thought of children as most people thought of warts. One makes a trip to the doctor's office, has it removed, and one is as good as new. The only other fear of not using a condom was--oh fuck.

The air seemed to be sucked out of the room.

Pregnancy!

He stared at Ivy, speechless. His eyes automatically fell to her flat stomach. She would be at least--he calculated the time in his head-- nine weeks. Did women show by nine weeks? Didn't most women look different when they carried a child? He examined her closely. She looked the same, except more beautiful, although he knew he was biased. She was tan from being in the sun.

"Say something." She shifted from one foot to the other.

"You're carrying a baby?" The word sounded strange coming from a man who had never said *baby* aloud, as far as he remembered.

"Yes." She laughed.

The room turned and he decided he needed to sit down. "Are you sure? I mean, that you're pregnant?"

"After five home pregnancy tests, a blood test in the hospital lab, and an ultrasound that confirmed the due date, yes, I am most definitely, one-hundred-percent sure."

He stood and went to her. "My baby?" Seeing her warning expression, he realized how it must have sounded. "No, what I mean is, we're having a baby?"

"Well, it's not a piglet." She laughed again.

"Ivy, I've been such a fool. Can you ever forgive me?"

Her eyes misted. "It's not about forgiving you, Max. I don't expect you to be a part of the baby's life unless you whole-heartedly want to be."

"I not only want to be a father to our baby, Ivy, but I want to be your husband. That is, if you'll have me."

One corner of her mouth drooped. "It's not that simple. We have to trust one another. We would no longer be two, but one. And what about fidelity? When you're married to me you make love with only me. Bimbos and whores are forever off the menu. Have you even thought about that?"

Did she actually think he would look at another woman, let alone be interested in another? "Sweetheart, my heart is only for you. I can promise you there will never be another woman who will turn my head."

"Okay, we have that settled, but what about your work?"

"What about my work?"

"You're traveling all the time. When a man has a wife and child he has to set his priorities."

Without hesitation, he asked, "Should I give it up?"

She shook her head, sending shiny tresses around her face. "No, I'm not asking that. What I'm saying is, you'll have a home, with us." She palmed her belly.

"There comes a time when a man needs to switch gears and try something new. You and the baby will always be my priority. And home--there's no place like it," he said as he took her slender hand and pulled her gently against his chest. He couldn't resist the urge to hold her another minute.

"Switch gears? Something new? I have missed your touch, your warmth and manly scent. I couldn't have fought you if I tried."

He bent down to plant kisses on her neck and she moaned, which sounded close to a kitten's purr. He lifted his head to whisper into her ear. "I'd like to try this job called 'matrimony and fatherhood.' I hear it's hard work, but rewarding."

She let her head fall back as he pressed his lips on her exposed collarbone. "It is hard work. I mean, from what I hear. It won't be easy. There will be arguments, diaper changes, sleepless nights, weeks of celibacy."

He snapped his head up at the last word. "Celibacy?"

"I'll be fat and ugly and tired."

"My sweet love, you'll never be ugly in my eyes."

She squinted. "But fat?"

"It's called baby weight." He looked deep into her blue eyes and his heart skipped a beat. "Do you love me, Ivy?"

"With every ounce of my being."

"And I love you. So will you marry me?" He couldn't wait another second. He needed to know her answer.

"Yes, and when?"

"Is tomorrow too soon?" He was ready now.

Elaine stepped back into the room, happiness evident in her glowing eyes and smile. "I'll call the minister from my church. He'll be ecstatic. I better grab my pen and paper." And she dashed of the room, probably to start making a list.

Ivy and Max broke out into laughter. Their life had come full circle. They loved one another, she was carrying his baby, and they would become a family in their dream house.

"I have a feeling that Elizabeth and Marcus are smiling down upon us."

He popped his head up, his eyes narrowed. "And by the way, how did you find out that I was a descendant of the Thorntons? The only record was the name on the adoption papers that were closed documents."

She smiled with the pride of a Cheshire cat. "I have my secrets, Max."

"Secrets?" His brow snapped up. "I didn't think we were supposed to have those anymore."

She kissed him on the tip of his nose. "You left the assistant's number on a piece of paper and you dropped it, I'm sure by accident. I called her, and with a bit of sweet talking and explanation, she was more than ready to help me out. In case that didn't work, I sent Jimmy to find out anything he could about your grandfather, Samuel."

"I can't wait to read your book. I have a feeling you're going to fill me in on a lot about my family tree, whether I want to know or not."

She nodded. "And with your contribution, it will be worthy of a Pulitzer."

"One will never know what they can accomplish unless they dream the impossible." Max kissed her on the neck and she giggled. "My dreaming Ivy."

Meet the Author

Suffering from years of hopeless romantic notions and sexy, sassy heroines and bad-ass heroes taking up residence in her mind, Rhonda decided to write and bring the stories to life. With baby on hip and laptop on the other--and two years later--Rhonda is a published author with a handful of spicy love stories waiting for the final touches. When Rhonda isn't crafting edge-of-your-seat, sizzling-ink novels, you will find her with her children, spending time with the ONE, watching soccer, watching a breathtaking movie, doing (or trying) yoga, and finding new ways to keep her smile bright.

Rhonda thrives on making her readers happy. She believes everyone deserves romance--one page at a time…

Turn the page for a special excerpt of Rhonda Lee Carver's

Delaney's Sunrise

Can a past love become their future?

The Thorntons' mansion is full of timeless secrets waiting to be unraveled. When small-town journalist Ivy and ghost hunter Max are stuck in the forgottena, dilapidated house, they find more than just a haunting. Ivy finds herself dreaming of the former owners, Marcus Thornton and his lovely wife, Elizabeth. Their profound love was once the talk of the town, and the cause their mysterious, untimely deaths never found. When Ivy's dreams begin to become reality, the mystery starts to unravel and sheds truth on more than just the past.

WARNING: Graphic language, naughty ghosts, a non-committal male, and a love that endures beyond time and death.

On sale now!

Chapter 1

Dee Crawford switched off the radio as she passed the road sign. *Willow Creek, One Mile Ahead.*

Anticipation and apprehension slithered up her spine like chilly fingers. Beads of sweat broke out on her forehead and between her breasts, so she rolled down the window of her Jeep. The brisk breeze cooled her feverish skin, but did little to diminish her uneasiness.

Taking a much-needed breath, slow and measured, Dee counted to ten, one of many relaxation techniques she'd absorbed from motivational CDs on the long drive from Chicago to Ohio's farmland. She'd need every last trick to manage her rolling stomach. She'd stopped at a greasy diner two hundred miles back and packed away more than a thousand calories worth of cheeseburger, fries, and strawberry milkshake. She hadn't had a good burger in at least five years--not since she moved away. Thinking back, she couldn't believe she'd once attempted a diet of tofu, bean sprouts, and eggplant.

More than once friends had called her crazy for her impulsiveness, yet Dee considered herself fairly level-headed. On the other hand, coming back to Willow Creek was probably downright nuts. Since she'd decided to return to the small-town home she'd hastily abandoned, she'd questioned her sanity repeatedly.

Past experience told her nothing but trouble waited in Willow Creek.

Dee pushed her thoughts into the back of her mind and kept her attention on the road.

A few miles later, she passed a familiar run-down barn and on the next curve, Dee turned onto the bumpy country road. For the next five minutes, she dodged cracks and potholes until she finally passed under the large *Delaney's Farm* sign.

One dark, dreary night, she'd pulled out of this very road and bid farewell to country living and everything that went with it. At the time, she'd thought leaving was the only way to rid her life of the guilt and sadness that had filled her.

And the only way to forget Abe Delaney.

Dee studied the scenery as she drove along the narrow gravel drive. She slowed the Jeep as she passed layers of thick, lush pine trees as green as if a painter had painted them that very moment. She breathed in the tangy, fresh scent. A tingle of awareness swirled in her chest. She'd yet to find a sweeter smell.

Dee glanced past the line of foliage to the sweeping view of the large pond. Ducks floated by an old gray fishing boat. A fishing rod stood propped against the hull.

She drove past red barns. The smells of hay and cow dung wafted on the breeze. A city girl's worst nightmare--or maybe not. Better than car exhaust fumes. Spotting a regal stallion trotting along the white fence, Dee smiled. One didn't see that in the city.

Reaching the north side of the property, she gazed across the blueberry grove and, beyond that, a section of green pasture. "Beautiful," she said aloud.

The solitude and peace of the landscape comforted her. She could feel her blood pressure drop and her anxiety float away.

The large white farmhouse hadn't changed a bit from what she remembered. It was still lovely enough to be featured on the front cover of *Country Home Magazine.* Large windows were framed in pristine curtains. The traditional wraparound porch was lined with rockers, welcoming someone to sit with a glass of iced tea as the evening passed.

Delaney's Farm was the most pleasant, dreamy place she'd ever seen. Built in the 1800s, it had started out as the town's first school. In those days, it was a one-room structure. Soon after the Delaney family bought it, they built on rooms and turned it into a comfortable home.

Dee parked, turned off the Jeep's engine, but didn't make a move to get out. She scanned the front of the house, looking for any sign of life. Not that she'd expected a red carpet welcome, but simple acknowledgement of her arrival would have been nice.

Abe had driven her away five years ago, and his sentiments probably hadn't changed. She had written to tell him she was arriving, but he hadn't responded. She hadn't been surprised. When his brother, Jacob, had died in a tragic car accident two weeks before he'd planned to marry Dee, life had taken a severe turn for the worse.

Closing her eyes and taking a deep breath, she finally slid out of the driver's seat, stretching her tired muscles. The sun beat down on her skin, and she glanced at the bright blue sky. It was an unusually hot day for May in Ohio, and she expected it to get much hotter once she came face to face with Abe.

Dee removed her bags and dropped the three leather cases to the gravel, studying them with disappointment. It was somewhat debasing to realize everything she owned sat before her.

But this was her chance for a new beginning. It was time she made a change. Would Abe realize that?

Dee heard the squeak of the screen door opening. Her heart beat faster. She turned, expecting to find a tall man sporting a frown. Instead, she came eye to eye with a silver-haired woman wearing an apron. Dee dropped her gaze to the woman's hands, which clasped tightly against her large bosom. From the older woman's narrowed eyes and glower, Dee wasn't a welcome sight.

Planting a winning smile on her face, Dee stepped up on the porch and offered her hand. "Hello, I'm Dee Crawford."

"Yes, Ms. Crawford," the other woman replied with a curt nod. "We've been expecting you."

Dee pulled back her hand and hooked her thumb in the front pocket of her jeans. "Please call me Dee. I'm glad Abe received my letter. I'm sorry, but he didn't reply, so that kind of puts me at a disadvantage."

With a pensive look and a sideways tilt of her head, the woman said, "I'm Mrs. Graves. I've been the housekeeper here at the farm for four years. I do the cleaning and the cooking."

The woman's attitude grated, but Dee took it with a grain of salt. Mrs. Graves could have waited to find a reason to dislike her before jumping to conclusions. Dee didn't intend to step on any toes.

"Thanks for greeting me, Mrs. Graves."

"Abe asked me to show you in if you showed up."

She sucked in a breath and bit her bottom lip as she swallowed her trepidation. Retrieving her bags, Dee made her way back up the steps to the porch. Mrs. Graves stepped to the side and held the door open. As Dee passed, she lost her grip on the luggage. One bag slid down her arm, falling to the wooden floor with a loud *thump*.

Mrs. Graves's mouth thinned as she examined the floor, as if looking for damage. "Do you need any help?"

Dee looked at the woman. Was she serious? Biting back laughter, Dee shrugged. She turned her attention to the familiar decorations of the foyer. Framed pictures of family still filled one wall, and she glanced over generations of Delaneys with their coal-black hair, dazzling smiles, mocha eyes, and olive complexions.

Her favorite picture, positioned significantly in the middle, was surrounded by an arrangement of smaller snapshots. Five Delaneys stared back at her as she examined the family portrait taken more than twenty years ago.

Ted Delaney had a proud tilt to his chin, and his warm eyes reflected his love for his wife and three sons. Mary Delaney stood next to her husband with devotion beaming in her kind, gentle smile. Behind the couple stood three handsome sons who were very similar in looks, yet so different in lifestyle.

The middle son, Max, was also the tallest, with a square jaw, a short military buzz cut and a face set in stoic lines From what she remembered, he was a Navy Seal and didn't make it home often because of his many assignments overseas.

Abe, the eldest, had thick black hair with soft, silken waves. His deep, mysterious eyes reminded her of a warm pool of melted chocolate. The proud set of his jaw said he was a force to reckon with. She should know. She'd gone head to head with him on more than one occasion. Her blood pressure rose to scorching heights at the mere memory of their arguments. She resisted the urge to fan herself.

Her gaze settled on Jacob, the youngest, the man she'd met and intended to marry. He'd had boyish features, welcoming, friendly, and in the picture he wore a mischievous smile. Of the three brothers, he looked most like their mother. The Jacob she'd known opened his heart to everyone, but in the end his deeply-concealed secrets had destroyed his happiness.

Tears stung her eyes. She blinked them back. Five years later, and her raw emotions still stung her like needles of devastation.

The sound of rubber-soled shoes on the polished floor, followed by an intrusive cough, pulled Dee from her thoughts. She turned and offered Mrs. Graves a forced smile. "That photo always grabs my attention."

Mrs. Graves shrugged. "Can I get you anything? Lemonade? Tea? Something to eat?"

Dee shook her head. Tendrils of hair fell against her face, cooling her heated cheeks. She brushed them back. "No, thank you. I'll just get my things settled into my room."

"Abe asked me to show you into the guest room--"

"The guest room?" Dee blurted between tight lips.

Mrs. Graves's eyes narrowed into slits. "Is there a problem?"

"I planned to stay in my old bedroom." Dee didn't want to make waves, but she didn't consider herself a guest.

Several expressions flickered over the other woman's face, until indifference swept through her blue-gray eyes. "Then so be it. I can prepare the bedroom with fresh sheets."

Dee waved a hand. "No, no. I can take care of it."

With a brusque nod, Mrs. Graves turned on her heel and started out of the room. Dee caught the woman before she disappeared. "Mrs. Graves, is Abe home?"

Mrs. Graves turned. Her cool glare pierced Dee from across the room. "No. He's out."

Dee let her leave without further interruption. The older woman reminded Dee of her pinch-faced second grade teacher. Mrs. Halesworthy had worn thick-soled shoes that made swishing sounds as she walked through the halls of the school. The teacher had carried her pointing stick like a weapon. If a kid broke a rule, Mrs. Halesworthy could scare the child until they peed their pants. She didn't doubt Mrs. Graves could frighten kids, and probably most adults.

Now that she was happily alone, Dee couldn't resist checking out the first floor. She felt like a child on Christmas morning. She'd always found silent stories in the antique furniture Mother Delaney had collected from all over the country.

She felt like an intruder as she snuck a glance into the living room. The décor transported her back into the 1800s. Dark wood, polished and refined, trimmed walls papered in solid red. Years of gentle wear had softened the finish on cherry hardwood floors. The paisley brown rug centered before the fireplace was new--or at least to her. The colors complemented the beige upholstery of the couch and chair.

The built-in shelves were also new, and brimming with books. She could guess Abe had read each one, maybe twice, some three times. He was a complex man. Country living sizzled in his blood during the day, but by night he was a scholar who buried himself in books. He'd even given thought to writing his own novel.

Dee headed toward the kitchen for a drink, but decided against it when she heard the sound of clinking dishes. Mrs. Graves wouldn't appreciate her company. Instead, she lugged her bags up the staircase and down the long hall. Luggage-lifting would have made one kick-ass workout, because she was exhausted by the time she reached her bedroom. Maybe her personal trainer had been a waste of money

It didn't matter anymore. No more personal trainers, luxury gyms, gourmet coffee shops on every corner or fancy restaurants. Willow Creek was far from the city. Coming back to the quiet town, she'd given up all the lavish perks for a simpler way of life. She hadn't found a drop of happiness in Chicago.

Maybe country life would steer her toward contentment.

The closest thing she'd get to a gym in these parts was milking the cows, weeding the gardens and harvesting the crops. If she wanted gourmet coffee, she'd have to brew it herself. Fancy eating wasn't a concern, considering she'd worked as a caterer for ten years and could toss together a fine meal when the mood struck. She wasn't giving up anything in the long run, right?

She lingered in the hallway with her hand on the bedroom doorknob. Taking a calming breath, she pushed the door open and crossed the threshold.

It was still her room. Nothing had changed. The pale blue walls, the white trim, the black sleigh-style wooden headboard all remained. She'd picked out the thick white comforter and colorful pillows herself. The matching chest once held framed pictures, but she'd taken them with her. She'd have them returned by nightfall.

Apprehension knotted her stomach as memories filled her mind. She tried to nudge them away, but they burrowed deeper.

Outside she heard the crunching of tires on gravel, drawing her to the large bay window. Tossing the smallest bag onto the bed, she pulled back the sheer lace curtain, and peered out at the front yard and the twisting, narrow drive. Abe's black truck came into view, leaving a cloud of dust in its wake.

Dee watched with bated breath as Abe parked in front of the house. Seconds later, he slid out from the driver's side. The morning sun glinted off his hair, turning it almost a faint purple. Blue flannel drew attention to his broad shoulders, while worn jeans accentuated the length of his toned legs. An odd feeling washed over her. Abe lifted his head, looking directly at her. A moan escaped her lips. Her heart clenched, and butterflies flitted in her stomach. He stared up at her. His steely, dark gaze penetrated her through the window.

With a twist of her wrist, she let the curtain drop and jumped back. She brought a shaky hand to her chest and ordered her body not to betray her. She closed her eyes and forced her breathing to slow. Abe was a mere man. He had no control over her. Or did he?

It'd taken months of mental preparation, as well as exhaustive planning, for her to come back to the farm. When she had left, she'd sworn she'd never return under any circumstances. Not as long as Abe remained.

She had been engaged to Jacob for less than two days when he'd brought her to Delaney's Farm. She hadn't been ready to meet the older, tougher brother Jacob had told her about. Jacob never could have prepared her for Abe. She remembered all too well how he'd besieged her with his curious chocolate-colored eyes. They had burned a hole through her then--as they would now.

She brushed her clammy palms down her pants and fidgeted with the lace edging her top. She'd have to face Abe again, sooner or later. Time to get it over with.

Taking a seat at the vanity, she stared at her reflection in the mirror. It seemed as though the hands of time had molded her face with their cool touch. People said she was pretty. She supposed it was true, in a classic, delicate way. Her hair was a shade of light chestnut, natural--unlike her friends, who had to color theirs every three months.

Her skin was fair, and she never tanned. Her mother had told her a hundred times that wrinkles were never flattering. Her pale, freckled nose and cheeks were the legacy of her equally pale, freckled grandmother.

She puckered her lips. They were thin. Ever since she could remember, she'd wished for a supple, full pout. However, just like her breasts, her lips had never reached ample proportions.

Oh well. There was more to life than big breasts and full lips.

She did have an ample brain, at least.

With a glance down her clothes, she sighed. The pink, frilly, long-sleeved shirt, gray slacks and tall boots made her look like a professional attending an important conference. She knew Abe. He'd get a laugh out of her outfit. He would think she was foolish wearing high heels on a farm. She would stick out among the horse barns and greenery like a sore thumb.

She changed into a pair of dark denims, tight t-shirt, and boots. "Calm and collected," she repeated to herself as she emerged from the bedroom.

She found Abe in exactly the same spot where she'd met him five years ago: sitting on the front porch. He stared at the blueberry bushes as if searching for answers in the tranquil scenery. He was probably asking Mother Nature how he could get her off his land.

Some things never changed. Had Dee really believed Abe would? Men like him never changed. He made people come to him. No doubt he'd have sat there and waited until she made the first move.

Stepping through the creaky screen door, she made her way toward him. The summer heat brushed a soft breeze across her face, warming her. Sweat beaded on her upper lip, but she attributed it to frayed nerves more than the temperature. She wiped the moisture, paused and waited. He knew she was there, but made no effort to look at her.

Wasn't he the least bit curious? *Turn and look at me!*

She followed his gaze out over the blueberry grove. The cloudy sky promised rain, and a group of deer ate grass along the edge of the trees. She swept her eyes over him. His hair was longer, covering his ears and nearly touching the collar of his flannel button-down. A layer of stubble dusted his cheeks, and his jaw was set in a tight, grim line.

She silently urged him to acknowledge her. She wished he'd make this easier for them both.

He brought his hand to his mouth, sucking on the cigarette he clamped between his fingers. He inhaled and exhaled as if it were a ritual. Finally, he took one last, long drag and ground the butt out on the wooden post.

Without anything to keep him occupied, he turned and caught her with a piercing look. It shook her to the core. It was clear by his narrowed, hard eyes and the bitter scowl that he would be doing everything in his power to make her stay here a bad experience.

She wanted to turn tail and rush back into the house, to find solace in her bedroom alone, but she stood her ground. She controlled her body, refusing to quiver under his raw scrutiny, even while she turned into gelatin inside.

He was only a man. She told herself to not back down.

Holding her head high and her back straight as a rod, she endured the sweet pain as his gaze scoured every inch of her. He visually caressed her, from the roots of her hair to the very tip of her new, shiny boots. His examination was purposeful and exaggerated, as if he intended to unnerve her.

Unfortunately, he did. The strength in his menacing eyes, his high cheekbones, and large frame were enough to alarm anyone.

Time had worked its invisible hands on him, too. Lines etched the skin around his eyes and mouth, but age hadn't taken anything away from his striking good looks. Instead, he appeared more distinguished and breathtaking. She couldn't deny the attraction that drew her. He was desirable, and could be devastatingly charming when he wanted to be. He just never wanted to be.

She'd always believed Abe was born in the wrong era. He should have lived and fought with the likes of Jesse James and Doc Holliday. Seeing him sitting there with his worn, torn jeans, his old shirt and scuffed boots, one would never guess he was a man who'd once worked in a multi-billion dollar financial organization.

Dee hadn't known Abe then. But she'd heard he wore Armani suits, drove a fancy car and lived in a luxurious penthouse in Manhattan.

Their eyes met. His were icy. She reminded herself they shared common interest...and familiar pain.

"I'm glad you got my letter." Her words sounded weak, edged in fear, even to her own ears. "I didn't think it was fair to just show up without notice."

He kept his gaze steady, locking her in place with its intensity. "What the hell are you doing here?"

She swallowed, her throat dry. "Thanks for the warm welcome. I knew I could count on your hospitality."

"You didn't answer my question." His voice deepened.

Calm and sure, she ordered her nerves.

He wanted to scare her into running away. She'd given him that pleasure five years ago, but never again, even if it meant growing a thicker skin and an even thicker heart.

"Abe, do I really need to answer that question?"

One booted foot propped against the railing, and the other stretched out in front of him as if he had no concern in the world. He slowly eased himself up until he stood his full height, six foot two, and a good two-hundred pounds. She knew he didn't have an ounce of fat under his shirt and jeans. As he moved, his shirt clung to six-pack abs and toned biceps. She'd forgotten how intimidating his tall frame could be, especially compared to her five foot four, one-hundred-ten pound frame.

He crossed the short distance between them. The scuff of his boots deafened her. Rolling her head back on tight shoulders, she looked up at him, refusing to squirm no matter how heated his gaze grew. He stopped within inches, towering over her.

"You're not welcome here." His voice was a raspy whisper. His lips thinned, and one corner of his mouth dropped.

Dee brought her arms up and hugged herself protectively, placing a palm over her chest. Was her blood pumping from fear...or excitement?

Her lips trembled. She wasn't afraid of him, but panic whirled inside her. He'd always had that effect on her. She'd hoped maturity would give her the advantage in controlling her reactions. Obviously her brain was on a different track than her spiraling feelings. Five years hadn't dampened the rushing of her blood, the butterflies in her stomach or her trembling hands.

She knew all too well that underneath the harsh, brawny exterior existed a teddy bear's heart. Once upon a time, Abe had opened up to her. She'd glimpsed kindness and tenderness. If Dee had to guess, she'd say he didn't let many people see the softer side.

He'd just have to get used to the idea that she was back.

"Abe," she started, then stopped to moisten her lips. "I'm not here to cause problems. Can't we just let go of the past and start a new friendship?"

The muscles clenched in his neck. She waited for him to snap.

"Let go?" His words were laced with anger. "It may be easy for you to forget the past, Dee, but he was my brother. Dammit, Jacob was my brother!"

"And he was my fiancé."

"He was your fiancé for two months. He was my brother for twenty-six years." His hands clenched into fists, and the line of his jaw hardened.

She exhaled and tucked a tendril of hair behind her ear. The breeze picked up, carrying his scent to her nostrils. She inhaled the masculine smell. It brought back the familiar feeling of when his kisses had melted her. She moistened her bottom lip and silently swore as neglected muscles throbbed.

"This isn't a contest to see who has more of a right to mourn Jacob's death, Abe." She refused to look away. "We both loved him and lost him, and together we buried him. If we can't get along for any other reason, it should be for his memory." She rolled her next words around her mind before she continued. "He left me his share of Delaney's Farm because he wanted me here."

He laughed. "Who the hell do you think you're talking to, Dee? Last I looked, I didn't have *easily manipulated* written across my forehead." His lip curled. The explosion was coming, but she didn't back away. "Look at you, Dee." He ran his gaze over her frame. He should have just licked her from forehead to toes. It evoked the same feeling. "You don't belong here. You come here in your fancy clothes and your shiny shoes and place yourself smack dab in the middle of *my* life. You believe you belong here because my brother willed you his half of the farm? You have no rights." He turned on a booted heel and stalked to the railing, placing both hands on it. "Although Jacob owned half, he didn't have the right to give it to you."

"I offered to sign it over to you, remember? We were sitting in the attorney's office after the reading of the will and I told you I didn't want the farm. I knew it wasn't right for me to have it." Her heavy sigh seemed to slice through the tension. "You refused to let me sign my share over to you."

He gripped the wood railing until his knuckles turned white. "Are you here to make that offer again?"

Dee clasped her hands tightly. To Abe, she was just a lingering sign of Jacob's rebellion. If Jacob had willed her his half of the farm, it was--in Abe's mind--just another impulsive act in a long string of impulses that had centered around Dee. Jacob hadn't been thinking clearly, Abe had said. After Jacob's death, he'd accused her of clouding both their minds with her hypnotic poison.

He turned. His emotions seemed under control, and his triple-layered wall appeared back in place. "Are you going to answer me? Are you here to make that offer again?"

She narrowed her eyes. "No."

He pushed away from the rail and brushed past her. She kept her gaze on his back as he stomped off the porch. "That's fine," he muttered. "You'll run again. The sooner, the better."

www.ingramcontent.com/pod-product-compliance
Lightning Source LLC
Chambersburg PA
CBHW021243260626
47155CB00004BA/1290